LOGIE O' BUCHAN

An Aberdeenshire Pastoral

GAVIN GREIG

with a new Introduction by
William Donaldson

ABERDEENSHIRE CLASSICS

Republished from the original 1899 edition

James G. Bisset Limited
12 Upperkirkgate
Aberdeen
1985

James G. Bisset Limited
12 Upperkirkgate
Aberdeen
AB9 1BG

British Library Cataloguing in Publication Data
Greig, Gavin
Logie O' Buchan: an Aberdeenshire pastoral of last century.
— (Aberdeenshire Classics)
I. Title   II. Series
823.8 [F]   PR6013.R48/

ISBN: 0–948246–03–0

Printed by Fretwell & Cox, Keighley, West Yorkshire

Introduction

LOGIE O' BUCHAN is a tale of Jacobite intrigue and romance set in the North-East just after the '45, featuring the exploits of a real-life figure, George Halket, schoolmaster of Rathen and Cairnbulg, who was traditionally thought to have written the song which gives the book its title. It was first published as a weekly serial in the columns of the *Buchan Observer* (from 7 December 1897 to 19 April 1898) and later in book form with minor stylistic revisions, by D. Wyllie & Son, Aberdeen, 1899. The edition was limited to 500 copies and has long been difficult to obtain. The present reprint appears at a time of quickening interest in Gavin Greig, thanks to the long-awaited publication of the large and important folk-song collection that he and James Bruce Duncan made in Aberdeenshire in the early years of the century. It is only now that his full stature is beginning to be appreciated and the range of his interests and activities acknowledged. This introduction relates the novel to Greig's own career, and to the life of the North-East during the period.

Gavin Greig was born in 1856 at Parkhill near Aberdeen, the son of an estate overseer. His father's family came from Buchan, his mother's from the Mearns, and through her he traced a connection with the poet Burns. He was educated at Dyce parish school, the Grammar School of Old Aberdeen, and at Aberdeen University. He graduated M.A. in 1876.

Greig was a typical loon o' pairts, a bright boy scaling the education ladder into the professions and then achieving distinction there. In some respects he was lucky: the North-East was a good place to be educated in. Provision of schooling was the best in Scotland, thanks to a traditional regard for learning and the operation of an important trust fund called the Dick Bequest which aimed to attract able teachers into the area by paying them almost double what they could earn elsewhere. The main hurdle to higher education — its cost — could also be surmounted more readily in the North-East. The University of Aberdeen had a uniquely comprehensive system of bursaries to help pay for subsistence, books and fees. These were attainable by annual competitive examination. Greig came fourth, out of the whole north of Scotland, in 1872.

On graduating he took the usual next step on the career ladder, and attended the Free Church College, Aberdeen, to prepare himself for the ministry. After a while, however, he gave this up and took a post in teaching. He married in 1878, and the following year at the age of twenty-three, he became headmaster of the rural school of Whitehill near New Deer, where he remained until his death on 31st August 1914.

Teaching had just begun to established itself as a profession in its own right. Poor pay and conditions had long limited the quality of recruitment into it. The ministry was the traditional goal of the upwardly mobile, and the schoolhouse was usually just the first step towards it, something a licentiate might take on for a year or two while he waited for a kirk. Professional training and decent salaries were changing that and by the end of the century teachers, especially in larger schools, could be better off in education than they would have been in the ministry. Greig's own career reflects this. He took an active part in the work of the Educational Institute of Scotland to promote the general standing of teachers, being treasurer for many years of the Deer Branch of the E.I.S., and was later created a Fellow of the Institute in recognition of his services. He took a keen interest in many aspects of local public life, and seems to have been universally loved and respected. Indeed had he not written later that in fact he drifted into teaching and was never really satisfied with it as a career, we might be tempted to regard him as the very ideal of the learned and worthy country dominie in the golden age of the Scots parochial tradition.

Had he been merely this, of course, there would be little more to say; but Greig was an enormously creative man, who made a large contribution to the musical and literary culture of the North-East. He remained a practising musician throughout his career, an arranger, composer, and musicologist thoroughly immersed in the musical life of the region at every level from serious art-music to popular song. He composed musical dramas on historical themes, published his own arrangement of songs by Burns, edited a collection of fiddle music, *Harp and Claymore,* for James Scott Skinner, contributing to it an essay on the strathspey, and compiled a number of articles on the development of popular song in Scotland, all before he began his epoch-making research into folk-song.

During his lifetime he was also well-known as a man of letters, with a considerable, although largely local, reputation as a poet, novelist, and playwright. At first he concentrated on poetry, and had various pieces published in popular anthologies. He was inspired by a keen sense of local patriotism, an idea that Buchan was the great missing piece in the jigsaw of lowland Scottish letters. He felt that it had hitherto failed to make a contribution to national literary culture in any way commensurate with its weight, and that people like himself must do something to redress the balance both by original composition and by investigating the existing literary traditions of the region.

A similar urge can be seen in his attempt to revive — perhaps to create — a native drama. In his plays *Mains's Wooin'* (Peterhead, 1909; first performed in New Deer in April 1894) and *Mains Again* (Aberdeen, 1913, but written by 1897), he was a pioneer of the folk drama movement which flourished in the North-East at this time. The erection of public halls in country parishes provided a focus for the community and a natural arena for a popular drama reflecting its outlook and language. A whole series of short plays bearing local imprints and obviously intended for amateur production survive from the late Victorian and Edwardian period. Greig's own pieces contain a typical blend of realism and comic fantasy and introduce a range of characters drawn from contemporary rural society. They were very popular. *Mains's Wooin'*, indeed, became a local classic and continues to be staged to this day.

His novels were set in Buchan too. Three full-length stories have been located, all of them first appearing as serials in the columns of local newspapers: *Morrison Gray: or, Life in a Buchan Schoolhouse (Peterhead Sentinel* from 5 May 1896 to 19 January 1897), a contemporary story of love and betrayal set mainly in the New Deer district; *The Hermit of Gight: or, the Fatal Casket,* a neo-gothic tale dealing with the fall of a powerful branch of the house of Gordon, published in the *Buchan Observer* (from 13 December 1898 to 23 May 1899); and *Logie o' Buchan* itself, whose action covers much of the broad coastal plain of Aberdeenshire east of Mormond.

Greig has commonly been presented as an isolated figure, labouring in obscurity without acknowledgement or peer; but there can be little doubt either about his contemporary celebrity (he enjoyed a European reputation as a folklorist during his own lifetime), or his position as a repesentative of a wider movement within the North-East of his day. In Victorian Scotland, professional opportunity was distributed on a wide geographical basis and able people frequently remained within the local community. Following the expansion and improvement of the teaching force and the virtual doubling of the clergy after the Disruption of 1843, a large and vigorous intellectual community came into being within the North-East, and its members had ample leisure, income, and opportunity to further their collective interests. The publications of the Buchan Club — of which Greig was president — the Banffshire Field Club, and the New Spalding

Club of Aberdeen bear testimony to their energy, vision, and breadth of purpose. Contributions on statistics, economics, geology, linguistics, anthropology, botany, folklore and history of every description are to be found within their hospitable pages. It was a notable age of local scholarship.

The sense of cultural continuity is an important feature of the life of the region; there were folklorists in Buchan before Gavin Greig. The perception that the area might be a unique storehouse of traditional lore went back at least as far as Peter Buchan (1790–1854), the Peterhead printer and song-collector who also wrote popular drama and fiction and whose interests are intriguingly similar to Greig's own. More recently men like Walter Gregor and John Milne of Atherb, Greig's own early mentor, had been active in the field, as well as a number of other writers. The great folk-song collection was the crowning achievement of a movement which had been gathering momentum for almost a century.

Yet Greig was haunted by a sense of almost despairing urgency. The impact of modernisation — the spread of the printed word, the penetration of the rural areas by the railway network, the introduction of compulsory education — was disrupting the delicate tissue of orality upon which traditional culture was thought to depend. His own career spanned a period of rapid and far-reaching change. From his schoolhouse windows he could see little that was not in some sense man-made. The very landscape was raw and new, torn from the naked heath little more than a generation before to create one of the most advanced and efficient farming systems in Europe. The coastal districts were likewise in a state of ferment as the rise of the great herring fishery swept aside the accumulated cultural patterns of centuries.

A deep sense of insecurity possessed the "Buchan literawti". All around them traditional society was disappearing and traditional values were going down. They struggled, while there was still time, to define the essential qualities of the old North-East so that they could be transmitted to succeeding generations. On the one hand, was the view of Buchan as the fountainhead of traditional culture. On the other, was a historical ideal, ultimately political in inspiration. The North-East had been the heartland of episcopalianism and of the Jacobite movement in the lowlands, the home of Pitsligo, Glenbucket, the Earl of Mar, the Marquis of Huntly, the Earl Marischal and his brother General Keith, Lord Lewis Gordon, and many others. Jacobitism was felt to sum up the central characteristics of the place and its people, and to symbolise their deeply-rooted sense of difference from the rest of lowland Scotland.

There is ample evidence of this in the local newspaper press, whose own dramatic growth is one of the most noticeable features of the period. Until about 1850, the region was served by one or two big "county" papers, like the *Aberdeen Journal* and the *Banffshire Journal,* which had such a large distribution pattern that they could give merely outline attention to the localities and do little to promote an active sense of local identity. In addition, they only reached a section of the population. Because of various taxes upon the press they were so expensive that many ordinary people could not afford to buy them. When these taxes were repealed in the '50s, however, it became possible to run cheap local papers even in quite small towns: the *Fraserburgh Advertiser* (1852), the *Huntly Express* (1863), the *Morayshire Advertiser* of Elgin (1855), and the two Peterhead papers, the *Peterhead Sentinel* (1856) and the *Buchan Observer* (1863) all began about this time and they did much to foster a sense of common identity and purpose, leading to a powerful resurgence of local awareness and pride throughout the North-East.* Taken together, they had a dramatic effect upon the demand for local writing, because of their insatiable appetite for articles on local history, folklore, popular

* If one includes the city of Aberdeen, then between 1880 and 1914 some forty different papers were published within the area.

antiquities, memoirs and reminiscences, poetry and fiction, all of which they tended to publish in large quantities.

The reduction in price enabled the new papers to enter a wider market, one dominated by working-class readers with whom the North-East, thanks to the excellence of its education service, was particularly well-supplied. As the audience changed, the medium tended to as well; news could be displaced from the centre of attention, and some papers at least began to act as an important vehicle for the mass popular culture of the day. Fiction was regarded as a powerful weapon in the struggle for the market. The *Peterhead Sentinel*, edited by Peter Buchan's nephew David Scott, shows this particularly well. It carried short and serialised fiction throughout the second half of the century, some of it locally written, some bought in from national syndicates. Its most distinguished local contributor was Gavin Greig.

It may seem curious that a person of literary reputation might seek to publish his novels in local newspapers at all, but there were fairly strong inducements. As the century advanced it became more difficult for first-time novelists to break into the literary market, and many of them resorted to newspaper serialisation as a stepping-stone towards publication in book form. The serial market could be enormously lucrative: Wilkie Collins was paid £5,000 for the serial rights of his novel *Armadale*, but of course, this was with syndication — involving simultaneous publication by many periodicals — in view. In the local press, the returns were more modest, often perhaps twenty or thirty pounds. Indeed Greig may have published his stories without any formal financial agreement with the papers concerned. In an age when it could still be considered vulgar to write for money, there may simply have been a tacit understanding about an "honorarium" if the story proved popular. And Greig's did.

Logie o' Buchan was specifically designed to meet the requirements of the new popular fiction market which had sprung up in Scotland following the explosive growth of a mass press during the previous generation. The Victorian novel fell into three distinct types: the serious art-novel, which would achieve book form at some stage of its publication history; middlebrow fiction, which might appear in book form but which was also printed in large quantities as serials in magazines, and the new mass fiction which tended to appear serially in newspapers and large-circulation popular miscellanies and might never reach book form at all. Each had its own particular conventions. In popular serial fiction, the most obvious of these was the overriding importance of the plot. Serial publication turned novel-reading into a marathon experience, and in order to sustain the interest of readers over a period of perhaps several months, it was necessary to manage the plot with much resourcefulness and ingenuity. The requirements of character construction and setting diminished in relative importance.

Characters in any case tended to be highly conventional, and to be derived from two main sources: the Scots realist tradition with its fondness for accurate detail and vigorous vernacular dialogue — and an imported vein of high Englishry whose extravagance of gesture and ornate, abstract language ultimately descended from popular melodrama. Lower-class characters were usually drawn from the first of these, upper-class ones — often with scant regard to social or historical probability — from the second. If they played an important part in the story, even lower-class characters might be shown speaking formal English throughout. The whole story of popular fiction in 19th century Scotland can be seen in the ceaseless pull between these two linked but ultimately incompatible strands of the popular narrative tradition. There are obvious signs of this in *Logie o' Buchan*, in Fred Clark and Jamie Robertson's use of English, for example, and the way Halket fluctuates between Scots and English in a manner more likely to be found in a late nineteenth than a mid-eighteenth century Buchan dominie. Nobody managed to resolve this problem satisfactorily; most writers ended up with a more or less uneasy compromise. The contemporary reader may well feel inclined to echo Halket's sentiments, however, when he declared "Nae man can dee himsel' full justice except in his ain mither tongue." (p.44)

Although the framework of Greig's novel was derived from nationally current conventions, he addressed himself to a specific local audience, and he deliberately used the most popular of available literary forms in order to reach a large readership within it. The novel itself tells us why. *Logie o' Buchan* is steeped in folk-culture. It opens with a passage in praise of innocent superstition, and closes in rapt contemplation of the power of traditional song. In between there are references to ghosts, halloween customs, a "wise-woman", dreams, pagan mythology, druids and standing stones, and, of course, that perennial folk-symbol the "broken-token" — in this case two halves of a sixpence which enable the lovers to reclaim one another at the climax of the story. The main narrative itself is an expanded version of a song. In short, *Logie o' Buchan* is an attempt to feed some appreciation of the area's distinctive folk-culture back into the mainstream of Buchan life, and it takes the form of a popular novel because that is perceived as the most effective possible channel of communication between the intelligentsia and the people.

In the classic pattern of nineteenth century European Romanticism, the bourgeoisie appropriated elements of folk tradition in order to weld them into the basis of what they saw as a new national culture. This was one of Greig's express aims in the great folk-song collection: he spoke of "reconstructing Scottish song" in the light of it. But in *Logie o' Buchan* he attempted something different. The novel marks a climax of the movement to re-establish Buchan as a country of the mind and to fix the main features of its terrain. Earlier in the century there had been a general readiness amongst the people of the North-East to accept their own remoteness and peripherality. Peter Buchan was perfectly capable of quoting approvingly from a southern review of his work which began: "There is a desolate sea-port of North-Britain called Peterhead, visited only by storm-tossed whalers, or home-returning voyagers to the Pole. In that desolate sea-port lives Mr. Peter Buchan, the upright and indefatigable collector of northern song, a man worthy of a more genial residence . . ." (Peter Buchan, *The Peterhead Smugglers,* Edinburgh, 1834, p.7). By the end of the century, however, thanks to decades of economic expansion, population growth, and a revolution in internal communications, Buchan people had become more accustomed to living at the centre of their own mental world. This was an act of reclamation as important as that which wrung the rich and productive farmland of Aberdeenshire from a wilderness of moss and moor, perhaps more so; and one of its chief architects was Gavin Greig.

October 1985   William Donaldson

LOGIE O' BUCHAN

An Aberdeenshire Pastoral

of Last Century

BY

GAVIN GREIG, M.A.

ABERDEEN

D. WYLLIE & SON

1899

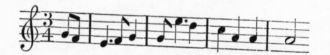

CONTENTS

ABERDEENSHIRE CLASSICS

James G. Bisset hope to publish at regular intervals
the following titles in this series:

Already published, uniform with this edition of LOGIE O' BUCHAN is:

LOGIE O' BUCHAN.

PART I.

CHAPTER I.

HALLOWE'EN.

IT was Hallowe'en in the year of grace 1746—Hallowe'en over broad Scotland : Hallowe'en in Buchan.

The dull short day had closed.   There was no moon, and the stars were hid behind the thick vapours that brooded over the dank dead earth.

But soon the landscape begins to be lit up.   Here and there, now to right, now to left, leap up through the gloom the flames of Hallowe'en bonfires—those piles of whin that eager young hands have for weeks been collecting to honour immemorial custom.

And the fairies were abroad that night.—Ah, those fairies!   People believed in them then ; but our scepticism has banished the wee folk from the land ; and oh, how much of the poetry of pastoral life has gone with them !

This night too all kinds of spells could be tried. Happy were the lads and lasses then.   For them indulgent Fate granted this annual occasion whereon all who dared might approach and consult the oracles of Love.

But science has abolished all this.   We are so much cleverer than our fathers that we can afford to laugh at

I

their lore. It was all nonsense, those beliefs of theirs. Of course, of course. But then are we so much happier for this superior knowledge of ours?—or better?

It was, as we have said, the year 1746—writ red in British history as the year of Culloden. That disastrous battle had been fought some six months before ; and the country was beginning to recover somewhat from the paralysing blow. Most of the trials and executions that had followed were now over, and the stream of blood was on the ebb. The rule of military violence too, that had been in such painful evidence for some time, showed merciful signs of abatement.

Buchan had had its own connection with the Jacobite rising, and had lent its quota of support to Prince Charlie's cause. Some of its leading men had followed his banner, and had shared his reverses. One or two indeed had had to flee for their lives ; and many had suffered in varying ways and degrees. But the community at large was beginning to forget these things,—so fast do even the most dreadful experiences fade from the general memory.

And now to-night it was evident that a good deal of the old happiness of social life had returned.

As the evening fell a lonely traveller might have been seen trudging along the road that leads northwards through the parish of Lonmay. Somehow or other he was to any one that cared to look at him a bit of an enigma. His long gray locks and beard seemed to be-token an age which his alert frame and firm step in turn belied ; while ever and again he carried his staff in a way that showed it was not needed for support. His dress and wallet would have labelled him mendicant ; but his features, as far as they could be seen, were much too intelligent and refined for the ordinary gaberlunzie.

As he pursued his leisurely way the night closed in. Occupied with his own thoughts he was paying little heed to anything by the way; but when the flames of the Hallowe'en bonfires began to light up the landscape he looked round with pleased interest; and, when away to the left a blaze kindled by some enthusiastic Strichen loons was spreading over and up the slopes of Mormond, his face too lightened up, and he muttered,—

" Ay, ay ; and puir auld Scotland is beginnin' to look some like hersel' again. . . . It's a sicht for sair een."

Then after a while he added, quoting the burden of an old Jacobite strain,—

" But there'll never be peace till—*somebody* comes hame."

At length he struck off to the right. By this time it was getting rather dark ; but the gaberlunzie (as we may now call our wanderer) seemed quite familiar with the country. He did not appear to have any very definite destination in view ; but his way lay in the direction of Logie, situated on the borders of Crimond and Lonmay.

As he walked slowly along, skirting some waste ground on which grew a profusion of broom, he heard a faint cry as of a babe. He stopped and listened. Soon there came another similar cry, followed by a rustling among the broom and a crooning moan.

It was now pretty dark, and the gaberlunzie, though not by any means a nervous man, did not care to proceed to explore the mystery in any precipitate way. It might be something uncanny—on a Hallowe'en night.

"Anybody there?" he asked in a tentative way.

A feeble moan was heard, followed by some inarticulate mutterings.

Concluding now that it was a case of distress he crossed the ditch that lay between, and, cautiously advancing a few steps further, peered in the direction whence the sounds seemed to proceed.

He saw a dark object huddled up among the broom.

For a little he hesitated. Just then, however, a bonfire kindled on a rising ground only a few hundred yards away lit up the scene, while the shouts of the merry youngsters who had fired the pile rang out on the evening air.

At the strange glare and the sudden noise the figure sat up and looked round with a kind of dazed terror. It was a woman with a baby in her arms. She was evidently a stranger, and had presumably crawled there for rest and shelter.

"What are ye deein' here?" queried the gaberlunzie.

With a slight scream she turned towards the speaker.

"Dinna be feart, lassie," he said in a kindly re-assuring tone that somehow seemed to reconcile her to his presence.

She looked as if she meant to speak, but soon her head drooped again. She was evidently exhausted or ill.

"Ye'll be better o' something. Tak' a drap o' this," he said, producing a small bottle from his wallet and kneeling down to her.

The woman obediently took a drink. The effect was quick and beneficial. Then he asked if she was hungry.

"It's my baby," she cried, finding voice at last, and clasping the little creature to her breast.

"Can you take me—anywhere?" she went on. "My pet—my dear wee Fred—he'll die!" And with head bent over her baby she rocked herself to and fro.

She was evidently a woman of some refinement, and she spoke with a good south-country accent. The gaberlunzie instinctively discarded his own doric.

"No fear of your baby," he said, cheerily. "Come along to some house."

She hardly seemed to notice what he said, but now with sudden eagerness as if recollecting something she exclaimed, looking wildly and appealingly to him,—

"O, can you take me to Fred?"

"That will be your husband?" said the old man interrogatively.

Then, as if getting hold of a further idea, she went on,—

"O, but he is dead. . . . I'll never see my Fred again. . . . They have killed him!"

And she wailed piteously.

"But where was he?" asked the gaberlunzie.

At the question, however, she grew suddenly calm. An access of caution seem to check her speech. But her interrogator thought he understood the situation.

"Was he—at Culloden?—with the Prince? . . Never mind telling me. . . . I'm on his side myself." But still she looked suspicious, and said no more.

"Come along just now at anyrate," he said. "We must get you to some house. Give me the baby to carry, and you may be able to follow."

Kissing her child she let the man take it from her arms. She could hardly stand from sheer weakness; but the stimulating effects of the liquor and the near prospect of help for her poor babe nerved her, and she staggered on after her guide.

The gaberlunzie was more and more gaining her confidence, and when on the way he returned to the subject of her antecedents he managed at length to extract from her certain particulars, of which the summary was,—that her young husband had followed Prince Charlie; that, having never heard from or of him since the army left Falkirk on its northward march, she had judged him fallen in battle; that, her father having been put to death, her brother banished, and their home desolated by the soldiery, she had set out to seek her husband's country, which she knew was Buchan, and then if possible find his friends, of whom, however, she knew nothing.

Ere long they approached the farm of Millbog, which was a good half mile from Logie. The sound of a fiddle came borne on the quiet evening air.

The gaberlunzie with his habitual caution did not make for the door, which was slightly open, but led the way through the cornyard so as to reconnoitre the inside from the uncurtained window.

His companion, who had followed, leaned wearily against the wall, while he stood looking in and noting the occupants of the kitchen.

Now, as the individuals there assembled are destined to play important parts in our story, we shall tell what the gaberlunzie saw, adding such supplementary notes as may seem necessary at an introductory stage.

The central figure that caught the eye was that of a young man standing up with his back against the dresser, and playing a slow air on the violin. This was Jamie

Robertson, apprentice gardener at Logie. He was physically a fine specimen of manhood, tall and well-proportioned, with an elasticity of movement and grace of bearing that seemed inborn and quite marked him off from the generality of rustic youths. His features were regular and clearly cut; and now, rapt and exalted with the inspiration of the moment and suffused with the light of a fine pathos, they stamped him a young Apollo. The note of the whole presentation was that of one reaching away from his surroundings, and straining after other and higher ideals that his present environment would recognise or allow. And this, as we shall see, was the note of his whole life and fortunes.

On a low creepie sat a girl of some eighteen summers —the daughter of the house and known as Bell, though fond and not unambitious parents had christened her Isobel. Rather under the average size, she was now budding into a plump and dewy womanhood—clear of complexion and bright of eye, and radiating a certain unconscious and undefinable fascination. She was listening to the music and looking at the musician, although occasional blushes and movements of the head, sometimes affectedly impatient, showed that she had also an ear for the remarks addressed to her in a low tone by a young man who, dressed in the fashionably fast style of the day, was sitting with easy carelessness on a table and ostentatiously tapping his toe with a riding-whip. This young fellow was the son of a bonnet laird in the neighbouring parish of Rathen. Fred Clark was his name; but among familiar friends he usually passed as "the laird." Although young he had already had a bit of a career—not quite fully known; and there were not wanting wise people who prophesied further developments.

Old John, the farmer of Millbog, or "Bogie" as he was generally called, sat in his customary chair by the fireside. He had just been discussing markets and prices with his neighbour Sandy of Clyacksneuk, an exceedingly well-to-do middle-aged bachelor. Both had stopped to listen to the music, which was compelling some attention even from Jockie, a restless urchin of some thirteen summers, who had been holding a high time with Jip the collie.

The only person who was moving about was Marget, the goodwife—a short woman inclined to a stoutness which constant activity and bustling had pretty much kept in check. She was commonly irrepressible; but now the spell of the music made her move about with unusual quietness, and reserve for the present her store of admonitory remark.

The gaberlunzie waited till the music ended ; then stepping to the door he knocked gently but firmly.

Inside was heard the farmer's voice,—

" Rin, Jockie man, and see fa's chappin'."

" Na fegs," was the quick and decisive answer. " Gar Bell gang. . . . It's Hallowe'en. . . . And maybe—"

Here the baby which the gaberlunzie held in his arms began to cry.

" Maybe it's fairies or witches," laughed Fred Clark.

At the sound of his voice the woman who had been resting against the wall suddenly started, and in a moment was at the window.

Just as she looked in Fred had taken Bell by the arm and was raising her up, saying,—

"Come along with me, Miss Bell. In an angel's company I don't much mind though I have to face old Clootie himself."

The poor woman saw and heard; and with a wild cry she fell to the ground. . . .

A few minutes later the weary wanderer was lying in an apartment at the extreme end of the house to which Marget, seeing the patient was evidently of respectable connection, had made the gaberlunzie carry his unconscious burden—access to the place being gained by a separate door. The baby had been warmed and fed and laid beside its mother, who in a deep sleep had now forgot all her weakness and heart-sorrows.

A return was now made to the kitchen and the rest of the company. Jockie, who had been hovering around "to see the ferlies," as he put it, led the way, followed by the gaberlunzie. As the urchin entered he turned towards the ben end of the house, where he knew his sister's castock, which had been pulled that evening, was concealed; and the old man naturally followed.

Bell, however, who was not far behind, seeing the unwelcome omen, darted after them, and taking the man by the arm turned him sharply the other way. Then pursuing her little brother, who had retreated into the room, she gave him a resounding slap on the cheek.—

"I'll learn ye to tak' a puir man intil the room, ye young widifu'!"

"Weel than," whined Jockie in an injured tone, "he hid nae bisness comin' aifter a body. I didna bid 'im."

"Come awa in by, auld man," cried the farmer from the ingle-neuk as the gaberlunzie made his appearance. "Ye're some caul' like."

The old man muttered his thanks and took the proferred seat.

"Guidwife," the farmer added as Marget entered, "ha'e ye onything in your pig? The puir man wid be a' the better o' a drap o' something."

"O nae doot," said Marget, "and there's maybe mair puir men needin' a drap. Fowk's files mair hame-drauchtit than they wid like till alloo."

John just grinned; while his wife, producing the vessel alluded to, began to pour out for the company.

The gaberlunzie took his glass with readiness.

"Ye'll tak' a drap, Sandy?" Marget went on. "Noo dinna be makin' ony demurs—fin ye like it, ye ken."

Sandy murmured a protest in the approved fashion.

"And you, Mr. Fred?"

"Of course. Never refuse anything good."

"Are ye for ony, gairdener?"

"No, thank ye, mistress," said Jamie, who was taking out a tune *pizzicato* on the fourth string of his fiddle.

"Weel, I winna press fowk. And ye're maybe jist as weel nae to meddle wi' the hard stuff till your beard's a bit langer than your teeth at onyrate. But gang ben, Bell, for some o' oor hame-brewn ale, and bring the kebbuck wi' ye. We'll be better o' a piece."

"Hey, mither, ye're nae sayin' naething to young Bogie," put in Jockie from a distant corner, who was beginning to recover his spirits after the overhaul he had got at the hands of his sister.

"Nane o' your impudence," cried his mother with ill-disguised admiration for her young hopeful's sprightliness. "Ye'll get a waucht o' something fin the kye's milket, and syne pack aff till your bed."

When all had refreshed themselves in a hearty way Jamie was asked to resume the fiddle.

"D'ye ken a tune ca'd 'The Ripells'?" said the farmer. "It was a famous ane in my young days."

"Ay; it's a fine specimen o' the auld Scots style."

"O d——n your Scotch rubbish!" exclaimed Fred Clark. "Give us something worth listening to—something from the operas."

Jamie coloured, but declined to notice the interruption.

"I'll try it; but there's only ae man can play that air richt."

"And fa micht that be?" asked the gaberlunzie, looking up with sudden interest.

"O jist my auld dominie, Maister Halket, that used to be at Rathen."

"Was that the old Jacobite devil that lampooned the King?" asked Fred. "It's a pity the Duke didn't catch the old rascal and string him up."

"O ay, maybe," interposed Sandy, "but he wisna sic an ill breet aifter a'—Geordie Halket. I kent him fine. He was born doon by at the Mull o' Crimon here, and him and me wis at the school thegither. He wis a clever chiel, Geordie; and aye his ain warst frien'."

Nobody noticed the fierce light that gleamed in the gaberlunzie's eyes as Fred Clark spoke, nor the way in which it died down into soft tenderness as Sandy interposed his kindly tribute.

But Jamie, having now retouched his strings, began the old air, then known as "The Ripells," but now for ever associated with the imperishable lay of "Logie o' Buchan."

The old man watched the performance with growing

interest; and by the time Jamie had got to the end of the second measure he was on his feet.

"Na, Jam—laddie," he burst out, "ye're nae bowin' the A's and the C's richt. Lat's see the fiddle."

And he took it with an air of authority that made Jamie defer to him at once.

With a vigorous stroke he drew the bow over the strings; altered the first a little; and then, ere the company had recovered from their astonishment, the place was resounding with the music, rich, full, and expressive— now swelling up with that inflected wail which only the violin can produce, now ringing forth in tones level and liquid as the note of a fine flute.

Jamie was spell-bound and remained silent, while the rest uttered their comments—all highly flattering except that of "the laird," whose opinion was conveyed in an impatient and somewhat irrelevant oath.

Jamie found his tongue at length.—

"That's grand! . . Maister Halket couldna ha'e deen't better himsel'. . . I could near hae sworn it wis him."

"It maybe *is* him," whispered Jockie to Fred, his mind full of all sorts of supernatural possibilities on a Hallowe'en night.

The remark seemed to strike his hearer. He looked keenly at the old fiddler, and a sudden flash as of recognition gleamed for one moment in his cruel eyes. Then, instantly assuming a careless look, he got up with an affectation of ennui, and strayed out with the air of a fellow who is above ceremony. The company in fact didn't know that he was gone till they heard him whistling his operatic airs as he walked down the road towards Crimonmogate.

Now that the gaberlunzie had shown his rare skill on the violin he was not allowed to lay it down in a hurry. He played many airs, slow and fast, rollicking and pathetic, to the growing delight of his auditors.

He was in the midst of a slow strathspey when he suddenly stopped.

"What's that?" he exclaimed, with a look of some alarm.

All listened, catching some of the gaberlunzie's alarm before they could detect its cause. But soon they heard a tramping sound.

"Some o' the beasts broken lowse," said the farmer. "Rin and see some o' ye."

But all sat still listening; and very soon a peculiar clanking sound as of bridle chains proclaimed that it was no chance unharnessed animal that had found its way into "the close"; and the alarm of an undefined apprehension began to show on all faces.

"It's the sodgers!" at length burst out Jockie in an awe-struck voice as he got behind his father's chair.

The next moment a loud rap at the door as if with the butt end of a riding-whip made everybody start, while a suppressed scream burst from Bell as she rose and ran to Jamie's side.

Before anyone could respond to the summons the door was unceremoniously pushed open.

"In the name of King George!" said an aggressive military voice; and Captain Campbell, booted and spurred, strode in sword in hand.

"Whom have you here?" he demanded of old John, who had risen from his arm chair in nervous haste.

John was not naturally glib of speech, and the

embarrassment of the situation made matters worse for him. He stood for a few moments helplessly regarding the captain, who repeated his question. Marget came to the rescue, as she often did.—

"Speak up, guidman. There's you there and me here.—Hing in."

John got a start.—

"There's me here and the guidwife there." Marget, who was looking from her husband to the captain, nodded assent.

"And yon's oor dother Bell," he added.

"Isobel as she was christened by the minister, Mr. Lundie, ye min'," Marget interjected.

"And syne there's Jockie yonder," the farmer went on.

His mother shook her head at Jockie to improve the occasion.

"Well?" said the captain impatiently.

"That's a' that's oors, sir," interposed Marget. "This is the young gairdener. He's wi' Captain Duff owre by at Logie here."

"O, that's all right," interrupted the captain; "but who is this old fellow here?" And he looked severely at the gaberlunzie.

"I'm Geordie Rogers, at your service, sir," said the old man rising and bowing to the captain.

"Indeed?" said the captain with a sardonic grin; "and where have you come from?"

Thereupon the gaberlunzie proceeded to give a voluble account of himself and his wanderings. It was evident that the captain did not believe much of it; but the old man was acquitting himself with such address that it seemed a pity to stop him. The captain hitched on to the table, and sat regarding the orator with an amused and even admiring smile.

At length the oration came to an end.

"And what have you got in that old wallet of yours?" asked the captain, touching the article in question with the point of his sword.

"O naething ava," said the old man, hastily; "jist a few odds and ends that a puir wanderin' body needs whase wants are sma'."

"Just turn them out, will you?"

"O I'm sure ye needna seek to see them. As I said there's naething worth lookin' at."

But the captain didn't answer. He simply looked and waited; and the gaberlunzie understood that the order was final. So he turned out the contents of his wallet on the floor.

Along with a quantity of miscellaneous and quite unsuspicious articles was a bundle of chap books and broadside ballads—such as used to be hawked in those days.

"What is that rolled up in paper?" asked the captain turning over the things with his sword.

"Only a—bit beukie."

"Hand it up."

This was done with some hesitation. When the paper was taken off it proved to be a small manuscript book; and the captain opened it.

"Poetry, begad; and original too," he said with a grin. "Whirry—Whigs—awa."

He went on reading, and his face took a severe expression. The company looked from him to his victim. The latter had the blanched look of one who is suddenly menaced by a grave danger. But as the captain continued reading the old man seemed to rally, and by the time he had to face further questioning he was wonderfully calm and collected.

"H'm! rank treason," said the captain at length, looking up and fixing a stern eye on the gaberlunzie.

"You made up this?"

"I wrote it."

"And who made it up, pray."

There was a pause.

"Who made it up?" thundered the captain, taking a step forward.

"It was a chiel they ca' Will Jack, wha has Corskelly boats in tack."

"No more of your rhyming nonsense here, sir! . . You are George Halket, once schoolmaster at Rathen, are you not?"

A sudden look of consternation appeared on the faces of the company, some of whom were betrayed into audible expression of their astonishment and dismay.

Quite calm, however, was the victim himself as with dignity he drew himself up and said,—

"Yes, I am George Halket, at your service."

The captain was somewhat taken aback by his bold bearing, which secretly he could not but admire.

"And you are the man that wrote 'A Dialogue between the Devil and George II'?"

"Well?"

"And you are aware that His Grace the Duke of Cumberland offered a reward of a hundred pounds for the author, dead or alive?"

"I understand he did so; but that was before Culloden."

"Yes; but we mean to see if the offer still holds good. . . . In any case you are a rebel; and I now arrest you in the name of the King. . . . George Halket, you are my prisoner. . . . Soldiers!"

At the word two troopers entered.

"Secure this man. He is my prisoner."

"All right, Captain," said Halket composedly as the men laid hold on him.

And here let us pause to give some short account of the man who had thus fallen into the hands of his enemies.—

Halket was a man of outstanding ability, being distinguished both as a poet and a musician. In character and disposition he was a strange compound, being at once astute and rash, generous and at the same time somewhat unscrupulous. He had proved so troublesome to the minister and kirk-session of Rathen, where he was schoolmaster and precentor, that they had been driven to take proceedings against him and have him removed from his offices. He had afterwards engaged in teaching at Cairnbulg. When the Rebellion of the Forty-Five broke out, Halket, who had been up in the Fifteen and was a keen Jacobite, became enthusiastic in support of Prince Charlie. Not that he cared so very much for the Divine Right of Kings, or was so deeply interested in seeing the Stuart succession restored, but the aggressive spirit of Jacobitism attracted him, and gave field for the exercise of his caustic wit and incisive pen. He attacked the house of Hanover in ballad and lampoon, and heaped unsparing abuse on the Whig party. His satire had culminated in the Dialogue to which Captain Campbell had referred. After the battle of Culloden had wrecked the fortunes of his party, he had found it necessary to get into concealment. For some time he had skulked about Inverallochy; and then, tired of this kind of life, he had set out on an extended tour, playing the role now of a gaberlunzie, now of a wandering minstrel; and after a few months of this Bohemian kind of life, he had been returning to his native Buchan, when, as we have just seen, he fell into the hands of his foes.

CHAPTER II.

HALLOWE'EN.

Continued.

WHILE all the company were deeply distressed at the turn events had taken, Jamie Robertson was in a kind of despair to see his old master in such imminent peril. There had been too many evidences of the blood-thirsty nature of the methods by which the Rebellion was being put down for any one to mistake the gravity of the situation for poor Halket. And Jamie, besides, had a good deal of sympathy with the cause for which his friend was suffering ; for, while too young to have any very pronounced political opinions—these coming with most people later in life,—he was sentimentally at least a good bit of a Jacobite himself.

"O sir," he said, approaching the captain and casting off the vernacular as he spoke, "it's a long time since, and he didn't mean much ill by it. He'll be a good subject now and obey King George.—Won't you Mr. Halket ? "

And he turned appealingly to the prisoner.

"It's very kind of you," began Halket, "but "—

"But it's no good," said the Captain impatiently. "He must go with us and stand his trial. . . I hope none of you," he added, turning to the farmer,—"I hope none of you knew that you were harbouring a rebel ; and that you are all good and true subjects of the King."

"O ay, we're a' that," said Bogie with unusual readiness.

"O, fairly that," assented Clyacks.

"Then, my good woman," said the Captain to Marget, "you might see if you have anything in which we could drink His Majesty's health—just to show our loyalty you know."

"Guidsakes," cried Marget, who had begun to recover from her fright, "it's whisky ye'll be wantin'? I dinna ken gin there's eneuch in the hoose the noo. And there's maybe an awfu' wheen o' ye at the door."

"O no, only a trooper holding our horses. And you needn't mind my men at all if your supplies are short."

"O, guidsakes, we'll seerly be able to gie them a' a drap in the bygaun.—Millbog's nae jist come to that wi't yet."

The jar was again produced.

Bogie led off.—

"Here's to the health of King George."

Clyacks followed suit.

When the glass was offered to Jamie he said quietly but firmly, "No, thank you."

"Come, come, sir!" said the Captain, sternly.

All looked alarmed; but Jamie was calm.

"I don't drink," he said.

"But you must now to prove your loyalty."

"What right have you to question my loyalty, or make me drink to anybody's health?"

"Dare you question my authority?" roared the Captain, raising his sword in a threatening way.

But Jamie merely folded his arms and stood erect, looking the other full in the face. The fellow was cowed.

"Well done, Jamie!" cried Halket.

"Silence, you miserable renegade!" shouted the

Captain, glad to have some one on whom to turn his baffled rage. "Come, sir, drink!" he added, as a glass was handed to Halket.

"Here's luck," said the latter, tossing off the liquor.

"That's not enough," roared the Captain, almos foaming in the fury of his passion.

"It's ower late noo. Ye sid hae spoken seener," said Halket, with the most provoking coolness.

"Another glass, woman," shouted the Captain, turning to Marget.

"Losh preserve's a'! Ye'll drink fowk oot o' hoose and haddin'."

"A half will do this time."

"O guidsakes, we're nae jist come to *that* yet. There's never been ony half measures in *this* hoose; and winna be as lang's *I'm* mistress."

And she filled the glass till it ran over.

"Now, sir, after me," said the captain.

"Weel," was the quiet reply.

"I drink to George the Second, King of the British nation," dictated the Captain.

"I drink to George the—fat did ye ca' him, Captain?" said Halket, waiting with glass in hand.

"The Second, King of the British nation."

"Ay, that's it—the second King of the British nation," said Halket, as he emptied his glass, and added *sotto voce*,—"And Charlie's the first."

"What did you say, you scoundrel?"

"Did I say onything mair than ye bade me?"

"Yes, you added something."

"Maybe I did. I'm an auld man noo, and fyles

speak to mysel' without kennin'.—But never min'; it's a richt, Captain."

Utterly baffled by his victim's imperturbability, the Captain was glad to end the farce with a peremptory order to the soldiers to bind him.

"Have you a rope, old man?" one of them asked the farmer.

"A rope!" burst in Marget. "O guidsakes, ye're nae to hang a man in a body's hoose? An' it Hallowe'en tee. His ghaist'll never leave the place.—Guidsakes!"

"Hold your tongue, you stupid woman," said the trooper.

A rope was produced. Halket submitted quietly while they tied his feet together. Then he got on the back of one of the soldiers, while the captain called to Jockie to bring the lamp to the door that they might see to mount.

As Jockie was taking down the cruisie from the ingle Jamie moved past him with his back to the soldiers.

"I say, Jockie."

"Weel?"

"Will ye dee fat I bid ye, and never lat on?"

"Imphm."

"Weel, when I cry 'wo' ye'll lat the lamp fa'."

But the Captain had darted a look at them which Jockie noted.

"Na, I winna lat it fa'. Ye think naebody can cairry a lamp but you," said Jockie in a complaining tone; and as Jamie turned and saw the Captain looking, he understood the youngster's remark, and, affecting to smile at it, followed the procession to the door.

Halket was to be mounted sideways on one of the

horses in front of the trooper. Jamie approached to assist in lifting him on, keeping his back to the light which Jockie was holding as high as his arms could reach. He secretly took a knife from his pocket, and, when the prisoner had been got into position, he managed to get its edge placed on the rope between his legs. Then, as the trooper was mounting himself, Jamie gave the horse a short sharp kick on the leg.

The horse started, and Jamie cried "Wo!"

The next moment the lamp fell ringing on the stones at the door, and everything was in darkness—all the more intense for the sudden quenching of the light. At the same moment the rope was severed; while, pushing Halket's legs apart to let him know he was free, Jamie pulled him from the back of the horse, and then flung his knife far off into the darkness.

The Captain shouted; the troopers swore; and there were many cries for another lamp.

Halket took in the situation in a moment, as he slid from the back of the horse and fell forward on his knees. He did not rise to his feet, but crawled quickly towards the wall of the house, and, keeping close thereto, he managed to get round the corner before the general hubbub had subsided.

Once round the corner, he rose to his feet and made for the cornyard. He slipped through among the ricks; but, judging it unsafe to attempt a flight right away over country which had nothing but low turf dykes to cover his retreat, he doubled round behind the steading and made for the mill.

And well was it for Halket that he didn't get right away, for Captain Campbell, realising that an ordinary cruisie was of little use now, bethought him of a way of getting a search-light that might prove adequate for the purpose in view. Ordering straw to be brought from the barn and peats from the hearth he soon had a fire started in the cornyard, which, in spite of the farmer's rueful protests, they proceeded to feed with sheaves from the dismantled ricks, till quite a big conflagration was raging.

"We must have a Hallowe'en bonfire too," said one of the soldiers, as the flames leaped aloft.

"Ay, and the best of the lot," added his comrade.

The country was lit up all around, and the Captain, sending his men to beat the immediate surroundings, stood looking in every direction for traces of the fugitive ; and, had Halket appeared in the open at this time, it is pretty certain he would have been descried and recaptured. But the illumination, the search, and the outlook were all in vain. Nothing could be seen.

Finding that his plan, of which he had at first been quite proud, was yielding no result, the Captain began again to storm and swear.

"You little devil!" he shouted to Jockie, "I'll behead you!" And he made as if to strike him ; but the youngster had disappeared in a twinkling. Then he turned on the adults and threatened all with gallows and faggot ; but everybody looked quite innocent, and the irate Captain felt perfectly helpless.

"He must have got into some of the outhouses," he said at length. "Hurry up and search them."

By this time the lamp had been re-lit, and John had to lead the way to the barn. It was thoroughly explored, the Captain driving his sword through and through the straw piled up in one end. Poor Halket would have fared badly had he been there concealed.

The byre was next searched, and afterwards some smaller houses. But they did not find their man, nor indeed any traces of him.

The Captain was in the worst possible humour; and now returning to the house he held a kind of informal court-martial, accusing some or all of the company of complicity in the prisoner's escape. But as all denied, and there was no evidence against any particular person, he had to give it up; which he did with a very bad grace.

" I shall find the devil yet," he said ; and then, turning to Jamie, he added with concentrated fierceness, "and you, sir—perhaps we shall meet again."

" Perhaps we shall," Jamie replied, meeting his opponent's gaze with a look of calm and dignified defiance.

Then the military party rode off, making their way back to Crimonmogate, where they had been putting up for a few days.

The reader has doubtless concluded, what was actually the case, that the information which had brought Captain Campbell and his men on the scene had been carried by Fred Clark. Pretty well convinced that the gaberlunzie must be George Halket, he had gone to Crimonmogate after leaving Millbog, and had communicated his suspicions to the Captain, expecting to share any reward that might accrue from the capture of the rebel, and at the same time pay off an old grudge that he himself cherished against the delinquent. The attempt as we have seen had miscarried ; and his chagrin on learning of the failure was even greater than that of the Captain and his men.

It was a great relief to the inmates of Millbog when the soldiers withdrew. Old John said little ; but he was much distressed that all this had happened in his house, and he, as he put it to Sandy, "an eiler i' the kirk"; while the destruction of his ricks was a keen grief to a man of his careful, not to say parsimonious nature.

The goodwife, repressed and overawed to some extent by the presence of the strong arm of military authority, had fretted and fumed in a more or less inarticulate way. Now when the restraint was withdrawn she burst forth, but, as any attempt to record what she said would fail to do justice to the volubility of her speech and its rare incisiveness, we must leave our readers to imagine the exhibition she made of her powers in this line.

After giving vent to her surcharged feelings in a storm of general invective, she became calm enough by-and-by to be able to address herself to the evening's duties. Then she seemed to discover that everything was in hopeless arrears, and fell out on Bell as if she were largely responsible for it.

Bell could at times "speak back" a little; but to-night she made no reply. Like the rest of the household she had been much put about by the untoward events of the evening ; but her mind was not inclined to dwell long on such things. It wandered away to other and more tender subjects, and soon she was in love's own sweet realm, weaving such phantasies as youth's bright spirit delights in.

She was thinking of Fred, and Jamie, and Sandy. The latter she could pretty easily dismiss from her dream. It was only parental hints and Sandy's own quiet attentions that brought the good-natured, well-to-do, elderly bachelor into view at all. Over the other two, however, she was strangely exercised—sweetly perplexed.

"The laird" was such a taking young fellow.—Women are always more or less taken with go and abandon in men, however much they may affect to discountenance such qualities. Fred knew this well. He had played the role of the go-ahead young man once or twice already with considerable success, until he began to have some confidence in his methods of attacking the female heart. By-and-by conquest for its own sake became the ruling ambition of his love-world. Now he had set himself to capture Bell's young affections; and it flattered his self-complacency to note that he was making an impression in that quarter.

Jamie, like all better and deeper natures, had too much self-respect and heart-reticence to try any arts of captivation, and thus laboured under a certain disadvantage when measured alongside an unscrupulous rival like Fred Clark. He had been at Logie for a year or two, and now at the age of twenty was finishing his apprenticeship. Bell and he had known each other very intimately all the time. Of late they had been more and more together, and their friendship appeared to be developing into something that would ere long merit a warmer name.

Somehow Bell felt that Jamie was more to her than the other young man who seemed to be aspiring to her affections. But then he had said or done very little that could be construed into any intimation or proof of special regard for her; while Fred, on the other hand, had quite clearly indicated his preference for her, and had gone out of his way to say many nice things. Again, Jamie was poor and had no prospects to speak of. Fred was a laird's son ; had seen the world ; and gave Bell to understand that he had a great future before him.

Poor Bell was in a very divided state of mind ; although the perplexity was by no means ungrateful, being of the sweet kind that comes from an *embarras de richesse.*

In the midst of her veering thoughts she remembered that it was Hallowe'en, and that there were several accredited spells by which she could that night resolve her doubts and settle the matter. Some of the simpler and more innocent ones, like pulling the castock, she had tried ; but, along with most other maidens, she longed to prove some of those intenser and darker ones which, demanding more nerve and daring, promised a response correspondingly more definite and final. It was a rather fearsome thing to think of trying any of these charms. There were stories of people getting great frights, every old grannie being able to quote instances that should scare any of the younger generation who might be thinking of invoking powers that were understood to be in some kind of alliance with the darker agencies of the universe.

There was one spell which seemed to Bell more manageable and less daunting than the rest—the winding of the clew in the kiln. She might try it when she went out to milk, and, if she could only get someone to accompany her, she thought she might be able to screw her courage up to the point.

Casting about for an ally, she very soon thought of

Jockie. Since the ear-boxing incident he had been " striven " with her. But she knew the way to his heart, and, having that night got a present of apples from Jamie, she did not anticipate much difficulty in conciliating Jockie and securing his services.

Decoying her little brother to the ben where she had secreted her present, she showed him the apples, and then began to unfold her scheme—at least as much of it as Jockie behoved to know to be able to render efficient assistance.

" Ye ken, Jockie," she said in a hesitating kind of way, " I wis thinkin' o' gaun to the mill to try something. It's Hallowe'en ye ken—an'—an'—jist for fun ye ken, I wis thinkin' o' tryin, something. Noo, Jockie, gin ye wid come wi' me—it's naething ava—I wid maybe gie ye some o' this."

Here she pointed to the apples, while Jockie's eyes sparkled and his teeth watered.

" I've jist to come wi' ye to the mill?"

" Ay, jist that—it's naething ava."

" An' foo mony aipples will ye gie me?"

" Foo mony wid ye like?"

" Wid ye gie me—sax?"

" Ay, I'll gie ye sax."

Bell assented so readily that Jockie wished he had asked seven. But he had a boy's sense of honour, and would stick to his bargain. But there was one point not yet settled.—

" And will ye lat me chise them mysel'?"

" Ay, will I."

" The noo?"

" Jist the noo.—But ye'll be sure to come, min', Jockie?"

"O, fairly that," said the urchin, who was already busily inspecting the store of fruit.

"And ye winna tell naebody, min', Jockie?"

"Naebody," answered he laconically.

Ere long he had his half dozen selected ; and the selection would have done all manner of credit to a professional fruiterer. Taking the biggest and best apple in his hand, and stowing away the rest about his person, he turned to his sister and said,—"Come on than."

But she explained to him that the thing was to be done when they went out to milking ; and Jockie undertook to hold himself in readiness.

"And min', Jockie, ye maun never tell naebody, min' ; never," said Bell with much impressiveness.

Jockie, whose mouth was now full of apple, nodded his head and then shook it, not being quite sure which kind of answer suited the case.

Just then was heard a voice,—"The kye'll be fair connicht the night ; I never saw the like a' my born days.—Bell, ye idle limmer, far are ye?"

Hastily whispering instructions to Jockie to follow after a little and wait her about the byre door, she slipped a small clew of worsted into her breast and hurried away to get her cog,—her mother being already on her way to the byre, addressing to the universe in general certain observations relative to the degeneracy of modern times and people.

Once settled down to her milking Bell began to think of the fearsomeness of what she proposed doing, and soon worked herself up into such a state that she resolved to abandon the project altogether. Again, however, the desire to know her fate returned. This was practically her only chance. Hallowe'en wouldn't return for a year ; and a year hence seems as good as never to a young ardent spirit.

She was now milking her last cow, and I am afraid in her excitement she didn't do the justice to the animal a good dairymaid should. She had finished before her mother, and, hurrying to the door, she found Jockie standing crunching his last apple. Instinctively she felt that she must hide her nervousness from him, lest he should take fright and fear to help in an enterprise that was scaring the principal.

" Come on, Jockie," she said ; and, feeling that her voice had a nervous ring about it, she added, as if to suggest an explanation thereof, " dinna lat oor mither hear's. She wid jist be scal'in'."

They went round to the mill together.

" Noo, Jockie, ye'll jist stan' at the door. Dinna shut it. Jist bide aboot it, and, gin I cry for ye, ye can come in. But min', dinna come in unless I tell ye. Min' that ; and dinna jist bide owre near the door, ye ken."

She wanted him near enough to give her courage and render assistance if necessary, but at the same time far enough away to prevent him overhearing anything.

Jockie began to feel somewhat eerie too, and after his sister had entered the mill he quietly got inside the door himself.

Bell now felt her heart beating wildly, and, thinking she heard something stir, she was on the point of retreating. But she would first try if an appeal to her companion would suffice to re-assure her.—

" Jockie," she whispered nervously, " are ye there ? "

Jockie slipped outside quietly and quickly, and then replied, " Ay, Bell, I'm here."

" Weel, weel," she said ; and, after listening a while and hearing no other sound, she proceeded to get her clew thrown into the kiln.   This accomplished, she began with nervous fingers to unwind it.   Quicker and quicker she wound, while her heart beat wildly—almost to suffocation.

She must be nearing the end of the clew.   Would anything happen ?—She couldn't stand the suspense. She must run away or drop.—The tension was terrible.

All at once she felt the thread was being held.   She nearly fainted ; her heart seemed to stand still ; and for a moment a wild thrill of almost delirious terror paralysed her.   With a desperate effort she rallied herself, and managed to say in a voice that sounded strange to herself,—

" Wha hauds ? "

" *Jamie Robertson*," said a voice from the kiln, deep, calm, and distinct.

.   .   .   .

Meantime the actual man whose name had been thus oracularly pronounced from the mysterious depths of the kiln-logie was standing alone and moody in the farm kitchen.   Clyacks had taken his leave when Bell and her mother went out to milk ; and old John had gone to give him a convoy and relieve his feelings somewhat by having a quiet talk in the cool evening air over the strange and distressing incidents of the last hour.

Jamie had also risen as if to take leave ; but he didn't like to go away without seeing Bell once more, and if possible getting from her some re-assuring word or look. So he remained in the kitchen after the others had gone out.

He was ill at ease. It wasn't so much the circumstances connected with the capture and subsequent escape of Halket that annoyed him. That episode, unfortunate and distressing at first, had ended in a way that called only for congratulations among the friends of the man in question, while Jamie himself could not but feel satisfied with his connection with the matter and pleased that he had been able to help so much in securing the escape from the hands of his enemies of an old teacher and friend.—It wasn't these things that annoyed him.

The disturbing thoughts had a different source. As so often happens with a young man, they had for their source and point of return—a woman. He had begun to realise for the first time how much Bell was to him He had known and liked her all along. The liking had grown with their growth. With special interest had he noted of late how she was developing in womanhood. But, young himself, he was mainly unconscious of the meaning and drift of his feelings. When we are young we feel much and reason little; as we get older we are glad to eke out our failing feelings with reasoning about them,—a sorry enough substitute in all conscience.

Jamie, we say, had never before admitted to himself that Bell filled so large a place in his heart and life; but to-night the truth was forced home on him; and in an unwelcome way. It was the attentions of a rival and the reception accorded to them that led to the awakening. Fred Clark was interesting to Bell; and Jamie didn't like it. His heart offered to tell him the reason; but he didn't just like to admit the impeachment in its full force. He wouldn't quite allow he wanted Bell himself. He tried to feel that a good deal of his dissatisfaction and ill-humour over the business was due to his conviction that Fred Clark was rather a shady character and not a fit and proper lover for Bell.—We all like to feel as virtuous and disinterested as possible.

Nursing such thoughts he was standing in the kitchen with his back to the wall and his eyes moodily fixed on the floor, when all of a sudden in rushed Bell, pale and breathless as if pursued by someone. He was startled and looked up in surprise—a surprise that only deepened when he caught sight of her face, for it exhibited such a strange blending of terror and joy that he was utterly at a loss what to think.

At sight of him a sudden development, almost amounting to a transformation, took place in her look. The happy element in it became a gleam as of love revealed and confessed, and the look of terror was chased from her eyes.

All this took place in a few moments. Jamie noted it all; but before he had time to say or do anything Bell had come quite up to him, and now with a low glad murmur she flung herself on his breast.

Jamie was completely taken by surprise. One moment before he had been feeling dissatisfied, almost angry, with everything. Bell seemed to be drifting away from him; and he was waiting to see if perchance he might secure one single word or glance that might suffice to keep hope alive in his breast. Now all was changed. He had got all he wanted, and greatly more. There had come suddenly and unexpectedly something far beyond his wildest dream. Bell, instead of merely looking kind and interested, had confessed her love,—had, in fact, revealed the uncontrollable passion of a conquered heart.

Jamie's surprise, indeed, was so utter and bewildering that there is no saying what its effect on him would have been, had not a sensation of delight supervened and challenged the supremacy of the other feeling. And a moment's experience of the situation made him ready to put wonder and speculation quite aside for the present— to leave, in fact, every kind of thought and reflection in abeyance, and surrender himself heart and soul to the pure ecstasy of the occasion.

A man likes to do the courting himself; but, just because this is the rule, an occasional departure from the established order of procedure is particularly stimulating and delightful. When a girl naturally modest and self-respecting so forgets herself as to act as Bell was now doing, the exceptional conduct lends a rare zest and rapture to the business; and the girl who on occasion thus forgets herself and the etiquette of courtship and takes the initiative in some demonstration and revelation of feeling may, by her action, give a fillip to matters that any amount of mere passive acquiescence in endearments would fail to achieve.

"Jamie," she murmured as she looked up in his face. In a whirl of fervid passion he kissed her warm panting lips. That acme of delicious experience brought a sudden re-action. Carried away by the intense and complex rush of feelings that her adventure had produced she had forgot herself, proprieties and all. But now the situation came home to her in all its force and meaning.

Here was she throwing herself into the arms of a young man who had never as yet avowed any decided love for her,—without warning or encouragement of any kind, in fact.

The dreadfulness of it all was instantly revealed. Disengaging herself in a moment, she ran out of the house almost as hastily as she had entered.

Between the house and the byre she met her mother and Jockie.

"Far hae ye been in a' the warld?—Jockie and me's been lookin' for ye."

Bell was relieved to see that Jockie hadn't given her away. This was the chief point. For the rest she managed to say something. No woman ever fails to do that.

Jamie had a minute to compose himself ere they re-entered the house. Bell followed her mother quite demurely, never once looking at him; and he felt more puzzled than ever over her strange conduct.

But now, explaining that he had been waiting their return only to say good-night, he took his departure. Bell merely returned his "guid-nicht" without looking up from the knitting to which she had now addressed herself. On former occasions she used to accompany him to the door.

Jamie was more and more at a loss how to explain it all. But that glorious if short-lived episode of a moment ago, nothing could ever blot *it* from heart and mind.

And it was the turning point in both their lives.

CHAPTER III

IN THE GARDEN.

NEXT morning Jamie rose to his work bright and early. The dawn had just begun to show faintly on the sea-line beyond Rattray when, having breakfasted heartily on good oatmeal brose which he had made with his own hands, partly through the necessities of the case and partly because he could get no other body to do it so well, he made for the garden.

The weather was still dull and lifeless, exhibiting the stagnation that so often obtains on the meteorological borderland between autumn and winter. Although there had been no rain for some time everything was wet and dripping. The dead leaves were dropping quietly to the ground, no breath of air deflecting their gentle fall. The burn of Logie was gurgling softly as it flowed past the garden and down the hollow by willow and alder to join the Ailie in its course to the eastern sea, from which came a dull continuous boom through the misty morning air.

A robin was sitting on a hawthorn near the gate as Jamie entered the garden—the last of the choir that used to wake the summer morning with bursts of jubilant song. Its thin hesitant twitter contrasted sadly enough with the glorious roulades that used to gush from the ecstatic throats of mavis and blackbird in those golden dawns.

Everything was sufficiently dull and depressing. But

Jamie's heart was light and his spirit gay. The robin's low warble, the gurgle of the burn, and the boom of the distant sea,—all were tuned to love in his happy ear. Cheerily he whistled up "The Gardener's March," the bright tune to which Burns a generation later wrote the song, "The gardener wi' his paidle"; and proceeded to his work.

Compared with the modern developments of the art gardening was then in a rather primitive condition. The first horticulturists had been the monks, and they seem to have carried the art to a considerable pitch of perfection, especially as regards the growing of fruits and culinary herbs, feeling that those who wanted to live a good life should see to live well. Since the Reformation gardening, like many other things, would appear to have gone backward. At best only the old methods were followed and the old kinds of plants grown, except about Edinburgh and the south of Scotland, where already some beginning had been made with newer and more advanced modes of floriculture. The Botanic Garden of Edinburgh was started about 1680, and in the early part of the succeeding century a gentleman, who had studied Continental methods, had a fine garden at Crichton, near Edinburgh, where the first pine-stove in Scotland appears to have been set up. As to the gardening of landscape and design, modern ideas and plans seem to have been introduced into Scotland about 1770 by the celebrated Lord Kames, who by his Essay on Gardening and Architecture, and by the illustration he gave of the application of the principles therein enunciated at his own residence, communicated the first impetus to this branch and aspect of the subject.

Aboriculture was in a still less developed state. Fruit trees, as we have said, had been all along cultivated since in the orchards of the early abbeys their sweet usefulness had been first demonstrated. But planting for timber is a thing of comparatively recent date in our country. The old forests of Caledonia had pretty much disappeared by the time of which we write. The wilder and more indigenous species of trees were still to be found, having mostly looked after themselves in the matter of propagation and growth. Such trees as the rowan, the saugh, the bourtree, the birk, and the hawthorn, are ever to be met with in old Scotch song and tradition ; but the more useful kinds of timber were hardly planted in Scotland before the beginning of the eighteenth century. The Earl of Haddington is generally considered the father of planting in our country, and he began the famous Binning Wood about 1705. Sir Archibald Grant began to plant in 1719. Dr Johnson, as everybody in Buchan knows, says, referring to his peregrinations in the north, that only at Strichen had he seen trees older than himself: and the doctor was born in 1709.

Logie was hardly a place where advanced ideas would be likely to show themselves in a hurry ; but gardening, according to the old school, made quite a fair show at the place, and Jamie was becoming a very competent exponent of the art, having that fundamental ability which enables a man to do well anything he may put his hand to.

At this season of the year Jamie had a good deal of digging to do, and was trying to make progress with it while the dull weather kept the ground soft and workable. His master had gone that day to Peterhead on some business; but Jamie was not tempted to indulge in mere eye-service, and he at once proceeded with all briskness to the corner of the garden where his work was for the time being to be prosecuted.

He had not long begun when a rustling was heard among some bushes on the left, and out stepped Halket.

"Good-mornin', Jamie," he said with the quiet restrained voice of one who is habitually on his guard.

Jamie looked surprised and delighted; but, before replying to the salutation, he glanced nervously round to make sure that nobody was within sight or hearing.

"O, good-mornin', Mr Halket," he said at length. "I'm richt gled to see you again safe and soun'.—Far hae ye been sin' last nicht?"

"O, I was aboot the hooses," he said in an easy tone. "But, man, Jamie," he went on with warmth, "I'll no forget it to ye." And he took the lad's hand.

"Say naething aboot it, Mr Halket," protested Jamie looking on the ground. "Ye did a hantle mair for me."

"I only wish I could hae deen mair for ye, lad. Ye were aye an apt pupil, and micht hae gane to the College and made a name for yersel' amon' learned men."

"Maybe, maybe," said Jamie with a bit of a sigh; "but my chance is past noo, and I'll jist hae to mak' up my mind to earn my breid wi' the sweat o' my broo.—But I'm thankfu' for the lear I got, Mr. Halket. It's been a great help and comfort to me. Ye gied me some insicht intil Laitin, and I hinna forgotten 't. I tak' oot my beuks mony a forenicht in my chaumer, and gang ower the bits ye pat's through at Rathen; and files I try some new bitties."

"That's richt, Jamie, man. I'm gled to hear ye keep

up your learnin'. Ye'll maybe fin' an eese for't some day ; and whether or no, it cultivates your mind, and that's the highest end that ony kind o' learnin' can serve."

" Syne I've my fiddle, and I'll maybe get the pipes tried again by-and-by. But sin' Culloden they've been awfu' doon on a'thing Hielan'."

" Ay, stick intil the fiddle, Jamie, man. It's a grand instrument, and ye're gaun to mak' a capital player."

Jamie blushed at the encouraging compliment. Compliments, while always more or less acceptable, take their main value and significance from their source; and Jamie appreciated Halket's good opinion because it represented the judgment of an expert, and all the more that on the previous night he had felt rather humbled over the fiddle-playing incident, construing Halket's action into a kind of reflection on his own powers.

And now they got on to the subject of national music and poetry. Halket had sought Jamie out that morning for practical purposes, and to make certain arrangements with him ; but all this passed from his mind. They were both enthusiasts, and had little difficulty in forgetting the work-a-day world and its concerns, although Jamie mechanically continued his digging. And, as became the subject they were discussing, they spoke mostly in good broad Scotch. In those days the vernacular was freely used by the educated classes in Scotland—ministers and even judges falling back on it whenever they wanted to compass a pithy remark or get into close touch with their hearers. Now-a-days such a thing is less common ; but there are some yet who allow themselves considerable liberty in this way. And, just as the wealthy man may most safely upon occasion wear a shabby coat, so the learned man may most freely without compromising his intellectual prestige use wide liberties in the choice of vocable and idiom. There may be at times through this a certain surrender of dignity; but there is on the other hand a gain in the range and elasticity of expression.

Halket began to tell his young friend of the musicians and poets he had met in his late wanderings. Speaking of fiddle-playing, he said :—

" Man, there's a young fellow ca'd Neil Gow gaun to beat a' the fiddlers in braid Scotland."

" Nae, Halket ? "

" Ay, Halket ; and Jamie Robertson tee."

Jamie laughed delightedly.

" Noo, Mr. Halket, dinna be makin' a feel o' a body."

" He's only saxteen," Halket went on, " and there was a competition at Dunkeld a few months ago, and young Neil licket them a' to sticks."

" Fiddlesticks ! "

And both men took a good quiet laugh.

The transition to Scottish poetry and song was natural and easy. Speaking of the prospects and out-look of native minstrelsy and its coming men, Halket said :—

" And there's ane o' the pedagogic brotherhood, a dominie ca'd Sandy Ross. He lives at Lochlee—the maist oot-o'-the wye romantic placie ye ever saw, i' the hairt o' the Grampians. He's a clever chiel, Sandy, and has a lot o' the nat'ral spunk and fire in 'im. Some o' 's sangs are fine, and he's workin' the noo at a pastoral poem."

" Is't ony like the ' Gentle Shepherd ? ' " Jamie asked.

"In some wyes, maybe. He read some bitties to me that nicht I spent wi' 'im. But in the first place his work will be in story form, while Ramsay's is a drama; and in the neist place—weel, Ross is nae sae guid as Ramsay."

"I could believe that," said Jamie. "The 'Gentle Shepherd' is jist perfect, I think."

"Yes," exclaimed the other with enthusiasm, "pastoral poetry has there said its hinmost word."

"Isn't it a pity," said Jamie reflectively, "that there's sae little feelin' for this kind o' thing in the north? There's oor ain Buchan country—hoo few bards we can muster! —What micht the reason be, d'ye think?"

"I dinna weel ken, unless it be that we are a kin' o' isolated up-by here. The Grampians seem to brak' the great tidal wave o' inspiration that the community o' bards and bardic sentiment has produced in the south. Syne, like a sma' inland sea, we hinna space eneuch to raise a wave o' oor ain o' ony consequence."

"I see," said Jamie. "I never lookit at it in that wye." And he paused to muse. But Halket went on.—

"A' the same we're nae jist destitute a' thegither. We hae oor poets, although they're maybe few; and, though they dinna maybe compare wi' some o' the great singers besouth the Grampians, they hae a note o' their ain."

"Ye think that?"

"Ay; and I ken a man that has't in him to tak' awa' a good bit o' oor reproach. That's Mr. Skinner, chapel minister at Linshart, owre by in Langside."

"Wis't his chapel that the sodgers burnt doon in the simmer time?"

"Ay; the Whig rascals!"

Halket looked fierce, but soon added with a grin,—

"But lat the scoondrels pass meantime. There'll maybe be bigger fires than that yet."

"He's a very learned man, isna he?"

"Very. He can write Latin verse amaist as weel's Buchanan or Johnston o' Caskieben. But I wish he would lat hexameters alane and tak' till guid braid Scots. Nae man can dee himsel' full justice except in his ain mither tongue. And when Skinner does that he'll write sangs that will live."

"And what aboot yersel', Mr Halket?"

"I dinna ken, Jamie. I've files thocht I micht dee something in this line mysel'. It has aye been my ambition to find a place, however humble, amo' the sons o' Scottish sang :—

> 'All hail oor native minstrel thrang !
> Unmeet am I to join your gang ;
> But toil and trouble sair and lang
> I'll never grudge it,
> Could I but add ae little sang
> To Scotia's budget.'"

"And ye'll dee't, Mr. Halket ; ye'll dee't !" exclaimed Jamie with confident enthusiasm ringing in his voice and beaming in his eye.

The garden gate was now heard to open, and both men, realising that they had begun to speak pretty loud, looked round with nervous alarm. Although the entrance to the garden could not be seen from where they stood, they could hear a light step coming along the walk, and Halket, whispering hastily, "I'll see ye again," disappeared in the direction whence he had originally emerged.

Jamie had quietly resumed his work when a fine bright voice was heard :—

"Good morning, James."

"Good morning, ma'am," said Jamie looking up and touching his bonnet.

Miss Innes, Captain Duff's niece, stood on the walk near him.

"Now, Jamie," she said with a low musical laugh, while the least trace of a blush appeared on her beautiful face, "you musn't call me ma'am. I'm not your mistress, you know, but only——your friend."

"Your pardon, Miss Innes," said Jamie with a chivalrous grace and blushing in turn, "I shall remember not to offend again."

"Well, see you don't. . . . And now I've come to see if I can get any flowers for the house this morning. . . . I fancy they are always getting scarcer."

"Yes they are ; but we should be able to find a few blooms yet."

And, sticking his spade among the soft new-dug earth, he prepared to lead the way to a part of the garden where some of the later flowers were making a wonderfully fair show—the mildness of the season materially contributing to this desirable state of matters.

As he plucked and arranged these, Miss Innes, after some references to the flowers, said :—

"Jamie, I understand you are fond of music."

"Well—yes."

"And you play on the violin?"

"It is the fiddle in our hands."

"Now don't angle for compliments, pray. . . . Do you play from the notes?"

"Yes—in a way."

"Have you ever heard the harpsichord?"

"No—I—can hardly say I have."

"I play it myself, and have got my instrument brought from Edinburgh. I don't think I could live long without it."

Jamie *had* heard the harpsichord. On several evenings of late he had posted himself under the parlour window of the mansion of Logie and listened to Miss Innes' playing, charmed beyond expression with the sweet ripple of notes in which had come to him the first clear suggestion and revelation of *harmony*, hardly to be compassed in a purely solo instrument like the violin. The music played was mostly strange to his ear, yet many beauties had therefrom dawned on him ; and when something familiar was rendered, deriving new meaning from the genius of the instrument and from its appropriate arrangement, his delight was intense.

"Do you know," continued his fair companion, "that the violin and the harpsichord can be played well together?"

"Indeed?" said Jamie.

There was silence for a little. She bent to pick up a flower which he had dropped, and went on ; but in a hesitating way—

"My uncle was thinking of having a gathering of the tenantry some evening about Yule."

(It was Miss Innes herself that had proposed this.)

" . . . And we were thinking that a little music would be a nice thing, just to entertain them a bit, you know."

(Her uncle had declared he didn't see the use

of this, but had yielded to his niece's opinion on the point.)

" . . Now if we could practise some pieces of music together—you and I—we could make the evening very nice and enjoyable for everybody, don't you think?"

(Of which proposal her uncle had not yet been told, his niece trusting to be able to talk him over when the time came for broaching the subject.)

Jamie, who heard only the remarks of his fair, sweet companion, and didn't share the information parenthetically vouchsafed to the reader, felt a strange sensation as of a new and embarrassing delight. He didn't well know what to say, and hesitated a moment.

The lady felt a little hurt and disconcerted that she had compromised herself so far, and added hastily—

"But if you don't care about it, never mind. It's of no consequence. It only came into my—our—"

"O! certainly, Miss Innes," Jamie burst in, "I should be more than delighted if—if you think it's right—and I could be of any use at all."

"Of course you could. Thank you, Jamie."

"And when might I come?"

"O, say—to-morrow night—about seven."

But now the bouquet was arranged.

"I am sorry the flowers are not better, Miss Innes," said Jamie, as with a graceful gesture he handed her the result of his labours.

"Thank you," she said, smiling sweetly. "If they are not so very beautiful in themselves the arrangement is."

"Thank you, Miss Innes," he said, bowing and blushing as he met her eye.

There was in Jamie's nature a high chivalrous element, which by a clear instinct threw off all clownishness, and responded to the appeal that grace and beauty in the person and presence of a fine woman made to it. And once again he felt the incongruity between his actual lot and the ideal plane to which under the spell and inspiration of the situation he had for the moment risen.

But now, with a sweet "good morning," Miss Innes had turned away, and was tripping lightly towards the house. Jamie watched her tall graceful figure till it disappeared, and then with a strange thrill turned to his work again.

"Ay, Jamie," said Halket, re-appearing, "and who may the fair lady be?"

Jamie explained that she was Miss Innes, niece of Captain Duff, who had come from Edinburgh to stay a while with her uncle at Logie.

"She's a fine lady," Halket opined.

"Yes," assented his companion, "and very frank."

"Captivating, I should say," added Halket, looking at the other. "Just you take care o' your heart, Jamie man."

"What do you mean, Mr. Halket?" exclaimed Jamie, looking up in surprise, although an involuntary blush showed that he understood the warning a little at least.

"O, nae muckle. But I hinna ca'd aboot the warld for naething, and I'm sair mista'en if yon fine damsel's nae mair interested in you than she ocht to be."

"O, buff and nonsense, Mr. Halket!—Me?—Forgie ye, man!"

"Weel, weel."

There was a pause. Jamie dug away, his companion looking at him with a quiet smile.

"Yon's a fine lass o' Millbog's," said Halket at length.

Another pause. Jamie dug hard.

"Ye mean—Bell?"

"Ay."

"Imphm."

"She's growin' a bonnie lass."

"Rale."

Another pause. Jamie dug harder.

"Ony word o' a lad for her?" pursued Halket.

"Hinna heard."

"Wid Clyacks be aifter her?"

"Couldna say."

"She widna care for yon scoot o' a chiel, Clark, d'ye think?"

James's face grew red, and there was fire in his eye; but he didn't answer.

"Come noo, Jamie: ye're aifter her yersel'—I saw't fine last nicht."

"O—I dinna ken."

"Ye ken fine."

"The auld folk widna look at the like o' me."

"O, hoo's that?"

"Weel, ye see they've siller; and Bogie and the wife's baith gey bigsy kin'."

"Toots; ye're as guid's them ony day, and a hantle better in mony wyes."

"Na, na, Mr. Halket; I'm but a poor lad."

"Ay, maybe meantime; but ye're jist beginnin' life. Hing ye in, Jamie, lad, and wi' your parts and perseverance I'm cheated gin ye dinna get as far

4

up by-and-by as ye can afford to look doon on *them*."

"Thank ye, Mr. Halket, for your good heartnin'. But I sair doot I'll never justify your kind opinion and prediction. I div think at times I could dee something in the warld, if I only got the chance."

"Mak' the chance."

"Ay, but puirtith's a teuch thing to fecht wi'."

"Nae doot, nae doot; but keep ye up your hairt; aim heich; and there's nae fear o' ye. Ye'll by-and-by get baith siller and place, and syne Bell's folk winna be jist sae ill to speak till."

"Weel, weel: we'll see."

"And, speakin' o' Millbog," Halket went on, "I had a favour to ask o' ye, Jamie; but wi' oor collieshangie and aething or ither I near forgot a' aboot it."

"Weel?" said Jamie, glad to be able to look up now that delicate and embarrassing subjects had been disposed of.

"In the first place, if yon chiel o' a captain has left my wallet and what was in't, ye micht bring't to me."

"An' far will I see ye?"

"O, I'll come back the nicht, say to this very spot, aboot aucht o'clock—would that dee?—Seven micht be better for an assignation wi' a lady; but—"

"O, that's a'richt," Jamie interupted with a smile and a blush.

"Syne there's the puir lass and her bairn that I brocht in aboot to the toon; I would like to ken hoo they're gettin' on. Puir thing, she fairly broke doon. I dinna richt understand what took her; but I maun be at the bottom o't if I can ava. You folk didna see very muckle, and I got things attended till rale quaet, nae wantin' to mak' owre great a stew aboot a place. But I'm interested in the lass and her history, and dinna want to lose sicht o' her and her wean."

"And fat dee ye want me to dee?" asked Jamie.

"Weel, I would like ye when ye're at Millbog the nicht seein' aboot my wallet to speir aifter the lass—hoo she's keepin' and what she's aifter deein'. And, Jamie, if ae thing or ither should keep me frae cairryin' oot my plans and deein' a' for her that I would like to dee, maybe I can lippen to you to help me?"

"Ye may that, Mr. Halket," said Jamie warmly. "Onything ye wid like me to dee—jist say the word, and I'm at your han'."

Jamie was very sincere in his offer to assist his friend, but it is doing him no wrong to hint that the chance the mission offered him of paying an early visit to Millbog did not detract from his enthusiasm.

It was arranged between them that Halket should meantime take shelter in a small house in the garden where tools and suchlike things were kept, and at dusk come to Jamie's "chaumer," where he could with more comfort secrete himself till Jamie should return from Millbog.

Jamie hardly knew what kind of reception to expect from Bell. He was, as he put it to himself, "in a swither." But he was to get another surprise. Bell was pretty much what she used to be. Since last night she had managed "to come till hersel'"; and now her attitude to Jamie represented a kind of mean between her best and worst behaviour on that memorable occasion.

Apprehensive to begin with, Jamie was relieved to find that matters were not so bad as he had expected to find them ; but very soon his wishes went beyond this negative kind of position. He could not now feel satisfied to have things *in statu quo*. So he set himself—in the diffident way that marks the young man—to make love to Bell ; and she, feeling that her self-respect was now sufficiently safeguarded, began to respond to a certain extent, and to exhibit unmistakable signs of interest, if not of actual warmth.

This little sentimental drama ran as an undercurrent through the more prosaic business that formed Jamie's proper errand ; but, as he managed to discharge his commission satisfactorily, we needn't grudge him the concomitant pleasure that the romance brought him.

The wallet was all right. Marget had put the things back in it, and laid it carefully aside.

Jamie's inquiries relative to the woman and child whom Halket had brought to Millbog on the previous evening elicited a little narrative, of which the following is the substance :—

The woman had got up in the morning. She was still in evident distress, but a firm resolve seemed to nerve her—spirit triumphing over bodily weakness and mental suffering. Marget, now interested in her charge, had tried to gain her confidence, but the woman was less communicative than she had been to Halket. She only said she had friends in Buchan whom she must find.

She rather attached herself to Bell, and in her company seemed to attain some brightness of spirit, although a keen observer might have seen that it wasn't very real at all. Referring to the incidents of the previous night, she hoped she hadn't disturbed the company. This led her on to speak of the young men she understood were then present, and to rally Bell on love matters, asking which of the fellows was her sweetheart. She encouraged her particularly to speak of Fred, asking all about him and his people, and—though more diffidently—trying to get at Bell's opinion of him personally, and her feelings towards him.

These things had occupied the forenoon. After dinner she suddenly declared she was going away at once. Marget and her daughter protested, not thinking her able for a journey ; but the woman was firm. All they could do was to induce her to leave the baby, to which they had already taken quite a fancy. She could return for the dear little creature when she had found her friends. And so she had gone, they did not know where.

CHAPTER IV.

RIVALS.

WHEN Jamie returned to his chaumer somewhat behind the time appointed, Halket, who had been waiting with an impatience that was in the circumstances not altogether unnatural, couldn't refrain from giving his young associate "a rub in the bygaun."—

"Weel, Jamie, ye're nae jist up to time; but we a' ken it's nae easy pairtin' wi' a bonnie lassie."

At which Jamie blushed, and hastened to report diligence.

The wallet was handed over to its owner, who, looking through the contents, was relieved to find his MS. book there and safe. He would have felt its loss very much, as all his recent effusions were written in it.

Having satisfied himself on this point, he seated himself on one end of Jamie's kist, and, motioning Jamie to take the other, said,—

"Noo, Jamie man, what aboot the lass and her bairn?"

Jamie retailed what he had learned at Millbog. Halket listened very closely, now and then interjecting a remark or a question. When the recital was over he sat silent for some time. He was thinking out the situation. His young companion, who still retained a certain deference towards his old master, waited until he should please to express an opinion on what he had heard.

At length Halket spoke.—

"Ay, ay. . . . There's something queer about that."

Which observation, being addressed reflectively by the speaker to himself, hardly called for an answer; and so Jamie remained silent.

At length Halket, sitting close up to Jamie, laid his hand on his knee.

"I say, Jamie."

"Weel?"

"D'ye ken what I'm thinkin'?"

"No."

"Weel, I hae an idea that—Clark—Fred Clark—that *he's* in this business."

Jamie, who hadn't reached the point that his companion had in his train of reflection, couldn't apprehend what Halket was driving at.

"I dinna understand ye richt, Mr. Halket," he said.

"Weel, jist listen; and I'll put the whole case afore ye as I ken't, and as it appears to me noo that I've thocht the maitter oot."

Here he gave a resumé of the woman's story as far as he now knew it; and then went on.—

"Noo, wisna Clark in the sooth last year?"

"Ay, and for a while afore that."

"Ken ye what he was deein'?"

"He says he was in the army; and he cam' north wi' 't. Then he blaws aboot bein' at Culloden and deein' great things there, although some folk say he was never near the battle ava."

Here Jamie stopped; and then after a little reflection continued.—

"But ye see he was on the King's—on the Government's side, that's to say; and your woman maks oot that her man was ane o' Prince Charlie's folk."

"Ay; but was Clark aye on George's side? Michtna he hae turned his coat when he saw that the Prince's cause was like to lose?—Hae ye thocht on that?"

Jamie admitted he hadn't; but the suggestion seemed far from unwelcome to him.

"He's the very man to dee't," he added emphatically by way of comment, inly glad to think that his own bad opinion of Fred Clark was corroborated by the hypothesis.

"Noo," continued Halket, warming to his task like some counsel addressing a jury, "he micht hae marriet this lass when in the sooth aboot Edinburgh. She's an attractive person, and her folk had been weel-to-dee. Syne we'll say he deserted her. Maybe nae jist intentionally at first. I'm nae sayin' that. Naebody comes to a hicht wi' their ill pranks a' at ance. But ance awa' and turned coat he couldna weel gae back, and of coorse his wife's folk he would expect would be a' ruined aifter Culloden; and he would only compromise himsel' by ownin' ony connection wi' them.—D'ye see?"

"The villain!" exclaimed Jamie, involuntarily setting his teeth and clenching his fist.

"Ay but, Jamie man," said the other, "we hinna a' thegither established his guilt yet. Things dinna look weel for him nae doot; but we maun wait till it's a' proved afore we pass judgment on him."

"Ye're richt, sir," said Jamie in a quieter tone. "I'm some hasty. I can see that.—But what wid ye propose to dee noo?"

"Weel, I'll jist hae to try to follow up the trail. It's

a pity she set oot without me seein' her. But we canna' mak' a better o't noo; and I'll jist hae to dee the best I can. She'll be awa' in the direction o' Rathen; and, if Fred Clark be her husband, she should hae little difficulty in findin' him."

"Unless he gaed under some wrang name in the sooth."

"Man, Jamie, I never thocht on that! Could he hae been sae far seen in his villainy as to dee the like o' that? Fegs, there's nae sayin'. He was aye a scamp. At the school he was aboot the warst loon that ever cam' through my hands. I've seen royt nickums often turn oot rale guid men; but their mischief was mair the oot-come o' animal speerits than ill-design. Fred Clark, ye wid hae thocht, did ill for ill's sake. I could mak' naething o' him; and in the hinner-en' had jist to expel him."

"And I suppose he never forgied ye for that?"

"Na; natures like his dinna forgie; and I'm jaloosin' he had some hand in last nicht's wark. There was naebody but him could hae looten Captain Campbell ken I was at Millbog.—Weel, weel, Freddie man; they gang far aboot that never meet; and we'll maybe hae a chance o' reddin' up that bit maitter wi' ye some day."

With the apostrophe Halket's face had darkened; but he wasn't the man to dwell long on subjects that prompted only thoughts of resentment and revenge. Very soon his mind reverted to the more practical aspects of the matter they were discussing.

"But I'll follow up," he went on. "I winna hae the freedom I would like noo that the sodgers hae scented me. Only I think that'll blaw by. The Government are tirin' o' the job, and Parliament will hae to pass an act o' indemnity afore lang. But, meantime, I'll hae to ca' canny."

"I hope ye're aye coontin' on my help," said Jamie.

"That's jist what I was comin' till. I'll lippen to you, Jamie, to dee a' ye can in this maitter. Ye'll aye ken what's gaun on at Millbog. Wi' her bairn there she's a kin o' anchored to the place, and will be sure to come back some time or ither. Syne I can come back mysel' if need be ; and we can lay oor heids thegither to see aye what's best to dee.—We only want to help the innocent and sufferin' and see justice deen.—Isn't that it, Jamie ? "

"That's sae, Mr. Halket."

And the two men joined hands over the project.

Early next morning they parted, Halket setting out on his way towards Rathen, and Jamie preparing for another day's work in the garden.

Jamie had nobody to talk to him that day, but his own thoughts were enough to keep him from " thinkin' lang."

At first he thought of Bell ; and his musings on that theme had a note of sweeter satisfaction and higher hopefulness than they had ever attained before.

By-and-by he remembered that this was the evening on which he was to visit Miss Innes and practise music with her. The prospect excited him, and soon sent him into day-dreams. Fair were the visions he wove. He was living in a grand house, had plenty of money, and was doing all manner of great and glorious deeds. And Miss Innes——. But he woke up from his dreaming ; and, blushing to think what his mind had been running on, he applied himself with renewed vigour to his spade, and resolved that he would dream no more.

As a kind of antidote he began to turn over in his mind the matters that Halket and he had been discussing, and to think out the problem of Fred Clark's connection with the business. And for a while he managed to keep his wayward fancy in check; but, as afternoon worn on and the evening approached, he found himself, in spite of his resolution, ever and again revisiting his fair dreamland, and building once more his airy castles.

O the time we thus waste! Could a man control his wool-gathering instincts and habitually concentrate his mind on fruitful subjects of reflection, what reaches of thought might he not cover, what refinements of mental discipline might he not compass! But fancy's vagaries are sweet; and we are all more or less "the fools of fancy."

The day's darg done and supper passed, Jamie proceeded to make himself as "snod" as possible before presenting himself at the mansion. He had no fine clothes to put on; but his tall erect figure and shapely limbs showed well in any attire. A douse in cold water was enough to bring out his fine clear complexion, and a few passages of a rough comb through his hair sufficed to send it into waving masses. He stood clothed in the dew of his youth, which nothing can quite overlay, and for which there is no substitute.

Then, taking down his fiddle, he sallied forth.

That same afternoon Fred Clark had walked over to Millbog. It was a fairly long walk according to our notions; but in days when people often went to Aberdeen on foot, a journey of this kind was nothing. He had called at Crimonmogate in passing, and had a private interview with Captain Campbell who was still there. He hoped to hear that Halket had been captured. But he was disappointed. The troopers had indeed been sent out next day in various directions; but, though they scoured the country pretty widely, and made many inquiries, they found no trace or cry of their fugitive.

Knowing that the Millbog people sympathised with Halket, he meant to conceal his connection with the affair; and, if any suspicion should have arisen in their minds that he was implicated, he thought, by putting in an early appearance and braving it out, to disabuse their minds of that impression.

He wanted to advance his suit with Bell; and, as he could see that he had a rival in Jamie Robertson, he felt it necessary to prosecute matters with energy and address, lest his opponent, who had the advantage of living near at hand, should steal a march on him.

He wasn't a bit serious, however. All he really wanted was to enjoy himself, and take all the fun he could out of life. And just now he was in pretty good humour with himself. Conscience didn't vex him much; and he was unaware of the special danger that now menaced him and his plans. So he whistled gaily as he walked along.

Approaching the farm, he found Bell outside, and blessed his good fortune. He could have a crack with her all alone. She had been searching for eggs, which were now scarce, and was making for the house with the few she had found in her lap when Fred hailed her. Not at all averse to a chat, Bell stood up, while Fred leaned over a gate in what he thought an attitude of ease and nonchalance that must be very fetching.

He rallied her on her henwifely qualifications and zeal, and asked, with an innocent air, if Clyacks kept a lot of poultry.

"Nane o' your impudence," said Bell, pretending to be offended. "I ken naething aboot Clyacks and his poultry ; and as little div I care."

After some more banter, he worked round to the point that he felt was more vital, and accused her of caring for "that delver fellow, Robertson." Again Bell repudiated the idea, but blushes came in spite of her. Fred noted it, and was irritated.

"You needn't care in any case," he said. "The fellow has another girl in his eye, and will throw you off whenever he succeeds with her."

"It's a lee, Mr. Clark !" exclaimed Bell, flaring up.

Fred now saw, with some dismay, that Jamie had a strong hold on the girl's affections. He was casting about in his mind what tactics to adopt next, when Bell, discovering that she had duties waiting her inside, turned to go towards the house. Fred had to follow ; and thereafter he got no further opportunity of pursuing the subject with her.

The old folks were very glad to see him again ; and Fred was relieved to note that nobody seemed to suspect him of having prompted the military raid that had so distressed them all. Marget, especially, who had a good deal of ambition, thought it wouldn't be such a bad thing if the young man's choice should fall on their Bell. Clyacks she admitted would be a good alternative match ; while of poor Jamie Robertson she never once thought in this connection, having quite failed to notice such signs as there were of a liking between Bell and him. So often do people see what they want to see, and ignore what would be distasteful.

Fred stayed supper with them, which was then, as now, a comparatively early meal among the agricultural population. But, as there was nothing specially exciting that evening about Millbog, he left early, and strayed away down towards Logie.

He had had no intention originally of going there; but since coming to Millbog that evening, he had begun to feel a deep interest in the young gardener at Logie—to wit, Jamie Robertson; and somehow or other he felt drawn towards the place.—Nothing more interesting to one than a formidable rival.

As he neared the place he managed to get hold of a more definite purpose than that wherewith he had started. If he could find out something on the spot about Jamie Robertson which, having a foundation in fact, might be twisted, and told to his disadvantage, he might succeed in prejudicing Jamie in Bell's eyes. For, without damaging his rival, Fred saw that his own chances were not by any means strong. Best of all if he could get hold of any little story that would give colourable existence to the sweetheart he had extemporised to bluff poor Bell. Of this, however, he wasn't just very sanguine, Jamie appearing too high-toned and sincere for flirtation.

He had a slight acquaintance with the coachman, and so dropped in on that functionary. Calculating that there would be as much rivalry and jealousy among the servants about a gentleman's place as would make them quite ready to reveal things adverse to each other, he led the conversation to Jamie Robertson, and adroitly invited the coachman to support with fact and instance his own impression that Jamie was a bit of a sneak. From this he meant to proceed to other points in his character; but he was soon delighted to find that he had struck oil at once.

The coachman almost immediately dragged in Miss Innes' name. All the people about the place, it had appeared, had noticed that Jamie was a special favourite with her. Her frequent visits to the garden and conversations with Jamie had all been observed and commented on; and somehow it had leaked out that Jamie was going that night to "The House," as they always styled it, to play music with Miss Innes. This, as a kind of climax, had called forth the most sinister comments among his fellow-servants. All which the coachman related with an acerbity that delighted his hearer.

So Fred had succeeded ever so much better than he expected. He had got hold of something—and that of the right kind too—which he could work up. But just to fortify himself with facts gained through personal observation, so as to curtail and reduce as far as possible the necessity of quoting second-hand information, he resolved to stroll over to tne mansion house himself, and reconnoitre.

As he left the stable a horseman rode up, whom, being quite near, he recognised as Captain Campbell. Giving his horse to the coachman, the Captain walked away over the little bridge towards the House, while Fred stood among the shrubbery till he passed, and then followed leisurely, speculating the while in a mild way as to Campbell's errand. Hanging back till the latter had been admitted, Fred approached with stealthy steps. The sound of music guided him to the window of the room whence it proceeded. Here he planted himself, and, with ear placed close to the sill, he could hear pretty well what went on within.

When Jamie had presented himself at the House, Miss Innes had met him at the door and taken him in, manners in those days being simpler than now, and the appointments of houses less elaborate and pretentious. Jamie felt awkward and somewhat abashed at first, never having entered his master's residence on the same kind of terms before. But the lady did her best to put him at his ease, and he was not the man to fail in giving an adequate response to such treatment.

Captain Duff had now been informed of the little arrangement. He had given an equivocal grunt when his niece hinted to him what she proposed doing; but, having the bluff, unconventional nature of the naval man, he was less inclined to stickle for the observation of caste distinctions than the ordinary landed gentleman would have been. He did think, however, that his niece was just a trifle free in her ways; but he consoled himself with the reflection that women are strange inexplicable creatures, and that he was not so closely responsible for his niece's actions as he would have been for the conduct of his own family. He did indeed recognise that his young gardener was a fine-looking and most intelligent fellow, and had himself taken a fancy to him; but he didn't see so far into these matters as female eyes would.

Miss Innes began by playing some of her classical pieces on the harpsichord. This instrument was the precursor of the modern pianoforte—the strings, however, being plucked instead of struck. The sound was comparatively thin, and didn't admit of gradations of tone. But the music was sweet; and the resources of the instrument were adequate in a general way for the interpretation of the complex effects that the science of harmony and counterpoint suggests and evolves.

Jamie listened to the playing with growing delight. Then, getting him to tune his fiddle in accord with the pitch of the harpsichord, Miss Innes suggested that they should try to play together such airs as they knew in common. And soon Jamie was mightily pleased to find that they could get along together—that the strains of his fiddle were dove-tailing into the more complicated structure of the arrangements his companion played. The experience was wholly delightful, his artistic sense simply revelling in the new and thrilling effects.

In the midst of their playing Captain Campbell was announced. As he stepped forward, Miss Innes rose from her seat at the instrument. He shook hands with her, and glanced inquiringly at her companion. Jamie turned towards him, and, as their eyes met, a haughty and defiant look appeared on the faces of both men, which puzzled Miss Innes to explain.

"You have company, Miss Innes?" said the captain with some stiffness.

"Yes, Captain Campbell," she hastened to say by way of explanation, "this is a young musical friend of mine who has come in to practise some pieces."

The Captain gave an impatient grunt.

"Think I may have seen the fellow before, perhaps; but I didn't quite expect to—find him—here."

"O, he is quite fit for my society, I can assure you, Captain Campbell, if that is what you mean—at anyrate we are quite pleased with each other."

Here she looked at Jamie, who blushed and bowed. Then, drawing herself up with dignity, she looked defiantly at the Captain, who was a bit cowed.

"O, I beg your pardon, Miss Innes," he said. "Only, you see, though divinity may itself condescend, we who are its worshippers cannot help feeling jealous for its dignity."

"A fine speech," said the lady archly, "and for that you are forgiven, Captain."

Jamie was waiting a chance of retiring with dignity. Like other proud natures he could remain in the background patiently enough, but didn't quite like being put into it. His look and attitude exhibited a fine mixture of defiant pride and due sense of the proprieties of the situation; and, as Miss Innes looked at him, her admiration for the young man grew. Reared and educated in the best Edinburgh society herself, she wondered where and how this young rustic had caught his fine instinct and delicate appreciation of things.

"Will you excuse me if I go now?" he said, when a lull in the duel between Miss Innes and Captain Campbell afforded him an opportunity of setting himself right in a dignified way.

"Well, Mr. James, you might have stayed and let Captain Campbell hear the result of our practice . . . But we may be able to give a better account of ourselves after we have had further opportunities of playing togther."

The last remark was meant for the Captain. He bit his lip and began again to frown.

Jamie bowed to him, and then turned away with Miss Innes, who accompanied him to the door and bade him good-night very cordially, adding that they would arrange afterwards for further practice.

Although braving it out before the Captain, Miss Innes did indeed feel the situation pretty keenly, and was in a sufficiently bad humour when she turned again into the room.

"Won't you give me some music now, Miss Innes?" said the Captain, trying to be as gracious as possible now that the cause of irritation between them had been withdrawn.

"No, I have had enough for an evening," was the stiff reply. "Let us go to uncle."

"O, I am very willing to remain here even without the music," he interposed hastily, looking fondly at her.

"But really I feel cold," she persisted, "and uncle will feel lonely if I stay too long away from him?"

Campbell looked disappointed, and tried a new tack.—

"That young fellow, Miss Innes,—what sort of a— fellow—would he be?"

"O, I thought you knew him," she replied mischievously. "He is the young gardener at Logie here."

"Oh!" And he affected great astonishment.

"But he is no common young man," Miss Innes went on,—"no common young man, I assure you. He only wants fine clothes to make him a gentleman outwardly, as he is inwardly one already."

"But, as it is, he will remain a clodhopper and a clown."

"He isn't a clown, Captain Campbell," exclaimed the lady, reddening with indignation, "and can't remain what he isn't. He has intelligence, native refinement, and artistic feeling, very much beyond—many gentlemen I have met."

" But he is bound to remain in his low surroundings and among sordid society,—such, for instance, as I saw him in a couple of nights ago."

' Indeed ? "—There was curiosity, along with suppressed resentment, in her tone and look.

" Yes, I met him at a farm along here ; and a fine young fresh country damsel had evidently attached herself to him. When we came in seeking a rebel we had heard was about the premises, it was good—awfully good—to see how she took the chance of getting very frightened, with her way of it, and nestling close to her fond swain.—Ha ! ha !—It was good."

Why was it that a certain pang smote the heart of his fair hearer at that moment ?—She felt ashamed to own it to herself, and would have almost died rather than let the Captain know or imagine she thought anything about it. She laughed, but it was in a certain hard, unnatural way.—

" You think we women are always throwing ourselves at men.—The conceit of you masculine creatures ! "

How she hated the Captain for that speech ! She knew quite well why he had made it, and she felt at once thoroughly ashamed and angry. But she dropped the subject, and now reminded Captain Campbell that she had proposed retiring, and in her own well-bred yet irresistible way she marshalled him from the room to her uncle's presence; and then, after seeing them settled with pipes and toddy, she withdrew to her own room.

When Jamie came out of the house, Fred crouched

down for the time being, lest he should be seen; but he soon got into position again, that he might hear the end of the business. It was interesting in itself—this tiff between Miss Innes and the Captain; but, as bearing on his rival Jamie Robertson, it was so important that he couldn't afford to lose a single word or incident.

When the two left the room, he slipped quietly away; and, as it was not so very late yet, he determined to call at Millbog again before going home.

How he chuckled as he walked along!—He was fit for Bell now. Her precious gardener—well! And how lucky he had been to lay hands at once on the very thing needed to crush his rival. Why, Providence seemed to have come specially to his aid. And how clever of him to think of suggesting that Jamie had another sweetheart!—He felt all the complacency of a prophet whose predictions had been triumphantly verified.

He wanted to see Bell again; but not alone this time. It would humble her all the more if the revelation he was about to make were made in presence of her parents. So, when he found all the household gathered round the ingle, he was not long in leading the conversation to Logie and Miss Innes. Then he dragged in Jamie Robertson; and, before he halted, what with facts, inferences, comments, and insinuations, he had woven a very sinister story indeed.

Poor Bell was cut to the heart. She did once or twice at the beginning try to protest or offer explanations; but, as she felt she was only likely to compromise herself without in any effective way combating Fred's assertions and inuendoes, she gave it up, and would fain have gone out. But no; she must hear it all; and so she sat, working busily at her spinning-wheel, but drinking in every word.

And that night, when Fred had gone and all the rest had retired to bed, she sat long by the "reested" fire, weeping bitter—oh, how bitter tears of chagrin, and wounded feelings, and disappointed hopes.

Her final resolve was that she would never speak to Jamie Robertson again—never!

CHAPTER V.

TROUBLES AND DANGERS.

THE woman who had come to Millbog on Hallowe'en and had got shelter overnight left, as we have already stated, on the afternoon of the following day. Her destination—undisclosed to the Millbog people—was Howemoss, the place where she had ascertained Fred Clark lived ; and she expected to reach it by evening.

Full of a certain overmastering purpose, she had nerved herself to repress her feelings and to dissemble, until she should get hold of the information which she saw was needed for the carrying out of her resolve. That accomplished, her feelings, like waters that have been long dammed back, began to swell up and over with ever-gathering force. No longer could she restrain them. Go she must. Further inactivity even was unbearable. The very confinement of a house she couldn't stand. She would choke if she did not forthwith get out into the wide open.—So forth she had hurried.

And, now that all restraint was removed, how surged the tumult in her breast ! It was like the raging of many waters, full of strange wild sounds, yet ever resolving itself into one dread resultant voice. And for her the awful burden ever rang—Fred was her husband ; and he was false !

When but a little ago she had thought that her Fred was dead, life seemed to have lost all its light and all its joy. Beyond that she did not think distress could go. But the revelation at Millbog on Hallowe'en was a second

and far worse death. And yet there was a lower deep
still. She had seen how Fred had deserted her and was
acting as if she had never existed ; but when on the
following day she discovered that to her he had all along
being going under an assumed name, she realised that
his deceit and falsehood had been deliberate and pre-
mediated—that he had planned her betrayal.—It was
dreadful !

Yet she loved this man ; ay, and loved him still.—
And *there* is ever the tragedy !

What wild thoughts flashed through her mind ! And
how mixed they were !

Why go to him at all ? Would it not be better to
crawl somewhere and die, and never let him know that
she had discovered his baseness and perfidy ? No ; she
must see him ; must speak to him. She would appeal
to him for the sake of the past. And, if he would yet be
true, she knew that her heart must forgive him. Perhaps
he would spurn her. Yet even that she would bear.
One thing she *cannot* do—cannot die till she has seen
her Fred once more.

She had walked along, keeping in a general direction
towards Rathen. Now as dusk began to come down, she
stopped at a cottar's house by the roadside to ask her
way more definitely. She got directions from a woman,
which she thought she apprehended, and pushed on.
She did not want to reach Howemoss till it was dark,
when she might have a chance of a secret interview with
the man she sought.

She was getting very tired, and her pace was ever
slackening, so that darkness overtook her when she was
yet a good way from her destination. No lights as yet

appeared on her way, and, as she trudged along, she began to realise that she was not so certain of her path as she would like to be.

She had to turn to the left at a certain point. Coming to a road that branched off in the required direction, she concluded it must be the one she had to take, and so struck off.

On she dragged — ever more wearily. The road seemed to descend into a hollow; and now she could hear the gurgle of a burn. Coming to it, she could perceive no bridge. It would have to be forded. So she stepped through, wetting her feet.

The road, now a pretty rough track, climbed a slope; and even in the gloom she could see that the surroundings were getting wilder and more desolate. At length she began to fear that she had lost the track altogether. And she had. It was indeed so poor that she was off it some time before she knew.

Now she stopped in despair. Then she turned as if to retrace her steps; but as she couldn't find the path by which she had come, she was helpless. Thoroughly tired and utterly miserable, she sat down on the cold, damp ground, and despair was fast gathering at her heart.

Wearily she looked around, when, all of a sudden, a twinkling light appeared away on the slope above her. Up she rose with fresh spirit, and made straight for the light.

The ground was getting ever rougher; she stumbled over big stones, and tripped on heather and whin. At times her feet splashed in boggy places; and once she fell into a place where peat had been dug. She was wet, and her clothes were all soiled. Yet on she struggled.

Her strength was now failing fast. She staggered and fell once and again, more from weakness than anything else. Yet the light ever beckoned her on, and oh! she must not give way!

Now she has reached the place whence the light comes. It is a little thatched hut, with but one little window and one low door. To the door she staggers. She cannot knock, but falls helplessly against it.

"Mercy on's! fa's that?" cried a voice from the inside, guttural and foggy, yet indubitably female.

Soon the door was opened, and our poor wanderer fell into the arms of a big, raw, elderly woman. . . . .

Betty Duncan, for such was the name of the individual who now carried the fainting girl into her humble abode, lived with her grown daughter Kirsty in this little one-roomed house, which stood quite by itself on the Rathen side of Mormond Hill. There was a small garden attached, which yielded kail and potatoes; and then Betty had her hens and pig. But all around for a considerable distance there was nothing but heather and rough uncultivated hill-ground.

Betty was a bit of a character, and was well-known. She had done some outdoor work in her younger days, but for many years she had managed to live without making any special exertion, although she and her daughter knitted and span a little, as was then the general custom. She had a good deal of intelligence and penetration, and, as people admitted, "kent the gate o' maist folk." She was always complaining of her hard lot; and charitable people, taking pity on her indigence and loneliness, vied with each other in their gifts to her, Betty taking care to reveal to each donor what the others had given, so as to induce a rivalry among them.

She also made it her business to get hold of the love-secrets of the young people, many of whom came to her to hint their experiences in this line, and—dearest of delights to the young heart—to be "bathered aboot it." In this way Betty came to have not a little influence with the young men and maidens.

Some people went the length of thinking Betty a little uncanny, and would not have cared to quarrel with her, or even deny her anything she might ask; and she took advantage in a certain way of this reputation. While careful to disclaim being a witch—it wasn't just very safe in those days to be known as such—she allowed her neighbours to suppose that she had a little more knowledge and power than belonged to most people.

Kirsty, her daughter, was, in the matter of outward appearance, a not altogether unattractive young woman. Large of limb and feature, she exhibited certain points physically that tell in rustic circles. Long residence alone with her mother, however, had made her, as the young fellows put it, "a wee bit gockit."

Betty had some feelings of humanity in her; and, when the weary wanderer fell exhausted into her arms, she called her daughter to her aid: and together they managed to carry the poor creature forward to the low peat-fire, where she quite fainted away.

There was but one bed in the house, an ordinary box one. Into this they prepared meantime to put their charge. But the poor creature was so soiled that it behoved them first to take off some of her dress. In doing so Betty spied some papers in her bosom, and quietly abstracted them.

"Fat's that, mither?" asked Kirsty, noticing the action.

"O, naething ava," her mother answered; adding, as she saw Kirsty inclined to betray some curiosity, "we'll see by-and-bye." And she laid the papers on the shelf.

When they had got their charge put to bed, Betty, in order that she might have an opportunity of examining the papers all by herself, as she knew her daughter couldn't always be trusted to keep a secret, sent Kirsty out for water and peats; and then, in her absence, addressed herself with avidity to a task that promised some spice of gossipy interest at least.

"O guid guide's!" she exclaimed, as she looked at the chief document, "a mairriage certificate, I declare! . . . . Weel, weel . . . And she's a wife, puir thing . . . Fred Jamieson . . . Lily Douglas . . . Ay, ay. . . . Mairriet at Edinbrugh. . . . That's maybe a gey bit awa' noo. . . . And far's this chiel Fred? . . . She's seerly left him. . . . He'd been a coorse breet nae doot, and she couldna bide wi' 'im. . . . They're nae guid aboot big toons, especially in the sooth."

Betty now took up the other papers, which proved to be mostly letters. As she looked and read she seemed to be struggling with an idea. She paused, turned the letter she was reading over in her hand, looked at the writing again; and then, in a kind of breathless astonishment, gave her deliverance.—

"I declare—it's awfu' queer. And the vreetin'—it's his. I could swear till't."

Then, with a malign light in her eye, she went on to moralise.—

"And this is some o' 's cantrips in the sooth? . . . Ay, ay; and syne he comes aboot ither fowk's bairns, and hauds a wark wi' them. . . . The scoondrel!"

But the return of Kirsty with her burden put an end to the monologue; and Betty hastily put the papers away between the leaves of an old family Bible.

Lily Douglas—for that we have at length found to be the name of our poor wandering and betrayed one—Lily Douglas was destined to remain in Betty Duncan's house for many days. A kind of brain fever developed; and for long she lay unconscious or raving, passing through a crisis that only youth and a sound constitution could have enabled her to surmount.

Betty soon saw that her patient was likely to remain on her hands for some time. In ordinary circumstances this would have been an unbearable affliction; but Betty felt reconciled to it. The episode promised her any amount of sensation in a general way; while, particularly and personally, she realised its significance,—and even value.

In the first place she said to herself that she had "a craw to pluck, and a gey teuch ane," with somebody. For that she could now wait.—Yet she hadn't long to wait.

The night after Lily's arrival Betty was dosing over the fire, while Kirsty was taking a turn of the bed, there not being room enough for three. A rap at the window wakened her up. She understood the signal, and, rising hastily, she placed the light so that it shone well on the face of Lily, who lay "at the stock."

The sneck was lifted, and in stepped Fred Clark, who had called, as he not unfrequently did, on his way home from Millbog,

" Ye're nae beddit yet?" he said, affecting a familiarity of voice and manner.

But Betty looked serious, and held up her finger, first as if warningly, and then pointed with it to the bed. Fred, not knowing what was up, came forward rather dubiously, while Betty watched his face with the utmost keenness.

The moment he caught side of Lily's face he involuntarily uttered a low oath, and, putting up a hand as if deprecatingly, staggered backward.

Betty had seen more than enough.

" Ye ken her?" she said, in her deep rough voice.

" No, no.—What do you mean?—Of course I don't. —I was just a little—a little taken aback at first. You see I never expected to see anybody there at all; and— really she's a bit like somebody I've seen before."

" Ay; I suppose that's jist it—ye've seen her before?"

" No, no,—not her; but she's like somebody I think I've seen. It was that that put me out a bit at first.— Very stupid of me of course.—But how did she come here, Betty?"

" And fa' micht she be some like?" Betty asked, ignoring his last question. " Wid ye min' her name?"

" No, really I couldn't; but it doesn't matter.—You haven't told us how she came here at all."

" Wis't Lily Douglas?"

He grew deadly white, and stared at her.

" I see ye min' noo," added his tormentor.

But he couldn't reply.

" And fin ye kent her ye was Fred Jamieson yersel'?"

But now he got command of himself, and vented his feelings in a perfect tornado of cursing and swearing. Betty wasn't a bit overawed. She simply waited.

" Noo, Mr. Fred," she said, rising from her stool, " there's nae eese o' a' this roarin' and rantin'. I ken a' aboot it.—This is Lily Douglas, and *she's your wife*."

" It's a black d——d lie!" he shouted. " Nobody can prove that."

" I can," said Betty. " I hae the 'lines.'"

" Where are they?" he demanded.

" Ay, ye wid like to ken that, nae doot. Never min' the noo. I'll lat them be seen fin the time comes; nae till than. And I've mair papers wi' vreetin' o' your ain on them, which ye winna be able to deny. Syne, to croon a', fin this puir thing gets weel again she'll easy be able to tell's that her Fred Jamieson's oor Fred Clark."

Thoroughly defeated and silenced, he dropped on the table, while Betty, pursuing her advantage, " gie'd him a gey dressin'," the worst element in her indictment being his " haudin' a wark wi' ither fowk's bairns."

Fred took it all very patiently. His conscience wasn't just very active, but his mind was. He was casting about for a way of escape from this the very worst scrape he had ever been in. He must gain over Betty at any cost; and so, when at last he got an opportunity of speaking he began very humbly to cringe and plead. This didn't seem to make much impression. Then he hinted at his willingness to enter into negotiations, and to come to terms that would be of advantage to them both.

Betty, who could see that only a barren revenge would be got by exposing Fred right away, was not unwilling to negotiate about keeping matters quiet meantime. She might thus turn the affair to present advantage, without surrendering the hold on him which the possession of the dread secret gave. The revelation would be none the less effective though postponed.

And so, when at length Fred offered her money, without committing herself to anything very definitely, she in a manner agreed " to keep the puir thing in the meantime, and say naething aboot it—till they saw."

.   .   .   .

But now let us return to Logie.—

Jamie, all unconscious of the mischief that had been wrought in his little love-world, was thinking of Bell, and longing to see her again. She used to come down to Logie occasionally of an evening—ostensibly to see some of the female servants ; and Jamie was always loyally in waiting to convoy her over the field to her home, fully half a mile away. Jamie was thus sure he would see her some evening soon, especially as she had not been at Logie for some time.

But he waited in vain. Bell never came ; and, as no good excuse for going himself to Millbog offered during those days, he began to feel the pangs of the lover's heart-hunger—that strange distressful yearning for the loved and absent.

He could bear it no longer. He *must* see Bell. It was the night of a Strichen market that he chose for his visit to Millbog. Bogie would be at the market,—and Clyacks too ; so that the coast would be comparatively clear.

One glance at Bell was enough to show him that

something was wrong—very far wrong. She never once looked at him ; but, with a face full of suppressed fire and temper, sat knitting by the fireside. Poor Jamie was nonplussed. Every time he had seen Bell of late she had surprised him for better or worse,—this night, alas, for worse. He was at his wits' end.

Marget spoke to him, but not very often ; and, then, in a certain cold way. Jockie was the only one of the three that was at all friendly. He neither understood what was wrong, nor would he have cared much though he had. He liked Jamie for his own sake, and, besides, found it to his own advantage to be on good terms with a gardener. " Man, Davie," he would say to a school companion who came from the neighbouring farm of Lumbs, " I like Jamie Robertson richt. He gie's ye fine aipples, and sometimes peers tee." And Davie was grieved to think that he hadn't a big sister to entice Jamie—and his fruit—over to Lumbs.

Unable to get a word from Bell, Jamie was on the point of leaving in despair, when, to his great relief, her mother went to attend to some of her dairy duties. Now was his chance, if Jockie could only be got rid of as well.

"O, I say Jockie, man," Jamie began, " I'm awfu' thristy. Would ye bring's a drink o' water—as fresh as ye can ? And I'll maybe min' on't till ye some time."

Jockie knew what " mindin' on 'im sometime" meant ; and he was wide-awake.

" I'll rin doon to the wall," said he promptly.

" That's a chap," said Jamie cheerily. " But ye needna' jist rin, Jockie. Tak' your ain time. I'm nae jist in sic an awfu' picherty as a' that."

Which Jockie also understood. So, taking a pail, he

6

set out. The well, which is there still, was about 150 yards from the house. It was bright moonlight, and early in the evening, and Jockie, less nervous than usual, managed to consume a good deal of time on the way. But Jamie, feeling there was no time to lose, addressed himself at once to the task of finding out what was wrong with Bell.

He gave a preliminary cough, hoping she would look up, now that they were alone together. But Bell ignored his cough, and himself too.

"Bell," he began nervously.

"Weel?"

"Fat's—adee?"

"Naething."

There matters stuck. Jockie would be half-way to the well by this time, and Jamie felt he had made no progress. He must make another and a more determined effort.—

"Bell!"

"Fat is't?"

"There's something adee wi' ye the nicht.—Fat's wrang?"

"Naething that I ken o'."

"Fat wye are ye nae speakin' than?"

"I've naething to say."

Another pause ensued. Jamie heard the beating of his own heart, and wondered whether it or the click of Bell's wires was the louder. Jockie would be at the well by this time. He could in imagination see him filling his pail. Now he was on his way back. Things were growing desperate.—

"Bell!"

" Weel ? "

" Look at a body, will ye ? "

" I hinna time."

" Ye eest to hae time ; and, when a body comes to see ye, it's little eneuch that ye say something to them."

" Ye needna come to me. Ye'd better bide wi' your gentry."

" Bell !—Fat d'ye mean ? "

" O, ye ken fine."

" No ; as fact's death I dinna ken ! "

" Weel than ye can gang hame and fin' oot wi' your learnin'."

Here Marget re-entered. Jockie, who had been waiting about the door for a little, now saw there was no use waiting longer, and stalked in, swinging his pail. In the passage he met Jamie.

" O, never min,' Jockie," said Jamie, as he moved to the door. " I'm nae sae thristy as I wis a file ago."

" It'll be Bell that's dry noo ? " said the youngster.

Jamie was in no mood for jokes. Yet, having regard to the possibility of future need for Jockie's services, he repeated his promise to mind on him ; and so went out.

Jamie's heart was aflame as he strode rapidly away from Millbog. In the wild turmoil of feeling that agitated his breast he was unable to think clearly or coherently at all, and so failed to understand what Bell meant. All that was present to his mind at first was the fact that Bell and he had got estranged. And the thought was wildly distressing.

Away over country he went, leaping ditches and fences, and hurrying on as if driven by some goading influence. But a few miles of this in the keen frosty air and under the light of a fine moon, served to calm his spirit somewhat; and at length he was able to formulate clearly what his mind had for some time been dimly working towards.—It was Miss Innes that Bell meant.

But how did she know even the little that was to know? And why should she make so much of that little? He felt first puzzled, and then angry and ashamed,—angry that Bell should treat him so unfairly, and ashamed that anyone should think of connecting his name with that of a lady like Miss Innes.

Still calmer thoughts supervened. The difficulty and trouble, being imaginary, would vanish. Bell might be in a bad temper for a little; but when she saw, as she must soon do, how preposterous her beliefs and ideas were, she would come to reason, and be as she was wont to be.

Having thus walked and reasoned himself into a pretty placid mood, he sat down on a stone by the side of a road, on which, as befitted his calmer condition, he had for some time been walking. It was a glorious night. The moon now rode high in the southern sky. The whole country sparkled keen with frost. And everything was so still.

At length he rose and set his face for Logie. After walking some distance, he descried a figure on the road ahead of him. He was gradually gaining on it, and at length he came near enough to assure himself that it was a man—presumably a farmer returning from Strichen market. Being in no mood just then for company, Jamie slackened his pace, and remained a few hundred yards behind, until the man, leaving the road, took a path that led across the fields.

"It'll be Clyacks," said Jamie to himself, and with the observation came a certain little heart-twitch. If he was driven off the field at Millbog, there was no saying how well Clyacks might succeed in his absence.

Jamie had proceeded about a quarter of a mile beyond the point where the man whom he took to be Clyacks had struck off, when he was startled by a cry as if for help. It seemed to proceed from about the place where the man, though unseen, would now be—about a couple of fields to the left.

Jamie stood and listened to see if the cry would be repeated. It was—louder and more urgent than before. With a bound he was in the field, speeding away as fast as he could towards the point whence the appeal for help came.

In the next field there was an old disused quarry, and, as the path lay past this, Jamie judged that the assault that led to the cry for help had been made there. As he neared the spot, he could see what looked like two people struggling together. Presently one of them seemed to go down, and the other bent over, and then kneeled on him.

But now the sound of Jamie's approaching footsteps seemed to be heard; and the one who was uppermost sprang to his feet. He looked towards Jamie, who was now within twenty yards of him, and then, turning, bolted away in the opposite direction.

Jamie reached the prostrate form, which had now sat up, although apparently unable to rise. It was Clyacks, sure enough; and Jamie, stopping, bent down to assist him. But Clyacks, pushing him off, cried out,—" I'm robbit !—Aifter the scoondrel, Jamie!—Never mind me!"

And, without a word, Jamie was off after the retreating figure of the miscreant who had done the deed. It was a tough race, and for a while the interval between the runners remained pretty much unchanged. But at length Jamie could see that he was gaining on his man, who soon began to lag, and, by his movements, appeared to be doing something else as he ran.

Jamie had now come pretty near his fugitive, and could see that he carried something in his hand. All at once the fellow stopped, and, wheeling right round, faced his pursuer.—

"Stop, you——, or I'll blow your brains out!" he gasped breathlessly, and Jamie could see that a pistol was levelled at himself.

The extreme danger of the situation flashed on his mind in a moment. But the ardour of pursuit was too keen for him to hesitate or pull up. Right in on his man he rushed.

Next moment a shot rang out on the stillness of the night air; and Jamie reeled and fell.

CHAPTER VI.

DISCOVERIES.

JAMIE was badly shot. Clyacks, though himself a good deal hurt in the scuffle which he had had with the robber, managed to pull himself together and follow up; and, with assistance from the farm which was not far off, Jamie was got home to Logie. His chaumer being unsuitable, and in fact, in the circumstances, almost inaccessible, the wounded man was taken into the coachman's house, and laid in a spare bed in the room end.

There was much consternation about the place. The news was forthwith carried to the mansion; and, although it was now pretty late, Captain Duff came over to "The Stables" to see the patient, pending the arrival of a doctor. Miss Innes, who was greatly distressed to hear of Jamie's untoward accident, insisted on accompanying her uncle, waiting anxiously in the kitchen while he went through to examine the nature and extent of the young man's wound.

The Captain's experience in the navy had brought him considerable acquaintance with surgery. After examining the patient, he reported him very badly hurt; which rather serious view of the case was afterwards confirmed by the doctor.

The whole district soon rang with the news, and Jamie was the hero of the hour. People sympathised with Sandy; but, as he was in exceedingly good circumstances, the loss of twenty pounds or so was not such a very serious matter. But Jamie's case was widely different. He had perilled his life, and that too in another's cause, and his pluck and courage were recognised and admiringly commented on in rustic circles for miles around.

All attempts to trace the robber failed. Sandy, although he had grappled with him, couldn't identify him, declaring that he appeared to be disguised; and Jamie of course was less able to contribute anything towards the solution of the problem.

The Fiscal was informed of the case, and an officer came to investigate it. But little could be disclosed, and detective methods were then of a pretty simple and unresourceful order, and, further, offences against the Crown and Government had of late so monopolised the attention of the authorities, that they were rather lax in dealing with matters that came under the scope of the general criminal code.

Thus the robber remained undiscovered, although there were one or two people who had certain theories and suspicions.

For some time Jamie lay in a critical condition; but youth and a good constitution carried him through. Miss Innes called to ask for him every day, bringing many dainties from the House, and in other ways showing her deep interest in his welfare.

To Bell the news of the affair came as a shock. Remembering how she had treated Jamie that very night on which it happened, she was struck with something like remorse, and suffered much mental distress until he was declared out of danger. But soon she heard of Miss

Innes' visits and attentions to Jamie, and the old feeling of jealousy surged up once more, overriding for the time being every other sentiment.

And during those days Fred Clark came more frequently than ever to Millbog. He saw the advantage that circumstances had given him, and determined to use it. The advantage told in two directions.—The coast was now clear for advancing himself in Bell's affections; and at the same time he could most effectually damage the position of his absent rival. Once or twice he went as far as the Stables, and, after a crack with the coachman, came back with a perfect armoury of envenomed weapons to use against poor Jamie.

So Bell grew ever more angry with Jamie, and more alienated from him. And, in spite of Fred's attentions, she was supremely miserable; for—

> "To be wroth with one we love
> Doth work like madness in the brain."

How she wished she could see him and have a talk with him! It would be some relief even to have an open quarrel. But this gulf of silent estrangement—it was growing unbearable.

She could indeed stand it no longer. She must have some communication with Jamie, and again she bethought her of little Jockie as a handy ally. Him she hired with gifts present and promised to go to Logie and ask for Jamie. He wasn't to say that Bell sent him, nor yet to pretend that she knew nothing about it. This was the general text of her instructions, but she enlarged on it to such an extent that Jockie interrupted the

harangue with an impatient "Ach!" and set out on his
errand, leaving her flinging all kinds of cautions after
him—to which, however, he paid little heed.

Jamie, who was by this time getting convalescent,
was overjoyed to learn that a messenger and a message
had come from Millbog—at last. Jockie was brought
through to the invalid's room, and with many smiles
and kindly words was encouraged to say his say. Just
then there arrived a consignment of delicacies from Miss
Innes ; and the urchin, being invited to partake freely,
had such a royal time of it that he determined so to
engineer matters so as to insure for himself a few more
visits to Logie. So he delivered his message in a way
that could hardly fail to lead to the protracting of
negotiations, and, with happy heart, promised himself
lots of more feasts divine.

He had, in pursuance of his plan, to tamper also
with Jamie's message to Bell. This he managed to do
with considerable skill and address ; but, unfortunately,
he committed the cardinal mistake of mentioning Miss
Innes' present. This was the red rag to Bell ; and poor
Jockie now saw with dismay that he had in a manner
wrecked the business that had up to that point promised
so fair. Bell had no more need for his services. She
didn't want to hear any more about Jamie Robertson.
She had no message to send him.

But Jockie was not to be baulked. If Bell would
give him no more commissions, he would go on his own
account. He felt it was almost a duty to go. Jamie
had told him that he was never able to eat half the good
things that came to him from the House, and had
appeared so grateful to him (Jockie) for his efficient

assistance in demolishing them that it would, he thought, be very mean of him to stay away. He didn't like people to think him a disobliging boy.

So Jockie went back. He had more difficulty than before in carrying the thing off; but he succeeded in a pretty fair way, although he allowed to himself that he was now " gey near the end o' 's tether."

Jamie himself could feel that the negotiations were making no real progress, and longed for such a return of health and strength as should enable him to go to Bell in person and put matters right between them, as he was sure he could now do.

One day towards dusk a strange gentleman called at the coachman's house, and expressed a wish to see " Mr. James Robertson." On being shown into Jamie's room and left alone with him, the stranger soon revealed himself as his old friend Halket, dressed so as to escape identification at the hands of the casual observer.

He had come to see Jamie in reference to the matters discussed and arranged between them at their last meeting ; and it was only on his arrival at Logie that he learned of his young friend's misfortune. His regret and sympathy were deep and sincere, but these feelings were now tempered by the joy of seeing the subject of them so well advanced in convalescence.

They had a long talk together, for both had a good deal to say. Jamie's story we already know. Halket's we shall briefly summarise.—

After leaving Logie, Halket had gone to Cairnbulg, where, having a number of friends, he was comparatively safe. One of these he sent over to Howemoss, to see what could be picked up in reference to the matter he was investigating.

No word or trace of the woman could be got. As far as could be ascertained, she had never turned up at the place at all; and, as Fred appeared to be coming and going quite freely, it was difficult to understand matters. But, as there was no clue on which to work, Halket had nothing for it but to wait. He had waited until his patience was quite exhausted, and now came to Logie to see if anything of interest or significance had in the interim there transpired.

Jamie had nothing to tell him that was of much use. He had never heard of the woman again. But, of course, a good few things might have happened that had never reached his ears, stowed away as he had been for a few weeks in a sick room. Possibly, however, the Millbog people could contribute information that might prove valuable.

Thinking the matter over, Halket determined to visit Millbog. He knew there was some danger in going there and disclosing his identity; but, counting on the sympathy and good-will of the inmates, he thought he would risk it.

When Jamie perceived his intention of going to Millbog, he decided to charge him with a little commission of his own. He confided to Halket his trouble and difficulty with Bell, and his friend, taking in the situation, at once undertook to explain matters to the lady in question, and disabuse her mind of such false ideas as she might have harboured relative to Miss Innes and her actions.

While charging himself very readily with the task,

he couldn't refrain from improving the occasion just a
little bit.—

"Weel, Jamie, ye min' I tell't ye to tak' care o' this
Miss Innes. I'll dee what I can meantime to put things
richt atween you and Bell ; but, unless ye tak' a firm
stand in the maitter, I winna hide frae ye my fear that
ye'll maybe hae mair fash yet owre this business."

"But," protested Jamie, "it's nae my wyte."

"Maybe no," answered his friend, "but the danger's
there a' the same."

And, with a hearty grip of Jamie's hand and a
cheerily expressed wish for his speedy restoration to
wonted health, Halket went away.

It was now evening, and moderately dark. He struck
through the fields to Millbog, and, making his way by
the corn-yard, paused a little to collect his thoughts and
rehearse his plan of action, before approaching the
house.

As he stood behind a rick, he heard a sound as of
subdued conversation, and, listening more closely, he
could catch the soft fall of stealthy footsteps. They
were approaching. He remained perfectly still, and
they stopped on the other side of the rick against which
he was leaning.

He now concluded it must be some love-tryst between
rustic swain and maid, and he was on the point of slipping
away, prompted by the honourable feeling that recoils
from playing eavesdropper, when the sound of one of the
voices arrested his attention. He seemed to have heard
it before. Now he recognises it.—It is the voice of
Fred Clark.

His anxiety to know what the fellow was about

made Halket lay aside his scruples for the nonce, and stick to his post.

He was next anxious to know who Fred's companion was. This was more difficult, for she—of the sex he had no doubt—spoke less freqnently, and in a lower tone of voice. But, disturbing as the conclusion was, he soon assured himself that it was Bell who was thus holding clandestine meeting with the young fellow.

Many a frown made still darker Halket's already shadowed face, often did he clench his unseen fist and set his silent teeth, as from time to time he caught the import of Clark's low-spoken sentences. Many were the mental anathemas he pronounced on his devoted head ; deep was the oath he swore to overthrow his designs and bring vengeance on the villain.

At length the two parted. Bell slipped away to the house, while her companion walked off towards the public road. Halket's first impulse was to follow Bell ; but soon he changed his mind. Matters were not ripe for interference. He must first see that he is able to prove his allegations against Fred Clark, before he attempt to expose him. He must have his weapons thoroughly forged and ready, ere he make the attack. So he will not say anything to Bell or her people to-night.

When he got on the road, he could dimly descry the figure of Fred Clark a little in advance. For a considerable way their road was the same, and Halket, as he walked along, without any very conscious intention, kept always at about the same distance behind. In this way he never quite lost sight of his adversary, who, on his part, however, had no suspicion that he was being followed.

After a few miles had been covered in this way, Fred turned off to the left, just at the point in fact where Lily had diverged in her unfortunate journey. Halket, though somewhat astonished, would, in ordinary circumstances, have held on his proper track; but the instinct to follow had so grown on him that, almost in spite of himself, when he came to the critical point, he too turned off.

And now he began to speculate with ever growing interest as to where Fred was going. He felt pretty much at a loss for some time, but, as they went along, the range of possible destinations narrowed down, until he was almost sure his man was making for Betty Duncan's cot away among the heather.

What was the fellow after?

At another time Halket would have admitted he had no business to inquire, and would have frankly acknowledged the meanness of thus shadowing a man; but, so intent was he on getting Fred Clark exposed and his base designs thwarted, that he felt no qualms of conscience in acting as he was doing.

It was not so very late yet, and Betty's light was still burning. Fred walked up to the little window, and Halket, expecting that his next move would be to enter the house, hung back till he should do so.

But Fred remained at the window, and very soon the door opened, and a figure appeared in the doorway. That it was a woman was all that Halket could tell; but he naturally concluded it must be Betty's daughter, whom Fred had invited forth by some understood signal. Which but deepened Halket's indignation and aversion. Here too, thought he, was the wolf prowling.

This was but another item falling to be added to the long indictment against the depredator.

The door was shut, and in a few moments the figure crossed the line of light that streamed from the window. Halket, who was familiar with everybody in the parish, now recognised it was Betty herself. This revision, while to some extent a relief, roused more curiosity, and brought his mind back to the track from which it had been momentarily diverted. Perhaps something would now emerge that would be of significance—something that would guide him in his hitherto fruitless search for a clue.

Nor was he disappointed.

The two, Betty and Fred, now adjourned to the rear of the house, presumably for the purpose of holding a consultation on some subject of interest between them ; and Halket, slipping up very quietly, got behind some bourtree bushes that flanked the little garden. Here he planted himself, and, although the wind whistled through the bare twigs, he could overhear most of the conversation carried on between Fred and his ally ; for, not suspecting that anyone could be near, they made no special effort to subdue their voices.

What Halket heard at first was to him quite enigmatical ; but very soon he got hold of a central idea, and, working out from this hypothesis, he managed to find an interpretation more or less plausible for most of the remarks that reached his ear.

The chief topic of conversation between Betty and her interviewer was some individual to whom they referred simply as "she." Could this be the woman in whom he was interested ? He would assume it was, and see how things to come would fit into this provisional theory.

It could be gathered that "she" was just now in Betty's house. How came she to be there? Fred had likely brought her. But how had he got her to stay?

Then they spoke of her condition, Betty saying that she was mending, but slowly. From which Halket gathered that the woman had been unwell. And this would explain her remaining in Betty's house. She hadn't been able to go away.

There followed references to money. Betty had apparently got some already, but wanted more. Fred must be buying her silence, or even co-operation. But, in passing, where had he got the money? He and his people were notoriously impecunious. Here was a side issue that might be worth following up, when the main one was disposed of.

At length it occurred to Halket to wonder why Fred didn't go in and see the woman himself. Why should he ask about her in this way? The conclusion to which this pointed was, that Fred had never yet shown himself to the woman, and didn't want to. But how then had she come there at all?

Fred and Betty had now moved away from their station, and, as Halket could hear no more of their conversation, he occupied himself following up this last line of thought and speculation. And, strangely enough, he was guided to an explanation that was in the main right, viz., that the woman had in her original journey towards Rathen lost her way, and landed at this place; and that Betty Duncan, having learned her secret, was now blackmailing her wayward husband, Fred Clark.

7

That young scoundrel was evidently straining every nerve to keep his poor wife out of sight and out of the way, so that he might, undiscovered and unchecked, pursue his dastardly courses.

This might do for the present. The woman, being unwell and unable to leave her present quarters, did not give so very much trouble just now. But, when she got well again, how was she to be suppressed? More drastic measures would certainly be needed to prevent a revelation that would crush her guilty husband. Would he shrink from taking such measures? After going so far in a course of sin and deception, would he pull up then? Halket had his own stern thoughts, and dark suspicions.

There was just one point on which he must first assure himself. It was the keystone of all his reasoning— the central aud ruling hypothesis of all his theorising. He must satisfy himself as to the identity of the "she" with the woman he was tracing. That established, he would be in possession of a body of facts and hints that should effectually equip him for meeting and overthrowing all the plots and machinations of the arch-villain, Fred Clark. Yes, he would run him to earth, sure enough!

He had now taken a cautious circuit, so as to command once more the front of the cot. By this time Fred had gone, and Betty had re-entered her domicile.

Halket waited for some time, so as to make sure that the coast was clear. Then he approached, and knocked at the door.

Betty wasn't a nervous woman. She answered the knock without any hesitation, throwing open the door and peering inquiringly into the gloom. Halket came forward. She could now see that her caller was a well-dressed gentleman, and she waited in some astonishment to learn his errand.

" Well, Betty ? " said he.

But she showed no sign of recognition, and then Halket remembered that he was to some extent disguised.

" Don't you know Mr Halket ? " he now added.

" O Lord's sake ! And it's you, sir," she exclaimed, holding up her hands, but making no movement to invite him in.

" I would like to see you for a little," said Halket ; and he made as if to come in, but she in a manner barred the way.

" Weel ; I'll hear ye."

" But I'm coming in."

" I've a——beddle in the hoose, and——"

" O, never mind, I won't disturb them ; but I must come in."

Then, when she couldn't make a better of it, she yielded, although with very evident reluctance. Half shutting the door, she said,—

" Weel than, wyte till I pit things richt afore ye come in."

Halket waited a brief moment, and then followed in. Betty, who was standing at the bed-side, now hastily shut the door by which these places used to be secured, and tried to look as if nothing were ado. But her visitor was not to be deceived.

" Whom have you there ? " he asked in a quiet, firm tone.

" Wid ye gang oot for the a' nicht things, lassie ? " said Betty, ignoring Halket's question, and speaking to her daughter Kirsty, who had risen from her seat at the fireside on Halket's entrance. The girl understood the order, and went away for water and peats. Halket waited till she had gone, and then repeated the question.

"O, jist a puir cratur that's bidin' wi's. She hisna been very weel, puir thing," was Betty's answer, delivered in an easy way.

"Who is she?"

"Fegs, Mr Halket, I dinna ken very weel mysel'."

"That's strange. Perhaps I may know." And he stepped to the bed, and threw open the doors.

Betty came forward with a haste that more than ever convinced Halket that he was right in his assumptions. She tried to prevent him looking into the bed; but he pushed her firmly aside.

Lily Douglas—for, of course, it was she that had been tucked away in the bed, and dared to say a word while the gentleman who was coming in should remain,—Lily raised her head and looked round. Halket saw and recognised her.

"Hillo!" he said cheerily, "you're here?"

"O, sir!" was Lily answer; and in it there was a note of trust and appeal that went to Halket's heart, and more than ever confirmed him in his determination to see her righted.

"That's all right, lass. I'm glad to meet you again."

Then he turned to Betty, who was now looking quite alarmed, and with an air of authority asked, "Who is this you've got here?"

"I dinna ken her name," Betty faltered.

"My name's Lily Douglas," said a sweet voice from the bed.

"Good!" exclaimed Halket, turning to the speaker once more.

"And how came you here, Lily?" he went on.

"I lost my way. . . . I was seeking Fred. . . . I think he stays at——O, I forget where it is: I am so stupid. . . . Can you take me to Fred?"

"She's rale ill," interposed Betty, "and has raved a hantle o' late. Ye needna mind onything she says."

"O, I have an idea how much to mind," said Halket drily. But, seeing that Lily was getting excited, he said to her soothingly, "Just you lie down, Lily, and be a good girl. I'll see that nothing comes over you."

And the poor creature, who had already contracted an instinctive trust in her original protector, lay down at the word, and was soon fast asleep. She was still very weak.

Halket, seeing this, gently closed the doors of the bed; and then, drawing a chair to the fireside, motioned Betty to take the stool. The old woman was now quite cowed, and submitted to the catechising to which he proceeded to subject her.

He let her see that he knew the main and essential facts of the case, and then made her acknowlege the rest. She made a pretty full confession, feeling she couldn't now help herself. The minister and the dominie exercised an authority in those days which the progress of democratic sentiment has now largely curtailed.

Nothing could well be done with Lily Douglas meantime. She was evidently too weak to be removed anywhere. This would tie up matters for a while at least. But he told Betty not to let her away without his express sanction. This he particularly and emphatically impressed on Betty. And, finally, she must keep his visit a profound secret, giving Fred Clark not a shadow of an inkling of any thing that might lead him to suspect that he (Halket) knew anything about this matter of Lily Douglas and his connection with her.

Threatening Betty with all manner of pains and penalties if she should in the slightest degree traverse his instructions, Halket went his way.

CHAPTER VII.

YULE.

THE end of the year was drawing on.

The dull weather of November had given way to keen frosts, and now, in the last weeks of December, a considerable fall of snow had taken place. It gave the country a picturesquely wintry look, without seriously incommoding people in their movements ; and, work being " weel forrit," the farmers were quite willing to take things easy, and prepare for enjoying the festivities of Yule. The general opinion indeed was that the weather was now " maist sizzonable."

Jamie was now quite recovered, and had returned to his work. He had, however, never been back to Millbog, or seen Bell. After getting his friend Halket to explain matters to her and assure her that there was " naething atween him and Miss Innes," he expected that she would admit she had done him an injustice, or at least give him some encouragement to renew his visits to Millbog, which her hard treatment of him had caused him to discontinue. When she gave no sign of an alteration in her attitude towards him, his pride forbade him to make any further advances ; and so they remained estranged, although each was ardently longing to meet the other again.—What mischief misunderstanding and pride together work in our lives !

Meanwhile at Millbog, while nothing wonderful had

happened, some things not altogether uninteresting were taking place.

Halket had returned to discharge the commission he had undertaken on behalf of Jamie. While not quite convincing Bell that Miss Innes' attentions to Jamie were due merely to courtesy and kindliness of heart, he succeeded in minimising their significance, and preparing Bell for giving Jamie, when he should next come to Millbog, a better reception than she had last accorded him. She fully expected he would follow up the overtures thus indirectly made through Halket by a personal call, when she would at least be prepared to hear what he had to say for himself. But he didn't come; and Bell felt sore at heart, though pride with her too kept her from making any advances.

Halket had also referred to Fred Clark, and warned Bell to beware of him. He wouldn't enter into particulars, or indeed make any definite charge against the young fellow; but he appeared so serious and emphatic in his warning that she was distinctly impressed, not to say alarmed. And next night, when Fred put in an appearance, she received him so coldly that he took occasion to get private speech of her, when she threw out such hints as made him quite nervous. He jumped to the conclusion that she had got hold of his dread secret. Of course he braved it out, looked very innocent, and swore a good deal. But he took care to discontinue his visits to Millbog until he should see what would come of it, and kept himself ready for action, should any revelation be sprung on him. Marget, who knew nothing of all this, did wonder a bit when Fred, who had of late been so assiduous in his attentions to her daughter, ceased to come near the house at all. But she was less inclined to remark it, or make any complaints about it, from certain other developments that began to show on the horizon.

Clyack's mother had lately died. She had been a worthy woman, kindly, prudent, and managing. Her son, who inherited some of her best qualities, was much attached to her; and, as he had never before wanted her presence and help, he felt very lonely now that she was gone. He came more frequently than ever to Millbog, where he could count on getting sympathy and the most sincere and friendly advice.

"I dinna weel ken fat wye I'm to get on," he would say. "Servant deems are guid eneuch fin ye've some wumman body o' yer ain to look aifter them. But they jist connich and blaud nae ordinar'."

"Ye'll need to get a capable hoosekeeper," was John's opinion.

But Marget ventured to revise this deliverance of her husband's.—

"A hoosekeeper—the very best o' them—they're nae like yer ain fowk."

To which Clyacks would assent. He and Marget somehow seemed to understand the situation better than old Bogie.

Much the same discussion was gone through each time Clyacks called. Marget had her own opinion as to what he ought to do, and she tried in a cautious kind of way to hint at a few considerations that might help to guide his mind in the desired direction. Clyacks had the bucolic nature—slow to apprehend new ideas, but tenacious of them when once apprehended. He didn't rapidly catch on to the ideas that Marget sought to instil, but every step he made in that direction was something gained. There was no fear of him going back on it. There wasn't a shadow of fickleness in his big honest nature.

Marget was encouraged in her little scheme by seeing that the subject of it was making progress, sure, if slow. Always as he came back with some other doleful tale,—now of the mismanagement of "the kitchen lass" or of "the deem that had the oot-wark," now of their quarrels, or again of the men's complaints "aboot the meat,"—Marget had good texts whereon to enlarge, and wherewith to enforce the recommendation she ultimately ventured to put into words, that he would "jist need to tak' a wife."

It took some time for this idea to reach his brain ; but by-and-by it did ; after which it was to him as axiomatic and incontrovertible as if it had been ordained of Heaven. He must take a wife. Marget couldn't well go further meantime. She could only hope he would have sense " to chise weel."

But during those days Bell noted a few things. Her mother scolded less than usual, and never when Clyacks was present. Nay, she even went the length of praising her work, and admitted that she was making good progress in the arts of dairying, baking, &c.

Bell could see what her mother was after ; but, not feeling any enthusiasm in the little game, she "never loot on." Then the old woman began to come nearer the point. Often, when they were alone together, she would lead the conversation to Clyacksneuk.—It was " sic a fine place—a big haddin' wi' a fine cover on't ; and a guid fu' hoose." And Sandy was " sic a fine man himsel'."—It was characteristic of the agricultural mind to regard the man as a kind of appendage of the farm. The latter was the thing to look at, although, of course, it was something to know that the *man* was not altogether unacceptable.

Bell assented to all this, but in such an uninterested way that her mother was driven to press her more closely. When, however, she could no longer pretend she didn't see what was meant, she tried to dismiss the subject by saying, " Ach, Sandy's ower auld for the like o' me." Whereupon the old woman buckled to the subject, and delivered a spirited oration, proving to a demonstration that a man should be at least fifteen years older than his wife, and, if he was twenty-five years older, so much the better. The girl didn't attempt to meet her mother's arguments, nor to provoke her by plainly resisting her will ; but she quite firmly decided in her own mind that she would never " hae a man that was auld eneuch to be her father."

Yule was now at hand ; and the social gathering of the Logie tenantry fixed for that date was becoming the great and absorbing topic of conversation in the district. The farmers with their wives were to be entertained to dinner in the House, and then in the evening there was to be a dance for the young people at the Stables. Captain Duff, who was leaving Logie in spring, wanted to make it a kind of farewell function, which might leave kindly recollections of his occupancy of the place.

The preparations for the occasion were extensive and thorough. There was just one item in the arrangements as originally proposed that had fallen through. This was the musical programme that Miss Innes and Jamie were to discourse. Miss Innes explained to her uncle why this would have to be departed from. Jamie's illness, she said, had so interfered with practice that they did not feel able to give a sufficiently good account of themselves, and would not run the risk of discrediting themselves by an indifferent performance. But this was not the main reason.

When Halket saw that he could not altogether disabuse Bell's mind of the ideas she had contracted in regard to the relations between Miss Innes and Jamie, and when he afterwards found from the latter that Bell had never given any sign of having changed or modified her attitude towards him, he decided to appeal to Miss Innes herself to help in the good work. It was a bold stroke. At first he meant to see the lady personally; but the delicacy of the situation so grew on him that he abandoned this plan, and set himself to put his appeal in writing. He rewrote the letter several times, and ultimately sent it anonymously.

It came as a blow to poor Miss Innes. She could see that it was no spiteful communication sent by some nasty creature to annoy her. Her anonymous correspondent appeared as sincere as he was well-informed, and put the whole matter so sensibly and well that she must perforce face the points raised, without any chance of finding cover or refuge from the cogency of their appeal. At first she was fain to treat the matter with a proud scorn. But she was too good a girl for this. Her better nature began to assert itself. Keen was the struggle and long ; but, when the storm and stress were past, victory remained with the right. With pride humbled and spirit bruised, she sat for some time in darkness of soul ; but erelong she began to realise that it wasn't to be all dark. There was dawning for her the light that Heaven vouchsafes to all whom duty leads into dark and lonely paths.

Miss Innes had gained the victory over selfishness and pride—substantially gained it. But she was still human. She would do what the writer of the letter wanted her to do; but we needn't wonder if she cast about for some way of doing it that would save her feelings as much as possible, and even contemplated the employment of the least little bit of dissembling. She would go to this peasant girl and laugh the matter off.—Such a preposterous idea that a lady like her should care for her uncle's gardener! Dear me!—And, to carry it well off, she must choose some time when she would appear to have encountered the girl by chance. Whereupon it occurred to her that the Yule-night dance would offer such a chance; and so she resolved to interview Bell on that occasion.

One thing was certain now.—She wouldn't carry out that pet little project of Jamie and her entertaining the company with music. No, no. It wouldn't do, now. When she came to this resolution she gave a little laugh, as if it were a small matter; but in eye and throat there were sensations that belied it all.

She took an early opportunity of letting Jamie know that she didn't now think it advisable for them to go on with their musical project. Of course she put a nice face on it, but Jamie thought he detected a certain change in her manner towards him, and was a good deal exercised over it. But he had got so accustomed to the change-ableness of female minds and moods, that he was prepared for almost any amount of the fickle and inexplicable when dealing with ladies.

And this was how there was to be no music at the dinner.

The eventful day at length arrived. The weather was quite propitious. The snow still lay on the ground, and gave a Yule-tide look to the country. There was a good deal of frost, and everything was dry and crisp.

With the dinner we shall not trouble very much. It was reckoned a grand affair by those who were privileged to be present. Some of the farmers who were good at figures set themselves to reckon up the number of pounds of beef consumed, and to calculate the price. But, as they couldn't so well put a value on the other viands and the general accessories of the table, they failed to strike a total with any confidence. It was, however, allowed that, "ae wye or ither the denner maun hae cost a hantle o' siller." And this was the nearest they could come to it.

We have much more pleasure in attempting to describe the evening gathering. It had been looked forward to with the keenest interest by all the young men and maidens on the estate of Logie, being considered the biggest affair of the kind that had taken place since the ball that was held on the occasion of the marriage of Mr Gordon, the late laird.

Buchan lasses a hundred and fifty years ago were in all essential respects pretty much what Buchan lasses are to-day. They were as fond of dressing well and looking well ; and, though their attire was simpler and less expensive, it was a matter of as deep and absorbing concern to them as are our more elaborate toilets to the damsels of to-day. And, when dressed, we may be sure they looked as charming to the lads then as do our present-day girls to *their* beaux.

Then there was just as much anxiety to be belle, and the same keen rivalry. It was something to gain this distinction at any dance ; but the honour of being belle on the present occasion was so great that every maiden did her level best to do herself and her charms justice, and, when the company were assembled in that big loft where the dance was to be held, good judges declared that never had there been seen in Logie such a display of youth and beauty.

Although there are no special judges appointed to decide on the rival claims of those who in such gatherings aspire to the honour of being considered "belle of the ball," yet, somehow or other, the opinion and judgment of the company soon get focussed, and in most cases a decision and award are soon made, which are as authoritative as if they had been delivered by some formal court appointed for the purpose.

Captain Duff and Miss Innes had come down to see the ball opened, and grace with their presence the auspicious occasion. They intended to stay a few dances, after which they would leave the company to enjoy themselves, as they felt sure they would do more unrestrainedly in their absence.

The opening dance was a good old-fashioned Scotch reel. The Captain took the floor with his niece, and, as Miss Innes stood up, fair of form and faultlessly dressed, and bearing herself with the dignified sweetness that comes of perfect good-breeding, everybody felt that she was queen, and peerless.

This was of course as it should be. For she was a lady born and bred, and no common person could hope to compete with her. While all noted her superiority, Jamie alone felt the full force of her grace and charm. The discipline that she had lately gone through had etherealised her look. He saw the effect, while never suspecting the cause. He was, along with other two players, providing music for the dance, and, as she moved through the mazes of the reel, his eyes never left her. He played for her alone. She was to him a kind of goddess, his feelings being more those of worship than anything else.

Miss Innes, however, had to be set aside when the question of who was belle came to be decided. She wasn't in the competition. Everybody recognised that ; and set themselves to scan the floor during the first dance to see who of the general company was worthy to win the prize.

Very soon it was felt that Bell was likely to carry the honours of the night. This was an impression while the dance proceeded ; and, when it was done, an informal comparing of notes resulted in a clear decision in her favour. Young, fresh, and fair, and dressed with great taste and neatness, she stood forth as the most charming of the rustic bevy. Jamie, who understood and endorsed the general judgment, could not help feeling proud, although the irritation he nursed kept him from enjoying the thing to the full.

When the second dance was announced, Captain Duff, as if aware of the opinion of the company and wishful to pay deference to it, took Bell as his partner. And now her triumph was assured and complete. She didn't know, however, that Miss Innes had something to do with it, that lady having prompted the Captain in the matter.

Having thus got her uncle to honour Bell with the first dance given to any of the general company, Miss Innes embraced the chance, when the dance was over, of sitting down beside the girl, ostensibly to congratulate her, but for the further and more real purpose of speaking to her about Jamie. By the time this subject was reached the next dance was in progress, and, as they were now left sitting pretty much by themselves, they had more freedom to converse together.

Hard as had been the struggle needed to come to the self-denying resolution, still harder did Miss Innes feel the task of carrying it out. Her pride and womanly reserve received a severe shock. Then it was so difficult to meet this girl on the common ground that had to be occupied ere the matter could even be broached between them. Bell too, on her part, was painfully embarrassed, blushing and protesting in the most awkward and shamefaced manner.

After the ordeal was over, Miss Innes remained a short time speaking to some more of the guests ; and then with her uncle left the ball, and walked back to the House.

When the Captain and his niece took their departure, there was a kind of lull in the proceedings, and someone suggested a song for a variety. In those days when songs and singers were fewer, a man would get identified with some particular ditty. He had always to sing it. His friends wouldn't let him off. He must sing when asked—and just that song. Nothing else would do. And his friends never tired of hearing it.

Among the more elderly people present was our friend

8

Bogie, and Bogie had a ballad that he had sung for many
a day.   His neighbour Lumbs now called for it, and, as
the company endorsed the request with hearty cheering,
Bogie had to yield.   He cleared his throat, and in a thin
and somewhat cracked voice began.—

THE BONNIE LASS O' FYVIE.

There was a troop of Irish dragoons
  Came marching up through Fyvie, O ;
And their captain's fa'en in love wi' a very bonnie lass,
  And her name it was called Pretty Peggy, O.

O come down the stair, Pretty Peggy, my dear,
  O come down the stair, Pretty Peggy, O ;
O come, come down the stair, kaim out your yellow hair,
  Take the last farewell o' your daddy, O.

O how can I come down, bonnie laddie, she said,
  O how can I come down, bonnie laddie, O ;
O how can I come down when I'm locked up in my room,
  And a well in below my room window, O ?

It's braw, it's braw a captain's lady to be,
  It's braw being a captain's lady, O,
It's braw to rove and rant and to follow with the camp,
  And to march when your captain's ready, O.

The Colonel he cries, Mount boys, mount boys, mount ;
  O tarry says the captain, O tarry, O ;
O tarry, O tarry another day or two,
  Or we see if this bonnie lass will marry, O.

Out then spak' our bold brother John,
  And O but he spak' angry, O ;
Says, If she winna go, we'll get sweethearts enew,
  There's mony a bonnie lass into Fyvie, O.

There's mony a bonnie lass into bonnie Auchterless,
  There's mony a bonnie lass in the Garioch, O ;
There's mony a bonnie lass in Fyvie's bonnie howe,
  But the bonniest o' a' is Pretty Peggy, O.

The first intown that we came to,
  Our captain was sick and weary, O ;
And the next intown that we came to,
  We got our captain to bury, O.

It was not the girl's beauty that I did admire,
  But she was my only fancy, O ;
My name is Captain Ned, I have died for a maid,
  I have died for the bonnie lass o' Fyvie, O.

After the song was over, Jamie, surrendering his fiddle
to another player who had just arrived, strolled out.   He
was standing on the little bridge that spans the burn,
listening to the music and dancing that had now been
resumed within, when a light foot, unheard till it was
close at hand, roused him from his reverie.   He started
to find Bell at his side.

"It's—a fine nicht, Jamie," she said, with evident
hesitation.

Jamie was still more embarrassed.

"Ay ; it's a fine nicht."

They stood a while, silent and irresolute.

"It's a fine nicht," said Jamie, evidently oblivious of
the fact that the observation had already been made and
assented to.

"Ay," was Bell's reply, as she looked away down the
stream.

Jamie looked too.

She was waiting till he should say something further,
and for that something he was industriously hunting.
But the inspiration was slow to come.

"It's a fine nicht," he said at length, but managed to
add—" for a walk."

And, by a kind of common impulse, both turned their

faces toward the garden. They stepped along in silence, and stopped at the gate.

"Wid ye like to—see through the gairden?" asked Jamie.

"Ay, fine," said Bell.

Now there wasn't much to be seen in a garden in December—especially at night. But really they didn't bother looking for anything. The path was narrow, and, as they had to walk quite close, Jamie was tempted to put his arm round Bell's waist, and, with a thrill, he felt her yield in just the smallest way. It was enough. He knew that she was his.

Jamie of course knew the garden thoroughly, and, with unerring instinct, he led the way to the point most interesting and appropriate at that moment. This was a bower at the far end of the walk they were treading. Honeysuckle hung in festoons about it. Of course leaf and bloom were gone, and the scent. But imagination could somewhat repair the scene and its accessories; and, though there was snow beneath and but the cold light of the stars above, they felt as if sitting in a leafy arbour on some divine eve in June.—Yes, youth and love are fit for anything.

"Bell?" said Jamie tenderly, as he seated himself by her side.

"Weel, Jamie?" was the soft answer, delivered in an easy tone as if there was nothing of any possible interest to her just then.

Jamie didn't know how to begin. A preamble would have been nice and appropriate; but he was too nervous for any rhetorical effort. He plunged *in medias res*.

"Ye mind Hallowe'en?" he said, with awkward suddenness.

But Bell steadied matters.

"Hallowe'en?" she repeated, as if trying to refresh an indifferent memory.—"Ay, I div mind something aboot it."

"Wis ye—wis ye—playin' a rig yon time?"

"Which time?"

"Yon time.—Ye mind fine."

But Bell didn't make any haste to answer, and he went on.—

"Yon time when ye cam' rinnin' in, ye min'."

"Och, dinna bother's!" was the reply.

The affected impatience Jamie knew quite well how to interpret, and, growing bolder, he went on.—

"Come noo, Bell, did ye mean't?"

"Mean what?"

"Yon.—Did ye raley mean't?"

"Maybe I did; but dinna bother's Jamie."

"Ye're sure, Bell, ye did mean't."

And Jamie leaned closer, and tried to look in her face. She made no reply.

"Some?—Jist some?" he said softly, as if to help her.

"Imphm," was the almost inaudible reply.

He clasped her in his arms. She didn't speak. She didn't resist. And once again their lips met in a fond passionate kiss.

It was no momentary, uncalculated ebullition this time. Each revelation and admission of love between two people grows more deliberate and full. This gradual widening and deepening of the range of consciousness

and confession provides a constant charm. When all
has been felt and confessed, though love may remain,
passion is well-nigh spent.

The evening was pretty well advanced when the two
left the arbour. And now self-consciousness came upon
them, and a sort of guilty feeling. How were they to
rejoin the company? They knew the kind of reception
they would get—the banter and the "raggin'" which
they would have to stand from their companions.

Jamie's first impulse was to retire to his chaumer, and
never show face at all; but then Bell would have to re-
appear alone, and the cowardice of the thing struck him
at once. No: they must go together, and together take
the "batherin'" that was sure to be their lot when they
presented themselves once more in the loft.

When they came to the foot of the stair by which the
place was reached, it was a relief to hear someone start
a song. It was sure to be followed by applause, during
which they would take care to enter, thus hoping to escape
a good deal of the storm that otherwise waited them.

The song to which they now listened was one of those
artless productions that find favour in rustic circles. It
was sung by a young woman, and was in praise of

THE PLOOMAN.

O weel I like a plooman lad,
  Sae weel's I like my plooman;
'Mang a' the lads baith near and far,
  Commend me to the plooman.

There's clever chiels at Rattery,
  They're unco braw at Haddo;
But O, it's Johnnie I lo'e best,
  My bonnie plooman laddie.

O weel I min' on Sandy Gibb,
    When first I fee'd at Essie ;
O Sandy was a lad to coort,
    He ca'd me his dear lassie.

And syne I liket Geordie Rae,
    He was a handsome fellow ;
But he gaed aff wi' Kirsty Broon,
    They're bidin' at Craigellie.

But noo I've Johnnie for my jo,
    And him I lo'e richt dearly ;
And we will mairry at Whitsunday,
    And syne we'll ne'er think weary.

For weel I like my plooman lad,
    Sae weel's I like my plooman ;
'Mang a' the lads baith near and far,
    Commend me to the plooman.

The applause on which the belated couple had calculated came off, and they managed under cover of it to get in without any general challenge. What they had escaped as a volley, came during the rest of the evening in single sallies from one individual or another. This, however, was much easier to bear—nay had a pleasant piquancy about it, just as a little spice adds zest to a dish, when a large quantity would make it unbearable.

For one thing Bell was particularly thankful, and that was the absence of her mother. The baby that Lily Douglas had left at Millbog always needed the attention of one or other of them, so that they could not well be both away from home at one time. After her mother's exposition of her views on matrimony, and the application of them to her daughter's particular case, Bell knew how bitterly she would oppose Jamie's suit. Of course the matter couldn't continue to be hid. It would have to be threshed out between them some time, but like most people she preferred to have the evil day postponed.

And now Jamie, who saw the fiddlers were managing quite well without his help, took Bell up for a dance.—It was the consummation of the evening's happiness for them both, being a kind of public acknowledgment and seal of their love and attachment.

After a few more dances there was a call for another song, and Jamie was singled out as the man to meet the demand. He would fain have declined; but the company, who knew his powers in this line, would take no denial.

He gave them

MORMOND BRAES.

As I gaed doon by Strichen toon,
  I heard a fair maid mournin',
And she was makin' sair complaint
  For her true love ne'er returnin'.

It's Mormond Braes where heather grows,
  Where aft times I've been cheery,
It's Mormond Braes where heather grows,
  And there I've lost my dearie.

Refrain.

Sae fare ye weel, ye Mormond Braes,
  Where aften I've been cheery;
Fare ye weel, ye Mormond Braes,
  For there I've lost my dearie.

O, I'll put on my goon o' green,
  It's a forsaken token,
And that will let the young men know
  That the bands o' love are broken.

There's mony a horse has snappert and fa'en,
   And risen and gane fu' rarely ;
There's mony a lass has lost her lad,
   And got anither richt early.

There's as good fish into the sea
   As ever yet was taken,
I'll cast my line and try again,—
   I'm only ance forsaken.

O, I'll gang doon to Strichen toon,
   Where I was bred and born,
And I will get anither true love
   Will marry me the morn.

The gathering did not break up till "the sma' 'oors o' the mornin'." Everybody declared it was the most successful thing of the kind they had ever been at ; and Jamie—well, as he took endearing farewell of Bell whom he had convoyed to the door of her home, he thought it had been the most glorious evening ever seen since lads and lasses and love appeared on the earth.

CHAPTER VIII.

SANDY'S WOOING.

No time of the year is as a rule so dull as that which follows the Christmas and New Year season. The year's festivity then reaches its height, and there follows the inevitable reaction. In the days of which we write the year began in March, and Yule had to bear the whole weight of the season's joy and rejoicing. And, as this particular Yule at Logie had seen something like a high-water mark in the festive line, the re-action was more keenly felt than usual.

At least two people, however, managed to contend pretty successfully with the dull feeling that was now abroad. They had got infused into their lives a joy and interest that, like a new-opened spring, would keep their hearts fresh and sweet for many days. Jamie and Bell, in short, were now enjoying "love's young dream," and everything, taking its colour therefrom, looked rosy and bright.

But no joys are perfect. Bell couldn't forget that her parents had set their hearts on her marrying Clyacks, and she dreaded the day when they should come to know of her love for Jamie; while Jamie, on his part, began to suspect, from the rather cold way in which they treated him, that he would not be regarded as a suitable match for their daughter.

These things troubled them a little; but they did not

touch the kernel of their joy. Secure in each other's love, they did not bother much about the future. Things that might prove obstacles to marriage do not greatly trouble young lovers, on whose golden horizon wedlock has hardly begun to dawn.

At length, however, the coldness with which he was received at Millbog became so marked, that Jamie was driven to appeal to Bell for an explanation; whereupon she admitted to him that Clyacks was coming about the house, and that her people wanted her to marry him.

"And will ye?" asked Jamie, in the foolish way of lovers who, like child-gardeners with their plants, are ever digging up their loves by the roots.

Bell, with a touch of feminine mischievousness answered,—

"He has never socht me yet."

"But gin he was to seek ye?"

"Jamie!"

There was any amount of tender reproach in the word. After which, of course, came fresh endearments; and they parted fonder than ever.

Jamie, nevertheless, ceased visiting at Millbog. His pride would not stand the kind of treatment he got. Bell and he nevertheless contrived to meet pretty frequently. She had resumed her visits to Logie, and Jamie usually managed to see her and accompany her home. And at times, when she had errands in other directions, she got Jockie to carry a message to Jamie that secured his attendance.

Meanwhile Sandy was coming more frequently than ever to Millbog. At length he summoned up courage to broach the subject of marriage to old John and his wife, asking the hand of their daughter Bell. Both gave their most cordial consent. With this Clyacks seemed to be satisfied ; but Marget who, having interrogated Bell, knew that he had never spoken to her on the subject, gently hinted that he would " Maybe need to speak to the lassie hersel'."

This was a new ordeal for poor Sandy to face, and it took him about a week to get his courage screwed up to the required tension. He was such a diffident wooer that he stood sorely in need of help to come to the point ; but Bell, so far from giving him any assistance in his courtship, made it as difficult as possible, being at one time shy, at another mischievous, and meeting all his hints with an innocence or a density that was most disheartening to the poor man.

One night he came determined to bring the matter to an issue.

" Weel, Bell, fu' auld wid ye be ? " he began.

" O, auld eneuch for a' the guid I've deen," said Bell with a laugh.

This disconcerted him a bit. He sat smoking a while and looking in the fire. The two had the place to themselves, Marget having, as usual, found a job . for every other body that would keep them out of the way a while. This Bell always noted, and silently contrasted the facilities afforded Sandy with the obstacles thrown in Jamie's way.

After a while Clyacks took the pipe from his mouth, looked half round, and spoke again.—

" Isn't it time ye were marriet ? "

"O fie, I'm but a lassie yet."

" But ye're aye growin' aulder. "

Sandy, who thought the reflection embodied in this last remark of his quite impressive and almost solemnising, was so distressed to find it greeted with merry laughter, that he didn't say another word that night.

The next time he came back he began where he he had left off.—

" Ye wid like to be marriet sometime, widna ye, Bell ? "

" O ay, but I'll be in guid time, Sandy."

Again, as before, there came a smoking interlude.—

" And fu wid I dee for a man, Bell ? " he said at last, but without looking up.

" O guidsakes, Sandy, nae ava jist !—Ye're ower auld for me."

" Fu auld wid ye think I wis noo ? "

" O, maybe fifty."

" Na, I'm only forty-sax. I cam' in wi' the century."

" That's awfu' handy. Ye'll hae nae diffeeculty in mindin' your age."

Poor Sandy was bound to reflect on the advantage to which Bell had referred, which carried him so far away from the point he had been making for that he couldn't get his mind into position again for renewing the attack.

And so he did no more courting that night.

But Bell's mother had overheard this little bit of conversation, and, when Sandy went away, she took her daughter to task about it.—

" Fat wye did ye say yon to Sandy, ye stupid limmer ? " she demanded, in unusually sharp tones. " Dinna ye ken a guid offer when ye get it ? "

But Bell was silent. She had learned the efficacy of this weapon of silence.

"My certies," her mother went on, "mony a lass wid jump at Clyacks."

There was no reply.

"Gin ye lat an offer like that by ye, ye deserve to want a' your days.—Sic anither coo 'll never low at your door again, I tell ye."

Bell's continued silence so irritated her mother that she went close up to her, patted her foot, and almost shrieked,—

"Fat d'ye mean, lassie?—Lat's hear ye!"

Bell had to speak. Her answer was sullen and short,—

"Weel, I'm nae for Clyacks."

"Fa are ye for than?"

"Naebody."

And Bell walked away, leaving her mother looking after her in anger, pity, and amazement.

Next night Bell was at Logie, and Jamie accompanied her home. They were standing in the cornyard, having a quiet crack before they should say good-night, when, as ill-luck would have it, Bell's mother, who had been taking a look round among pigs and poultry, happened to pass that way.

There was no missing the pair, or mistaking their relations. Full in the moon they stood, Jamie's arm encircling Bell's waist, while she leaned her head on his shoulder.

Marget saw, and stopped. It was some little time ere she took in the scene and situation, and, after that was done, she spent a few more seconds getting mind and tongue in line for action. The interval was a trying one for the delinquents, especially for Bell, who could best gauge the storm that was coming, and had most reason to dread its violence. Yet neither of them offered to get out of the compromising position in which they were being seen.

Which, while both honest and wise of them, only served to aggravate matters in the eyes of their censor.

"Bell!" she cried at length; and there was no mistaking the attitude and feelings of the speaker. The tone and inflection of voice bespoke uncompromising blame and bitterest rebuke.

Yet, not feeling called on to make any reply, Bell remained silent, while her companion, not being addressed at all, had still less call to put himself forward.

"Come to the hoose wi' ye—this meenit, see!"

There was something definite in this, and Bell instinctively made as if to disengage herself from Jamie's embrace.

"And you, Jamie Robertson," Marget went on, "gang hame wi' ye!—Comin' prowlin' aboot dacent fowk's hooses at a' 'oors o' the nicht!—Think shame o' yersel!—I'll tell the Captain aboot it."

Jamie had now stood apart from Bell. Disconcerted at first and almost dismayed, he was now getting nettled under the lash of Marget's tongue, and his feelings were fast sharping into resentment. But she went on.—

"Ye should bide amo' yer ain kin.'—Ye seerly ken Bell's nae for the like o' you.—She's bespoken for better fowk, somebody fit to gie her a richt kin' o' a hame."

Jamie now felt quite indignant; and there was a certain dignified defiance in his bearing, as he stood off. from Bell and assumed an attitude of interrogation that was unmistakeable, even without the "Indeed?" that accompanied it.

" It's nae true, Jamie," cried Bell, putting her hands on his shoulders and looking up fondly in his face. " It's nae true. They're wantin' me to mairry Clyacks. But I'm nae for 'im.—I'm for *you*, Jamie ! "

And Jamie again put his arm about her, while Marget stood almost paralysed with anger and astonishment. Her victims had turned the tables on her, and were acting their little drama with a freedom and unconsciousness that quite took away her breath.

" That's a' richt, Bell," said Jamie tenderly, " I'll trust to ye.—But gang awa wi' yer mither the noo.—And guidnicgt."

Then he strode away with that dignified step of his that came as natural to him as if he had been born a prince, while Bell walked quickly to the house, followed by her exasperated mother.

Into the house we shall not follow them. It isn't edifying to witness much of the kind of scene that was therein enacted. Suffice it to say that the mother was very bitter, and the daughter sullen and defiant, with the result that the cause of irritation and estrangement between them was deepened, and threatened to become permanent.

Bell's father was duly informed, and at the mother's suggestion he subjected his daughter to a lecture on the folly and sinfulness of her conduct. Although it was much less sharp than the maternal attack had been, Bell felt it more and treated it with greater respect, as her father so seldom intervened in matters of domestic discipline.

A night or two after Clyacks called again, and once more returned to the subject of marriage. Bell felt there was little use hedging any longer. She had better face the crisis at once and have done with it.

"Sandy," she said, "I canna be your wife. I like ye—rale weel; but —but I've anither lad."

"Yea?" said Sandy. And he sat silent a while, till he should get hold of the import of the words.

Afraid that he wasn't quite understanding the situation, she added,—

"An' I like him best."

"Vera likely," was the quiet response. Clyacks spoke in his slow sententious way; but feeling the thing very much more than one would have thought from his outward deameanour, which was stolid enough.

"And fa micht this ither lad be?" he asked at length.

"Och!—never min'."

But Sandy wouldn't be put off. He must know.

"Weel than, it's—it's—Jamie Robertson."

How difficult it was to say the name.

"Yea?" said Clyacks, and relapsed into silence. But he wasn't done with the subject. Somehow, when the conversation got off and away from himself, he felt more freedom.

"An' ye like him best?" he said, after a little.

"Ay," was Bell's brief answer, but blushing and simpering spun it out.

"And has he socht ye?"

"Ay,—a kin' o't."

There followed another and a longer pause. There wasn't much sign that Clyacks was exercising himself over the matter to any particular extent; but inwardly a struggle was going on, —and, for a man of his phlegmatic nature, a deep one. Bell suspected that he was

9

feeling more than he showed, and she was sorry for him.

At length he sat up, and Bell instinctively felt that he had made up his mind in some way or other.

"Weel than, Bell," he began, speaking with great deliberation, " I winna seek ye again. . . . Jamie's a guid lad. . . . . He ance did me a guid turn, and I hinna forgotten't till 'im."

" O thank ye, Sandy," Bell broke in, "ye're awfu' guid ! "

He took no notice of the interruption, but went on.—

" Noo, gin Jamie tak' ye, it's a' richt. But gin he *dinna* tak' ye, or gin ye dinna want to tak' *him*, ye'll maybe min' that I'm aye willin'."

Clyacks flourished in other times and circumstances from Barkis, but in their way of putting proposals matrimonial the two men seem to have approximated somewhat.

After this Clyacks never referred to the subject of marriage again. Yet, unlike most rejected suitors, he continued his visits,and remained on the best of terms with the woman who had refused him. Marget was puzzled. If Bell had accepted Sandy, he would no doubt have disclosed the fact ; and, if she had rejected him, it was strange to find him coming to the house as if nothing had occurred to disappoint him.

There was no use questioning her daughter, so she approached Sandy on the matter.—

" Fat's adee wi' you and Bell ? " she ventured to ask one evening.

" Oh, naething," said Sandy, in an easy tone.

She pressed him further, but all she could get out of him was the assurance,—

"It's a' richt, mistress: Bell and me understands ane anither."

This wasn't satisfactory, but it left room for a hope that it would all come right by-and-by.

In any case she couldn't well say anything further in the way of criticism or scolding, until she knew better how the matter stood. In this way Bell had rest for a little.

One may be sure Bell was not long in telling Jamie the good news. He was much moved to hear of Clyack's magnanimity :—

"He's a fine chiel, Sandy," he said, with enthusiasm.

His good opinion of his rival was destined to be still further enhanced. For one day Clyacks came to the garden, ostensibly to see if he could get "ony guid lang blue tawties for seed," but really for the purpose of interviewing Jamie.

He had difficulty in getting on to the subject that was uppermost in his mind, and spoke a lot about the weather and other irrelevant topics, before he managed to introduce it.

"Ye'll be gaun awa' afore lang, Jamie?" he said at length, with an effort.

"Ay, my time's aboot oot," Jamie replied.

Clyacks stood looking half away from the young man for a few moments, then, without looking round, he asked abruptly,—

"Wid ye be thinkin' o' mairryin' ony time?"

Jamie started, and blushed furiously. Which latter exhibition was quite wasted, as his interrogator continued to look away into the shrubbery.

"No,—nae— jist yet," was his stammering reply.

"Cause—I micht hae gi'en ye a bit help to tak' a placie. But I suppose ye maybe widna jist care very muckle for fairmin'.''

"O, thank ye, Clyacks; ye're awfu' kind.—I dinna think I wid mak' a guid fairmer. I'll may be jist as weel stick to the spad'."

"Weel, than, if I could dee onything to help ye, jist lat's ken.—Files a body's nane the waur o' the turn o' a few bawbees when they're settin' up hoose for themsel's."

Clyacks had chanced to hear Marget refer to Jamie in a disparaging way as being "as puir's a kirk moose," and this had dictated the kindly hint he now gave the young man. Jamie thanked him very warmly. He said he wasn't thinking of settling down just yet: he would like to see a bit of the world first. But he was happy to know that, if ever he should be in need of help, there was one good friend to whom he could in confidence go.—And the two men shook hands, quite understanding each other.

During those days Miss Innes felt particularly lonely. To one who had been accustomed to Edinburgh with its gaiety and stir, life at Logie was necessarily dull and slow. When she first came to Buchan, she had suffered a good deal from *ennui*, until she began to be interested in and attracted by Jamie Robertson. And, in passing, there is no saying how many attachments owe their origin to a certain vacuity of mind and heart at a critical juncture. In the midst of congenial society, Miss Innes had, in all probability, never given such an one as Jamie Robertson a single thought. Meeting him in Buchan where the people seemed to her dull, and life uneventfu she was glad to find one who was interesting and attractive, and erelong intercourse with him had established friendly relations, and ultimately produced an attachment, the strength of which she had not gauged until called on by the pressure of circumstances to break it.

Had Captain Campbell been an acceptable suitor, her life at Logie would have been much brighter; for, as we have seen, he paid her warm attentions, and, although she was still cold and distant, he continued his visits, coming frequently from Peterhead, where with a party of his men he was now stationed. But she had never cared much for the Captain, and, since they had came into collision over Jamie Robertson, her indifference had got accentuated into a feeling that approached dislike.

Her connection with Jamie had brought interest and brightness into her life; but it had to be enjoyed with a certain innocent unconsciousness. It was something that would hardly bear statement, still less examination. And, when circumstances had compelled her to look at it, she had been visited with a certain shame and self-reproach that, hard enough to bear in secrecy and silence, were aggravated by the fact that some other people shared the knowledge of her humiliation.

After her interview with Bell she had suffered much mental distress, and the night that had been the happiest of their lives to not a few at Logie was to her the most keenly miserable she had ever spent. Time and reflection of course helped to bring her into a calmer mood; but the wound to heart and pride remained, and she longed for the time when she would with her uncle leave Logie, and put all its associations into the perspective of the past.

Such were her feelings at first. She saw matters in but one light; and, as her mind took this direct and uncomplicated view of the situation, so were her wishes and intentions in regard to it marked by confident decision. But nothing is so simple as it at first sight appears, and Miss Innes was destined ere long to feel this episode in her life's drama complicated in quite unforeseen ways, and the moral problem involved burdened with new distractions.

She could not help seeing Jamie occasionally; but she came less frequently to the garden, and was much more distant in her dealings with him. This line of conduct was mainly dictated by a sense of duty; but there was just the least trace of pique behind this worthy motive, which showed that the mischief and the danger had been suppressed rather than eradicated.

Jamie couldn't understand the change in Miss Innes' manner towards himself. Of course he had wondered why Bell had so suddenly got over her difficulty in regard to Miss Innes; but he was content in such a matter to leave speculation alone and feel that all's well that ends well.

Not knowing, however, why Miss Innes should be different, he would at times offer to converse on the old themes that used to be so interesting to them both,—on music and poetry,—literature and art, and the wider outlook of culture; and, though at first unwilling to engage in such conversations, the lady would from time to time forget her self-denying ordinance, and be betrayed into an exhibition of the old interest and even enthusiasm.

After such lapses she would reproach herself, and record new vows; but, somehow or other, she had secretly to acknowledge after all that she wasn't making much progress along the path she had marked out for herself.

Next she began to wonder if it was all so wrong and bad as she had at first thought. Their conversations were always on most improving subjects. Sometimes, indeed, the talk soared away into ideal heights. And Jamie seemed so fond of these discussions, and confessed himself so improved and elevated by them, that it was surely a great pity that anybody's narrow and squeamish ideas should interfere with a course that produced such gratifying results.

Jamie was indeed a different man when in Miss Innes' company. He seemed then to get away from his poor surroundings and their narrowing influence—to rise above himself, to breathe a serener air, and to speak another and vastly more copious tongue.

As Miss Innes continued to note this reaching away from his environment on the part of Jamie, there began to stir deep down in her heart a hope, unexpressed at first and unconfessed, that thus perhaps would he ultimately leave the sphere where she had to surrender her claim in him, and join her on a plane where old attachments and affinities would lapse and perish. Whenever this idea offered to take definite shape in her mind, she was struck with something like remorse, and crushed down the temptation. But, though we may refuse to look at forbidden sweets, we can never quite forget that they are there.

CHAPTER IX.

BETTY'S DREAM.

HALKET returned from time to time to Betty Duncan's cottage, to see how Lily was getting on. He had several conversations with her, in which she confided to him a good many particulars relating to her past history. On these points her memory was clear enough; but, when she came to deal with her more recent experiences, she often forgot or mixed up things in quite a pathetic way.

She spoke at times about her baby, wondering where it was, but, strangely enough, never showing any anxiety as to its welfare. Of Fred she also spoke, but happily appeared to have forgot all about his treachery. Her mind had evidently been much affected by the distressing experiences through which she had passed, and had indeed come perilously near being quite unhinged.

Having forgot about her husband's treachery and double-dealing, she innocently disclosed one thing after another that more and more compromised the fellow, until Halket could see that only discovery and identification were needed to bring on him the very severe penalties that were being meted out to the Jacobites that had been specially bitter and outstanding in their opposition to the Government. But, just because it had been done in Prince Charlie's cause, Halket would keep the thing secret, although he thought that, as now a base renegade, Fred Clark richly deserved to suffer.

Fred also had come from time to time to interview Betty as to the progress her patient was making, and, when he understood that she was fairly well recovered, he proposed taking her away. Probably his intention was so to browbeat and intimidate the poor creature as to make her return whence she came. But he did not get the chance to carry out his intention; for Betty gave him to understand that out of her house Lily was not to go meantime.

He tried all kinds of weapons—threats, and flatteries, and promises; but nothing could move Betty. Nor would she give him any reason for thus thwarting his wishes. But Fred found out for himself.

One night he came to Betty's, and, looking in at the window, saw Halket sitting at the fireside conversing with Lily. At once he concluded that this man—his old dominie and natural enemy—was at the bottom of the business. He would be championing Lily against himself; and Betty was his ally. Doubtless, too, Halket had learned all his antecedents, and would be going to crush him. It was this same man, further, that had poisoned Bell against him. Fred soon ran it all up.

And now he was driven to contemplate more desperate measures than ever. No ordinary remedy need be tried in a crisis.

Thus do people go from sin to sin. No man can well bargain, on his beginning a course of crime and deception, how far he is to go. One step commits him to a second; and ever, as he goes, it becomes more difficult to pull up, until, in many cases, he brings ruin on his head. Things he would have shrunk from at first are now offered him as alternatives with exposure; and, while in other circumstances they would have been put aside with a shudder, now measured with utter ruin, they are embraced as the lesser of two evils. Happy he who never so entangles himself as to have to make the dread choice.

What Fred *must* do to begin with, was to get Lily out of their hands. This would be very difficult to accomplish; for Betty, knowing how anxious he was to get her away, was specially vigilant. He came frequently, but no chance ever offered. He thought of many plans, and tried some; but none of them succeeded. Their only effect was to increase Betty's watchfulness. Then he ceased coming, and Betty thought he had given up hope of accomplishing his purpose.

So January passed, and February came. It was now a particularly dreary time. The snow had gone, and the country looked bare and black. Rain and high winds were frequent.

One dreary night Lily sat by the fireside talking with Betty, while Kirsty slept on a "shake-down" in the corner, which had now been her bed for many weeks. Lily's mind had been reverting to past times, and she spoke much about Fred, exhibiting all the tender fondness of a devoted wife who is longing to rejoin her absent husband.

"Yes, he is going to come for me, my Fred," she said, "and I'm going away with him."

"Na, nae a fit o' ye," said Betty, in her hard unsympathetic voice.

The poor creature looked sad, but said no more. She sat gazing fixedly on the smouldering peats, while outside the wind howled along the bare hillside.

"Gang awa' to your bed," said Betty at length.

"I'm waiting for Fred," was the quiet answer.

"Havers! Ye'll never—ye winna see him the nicht. Ye maun—"

"Hark!" exclaimed Lily, with wild eagerness on her face, and holding up her finger. "That's him!"

Betty listened, but heard nothing. It was only some more of Lily's delusions, she thought.

"Ach, ye puir stupid cratur!—Gang awa' to your bed: I'm awa' to mine."

But Lily paid no attention to the order. She had risen to her feet, and was standing in an attitude of listening, her whole soul in her face.

"Hark!" she cried again; and now Betty herself thought she heard a voice in the wind, although to her it was perfectly inarticulate.

A great light had broken over Lily's countenance.

"That's him! It's Fred!" she exclaimed, and, with a wild cry of delight, she darted to the door.

So sudden and unexpected was the movement, that she had reached the door before Betty could bestir herself to arrest her.

"Come back, Lily! Far are ye gaun?" she cried, as she rushed after her charge. But by this time the poor girl was out into the night.

Betty soon reached the door, and, as the light streamed forth into the gloom, she caught one glance of a disappearing figure.

"Fred, Fred," came the cry, borne back on the wind, and the next moment Lily had vanished into the wild night.

Betty followed a few steps from the door, crying, "Lily, Lily!" But there was no reply. Only the wind was heard as it whistled past, and then went booming away into the infinite darkness.

There she stood in helpless despair. There was no use trying to follow. Even had she known the track by which Lily had gone, her old limbs would have had no chance in the race.

It was some time ere she could quite realise or believe that her charge was gone. For a while she tried to persuade herself that the girl would return. It must have been a delusion—that voice; and, after running a bit and finding nobody, she would be sure to come back.

So Betty stood, hoping against hope. At length she retreated to the doorstep, and stood there " in the lythe" a long time. But she waited in vain. Hope was dying in her heart; and, as it passed away, there came thought and reflection.

What was she to do? How was she to explain the affair to Mr. Halket? He would be bitterly disappointed to find Lily gone, and would lay all the blame on her. He would charge her at least with gross carelessness, and there was no saying but he might even suspect her of having connived at the escape. If she had even had Kirsty as a witness of the affair, it would have been something; but that young person had slept soundly through it all. Poor Betty was in great distress, and felt quite dismayed at the prospect of meeting Halket.

Reluctantly at last she quitted her post at the door, which, however, she left open so as to help, if possible, and encourage the wanderer to return. Advancing to the corner where her daughter lay, she shook her; and, when the girl appeared to be sufficiently awake to understand what was said, she told her of Lily's escape. Kirsty, however, did not share her mother's concern to any great extent. She didn't feel any particular responsibility in the matter, and, in any case, nobody could "gie her the wyte o't."

"O deil care, lat her gang!" she said, with impatience. "A body'll get back to their ain bed noo."

She was, however, too lazy to make any effort just then to re-occupy the place of which she had been, as she thought, unfairly dispossessed; but, turning on her side, was fast asleep once more. Nor did Betty go to that bed either. She knew it was useless. There would be no sleep for her that night.

With the earliest streak of dawn Kirsty was on her way to Cairnbulg, to apprise Halket of the events of the previous night. It was afternoon, however, before he appeared at Betty's dwelling. He had visited Howemoss, and some other places in the neighbourhood making inquiries, but found no trace whatever of the fugitive.

Halket, of course, was in great distress over the untoward event; but, to Betty's great relief, he didn't fall out on her at all. He was a shrewd man, and knew sincerity from sham pretty readily. Betty's account had the marks of veracity; and, things happening as they did, she could hardly be held in any way responsible for the occurrence, most unfortunate as it was.

The practical and urgent question was, where was Lily, and how was she to be brought back? Halket himself had little doubt that the voice that wiled her forth was real—and Fred's. The talk of the evening had stirred old associations, and, with sense preternaturally quickened, she had caught the import of the call that to Betty's duller ear had come as at best only an inarticulate cry. And, with the old ascendancy over her mind now re-established, there was no saying what Fred might not manage to do with her.—Halket alternately shuddered and ground his teeth in helpless rage.

With what light remained he proceeded to explore the immediate surroundings of the cottage, and then the hillside beyond for a considerable radius. Darkness brought him back, and he again sat down at Betty's humble hearth to talk matters over; after which, with head between his hands, he sat silent, gazing in the fire and thinking—thinking.

He was roused from his reverie by a tapping at the window.

" That's him ! " said Betty, in an excited whisper. " Weesht ! "

Halket didn't need to ask who was meant by the " him." It was Fred Clark sure enough. Halket sat up in sudden excitement, but quietly, in obedience to Betty's injunction.

Fred always looked in at the window before he gave the understood signal; but to-night, the cruisie being unlit, the " ingle-cheeks," at the further of which sat Halket, were in shadow, so that he failed to note the presence of his enemy. Betty was rising to go to the door, when Halket whispered,—

" Just wait ; I would like to see him myself."

" But he never comes in," said Betty.

" But he will if you tell him Lily's away.—Bid him come in till you tell him all about it, but never let on you suspect him at all."

Fred had of course come to put Betty off the scent, and, in pursuance of this design, pretended utter surprise and dismay when she told him Lily was gone. Betty, however, played her part quite as well, and at length got him persuaded to enter her house, which he did all the more readily that he saw the lamp was not yet lit and learned that Kirsty was "awa an eerant."

Halket had left the fireside and was standing in front of the bed, so that he could not be seen until Fred and Betty were well into the house. When Fred had got seated on the chair he himself had just vacated, he made a slight movement, so as to attract the young fellow's attention. Fred started violently, and looked towards the bed.

"Oh," stammered Fred. "You're here?"

"I am, as you may see.—And you?"

"Well, d——n it, I have about as much right here as you," exclaimed Fred, deeming it his best policy in the circumstances to get abusive. He could carry off his guilty embarrassment better in this than in any other way.

"Yes, I suppose we are both on the same errand pretty much," Halket said, as coolly as before. "Only you have the advantage of me in knowing fully more than I can pretend to do."

"What the d——l do you mean?" demanded Fred, in a loud blustering tone. "None of your blind parables here, man!"

"Well then, to speak plainly, I want to know what you've done with Lily Douglas, your wife."

Halket had come close up to Fred as he spoke. He got an answer, but it was as unexpected as it was sudden. With a fearful oath, Fred struck him a heavy blow full in the face, which made him stagger backward and fall

over a stool. Then, without waiting to see what condition his adversary was in, Fred strode out and was
gone.

Halket lay stunned for a few minutes. Betty had
run to his aid when he fell ; but, not getting him to rise,
she hastened and had the lamp lit; by which time
Halket had risen to his feet. He was disfigured about the
face and considerably shaken, but not just seriously hurt.

After resting a while and partaking of Betty's evening
porridge, he felt himself able to undertake the homeward
journey. So, giving her earnest instructions to do
everything she could think of to find Lily, and to send
him instant word if she should light on any information
about her, he set out, and proceeded at a rather slow
pace towards Cairnbulg.

With body shaken and sore, and mind irritated and
distressed, he was in a sufficiently wretched mood. Nor
did other circumstances help him to take a more cheerful
view of things. It had begun to rain, and he was now
quite wet. The hillside had been wild and dreary, and
now, as he crossed the stream that flowed darkly past
the castle, the wind was whistling with a new note of
eerieness among the reeds, while above him he could see
the battlements frowning ominously, as the rain-clouds
darkened overhead.

He passed a restless feverish night. All kinds of
strange dreams visited him, but somehow he never seemed
to get away from that castle. It was ever before him
with its dark frown, till it became a kind of nightmare,
and he was glad to be wakened by the man in whose
house he stayed calling to him to rise as somebody
wanted to see him.

He felt more stiff and sore than he had done on the previous night, and got up with considerable difficulty. It was Sunday morning, and he wondered who could be wanting to see him on such a day. Could it be Betty? And had she anything of importance to communicate?

His visitor had declined to enter the house, and so, getting on boots and bonnet, he hurried out—to find that it was just Betty, and that, from her excited look, she evidently *had* something important to tell. She beckoned him some distance from the door, and, without any kind of introduction, burst out.—

" Mr. Halket—I've seen her ! "

" No ? " said Halket, with overmastering eagerness.

" Ay.—It wis awfu' ! "

" Where ?—and when ? "

" Jist last nicht.—O me ! "

" But where ? "

" In my bed. I wis dreamin' aboot her a' nicht."

Halket's countenance fell.

"So it was only a dream," he said, with evident disappointment in his tone. " I thought you had actually seen Lily."

" Sae I did," protested Betty, with great eagerness, " sae I did. I saw her as plain's day."

Betty, like most people of her class and day, had implicit faith in dreams. All such things with them had a meaning, if only they could get at it ; but, when the visions were direct and plain, as in this case, they had no doubt or difficulty whatever in the matter.

With Halket himself education and reflection had gone a long way to emancipate the mind from the thraldom of such superstitions ; but no man can quite get away from the influence of the traditional beliefs of the people among whom he lives, and, in the present case, his mind had been prepared by his own experiences over-night to give more attention to Betty's narration than he would otherwise have done. At anyrate he judged it best to hear what she had got to say ; and so he led the way into a little yard, where their consultation would attract less attention, and invited her to tell him about her dream.

"Now," said he, encouragingly, "lat's hear ye.—Ye've been dreamin' aboot Lily ? "

"Ay ; and I couldna wyte till I tell't ye.—O me ! "

But Betty, now that she was on the spot, didn't seem to be making much speed with her errand. She had a woman's difficulty in coming to the point and parting with information that she felt was important and would be exciting. And so Halket would help her.—

"And ye saw Lily ? " he said.

"I saw her," was the reply, uttered in the most impressive manner.

"And where ? "

"She wis sittin' in a neuk—O me ! "

"And where was that ? "

"It wis—O me !—in a dark hole—a dungeon ye ca't—aneath the castle yon'er."

She pointed away towards Cairnbulg Castle ; then, covering her face with her hands, she shuddered as if she again saw the vision. Halket started, and turned pale.

"And the puir thing will never get oot," she added, with a moan.

Halket was getting more and more impressed. There

might be something in all this. His own dreams, although hazy and elusive, had hung around this same place ; and the coincidence moved him a good deal. Whatever might be one's theories as to dreams in general, there was no doubt that strange revelations had at times come to people through their medium.

" Do you mind where about it was, Betty ? " he asked.

" I hinna been aboot Kyarnbulg Castle for mony a lang day ; but I ken fine far aboot the place is.—I can see't at this vera minute, and Lily hunkert doon in that dark neuk ; but it's in aneath the castle, and hine ben a dark passage, and syne doon and ben again, and a' the doors is steekit close.—Ye'll never win till 'er ; and the puir thing will jist hae to dee—O me ! "

And Betty wailed in her anguish of spirit, while Halket, more impressed than ever, stood thinking over the matter. He was quite familiar with the plan of the castle, and knew its passages and retreats. If Betty's description of the place where Lily appeared in her dream tallied with what he knew, he would consider himself called on to take the matter up, and would do everything in his power to have the place explored that very night. The poor girl must be somewhere ; and what more likely than that the monster by whom she had been betrayed should decoy her into a place where all trace of her would be lost for ever ?—He almost sickened at the thought.

But now, restraining his feelings, he proceeded in as calm a tone as he could command to question his informant about the place she saw in her dream. In her excitement she became very voluble ; but he soon stopped her.—

"Stay, Betty, we must take more time. I can't follow you right.—Let me see."

Here he took a small stick that was lying near, and proceeded to draw a plan of the castle on the ground. Betty had some difficulty in understanding it, having never been accustomed to this way of representing places and directions; but at length, with the help of instruction and explanation, she managed to get her bearings. Then she proceeded to show where the dungeon lay, and how it was approached.

Halket, who knew of nothing just there that answered the description she gave, thought she must have misunderstood the outline plan to begin with, and tried to get her to alter the assigned locality of the spot she was referring to; but Betty was firm, and stuck to her first statement. It was just there, and nowhere else. At which his countenance fell, and the hope that had sprung to sudden life in his heart now died away.—It was no use: Betty's dream was a delusion. It didn't correspond with facts, and was thus discredited at the very outset.

He didn't like to tell her what he thought: she was so earnest and excited over the matter. He promised to see at once if anything could be done to reach and rescue Lily; and, thus assured, Betty, after a fresh exhibition of grief, and even horror, took her departure.

Halket returned to the house more dispirited than ever. When one, after being tempted to hope, falls back again into despair, their last state is worse than the first. He would taste no breakfast; but, after sitting a while in moody silence, he returned to bed, where he lay till the people returned from church; when he rose and partook of a little dinner.

They had just got through the meal, when in stepped Jamie Robertson from Logie. He had walked over from Lonmay Church after service. Halket was mightily comforted to see him. No other body in fact could have at that moment been so welcome.

After a little general conversation, Jamie and Halket strolled forth together. Very soon Jamie was in possession of the distressing incidents that had recently happened. His indignation against Fred Clark was such that, had he got hands on the fellow at that moment, he might possibly have done him fatal injury.

Then Halket proceeded to tell him about Betty's dream, and the disappointment he had experienced in connection with it.

" It was nae eese," said he, " her plan didna correspond wi' things ava. I was sorry for Betty, she was sae earnest aboot it, and sae sure that the hale thing was true. In fact," he added apologetically, "it was her bein' sae excited aboot it that made me pay ony attention to her story."

As the conversation proceeded, they had strolled into the yard where Betty and Halket had that morning had their interview.

" Jist look here," said Halket, leading the way to the spot where the plan he had drawn on the ground could yet be seen. " This was the place where she had her dungeon, but of coorse there's naething there."

Jamie had never spoken, and Halket now looked up. A certain wild eagerness in the young man's face arrested him.

" What d' ye think—Jamie ? " he stammered.

" She's richt," Jamie burst out, " Betty's richt aifter a'. There *is* something there ! "

Halket staggered back a couple of steps.

" Ye dinna mean't ? " he exclaimed, much agitated.

" Yes, there is.   I min' bein' aince in when I was a loon wi' ane o' the apprentice gairdeners. There's a secret door gaes in frae yon auld place like a stable. Folk say it was aince a kin' o' a chapel."

" Could ye get the place again, think ye?—the door —and then alang to the dungeon ? " was Halket's breathless question.

" I think—I maybe could," said Jamie, reflectively.

" And—are ye willin' to come wi' me and see if we can get the place, and— "

Jamie seized his hand.   He said not a word, but looked his answer in a way that words could never have expressed.

Thus assured, Halket grew more calm and resolute, and began to sketch the arrangements for the enterprise to which they had bound themselves.

" We maun wait till it be dark.   That winna be lang noo.   But oh! gin she be deid by that time! "

And they shuddered at the thought, and put up a fervent prayer to Heaven that they might be in time to save the poor girl.   They did not seem now to doubt the credibility of Betty's dream.   As it had been set aside when its alleged locality was thought to be inconsistent with actual topography, so, when this preliminary point had been settled in its favour, the rest of the dream was tacitly taken for truth.

They now set themselves, in as calm and deliberate a manner as was possible in the circumstances, to think out the situation, and devise the necessary arrangements. Then they proceeded to get together such things as they expected to need for entering and exploring the place. Quietly and unobtrusively they went about everything. They wanted of course to keep their enterprise secret; but, had it been as open and worthy an undertaking as might be, the very pronounced Sabbatarianism of those days would have looked doubtfully on any activities connected with it being engaged in on such a day.

They waited impatiently for nightfall. As the shadows deepened, they got more excited. A feeling of eeriness, too, laid hold on them, although neither confessed this to the other.

At length, when night had quite settled down, they slipped away across the fields towards the castle. They walked in silence. Their arrangements had been made. And their feelings were too intense and complex just then for utterance. Pity and horror, anger and aversion, apprehension and suspense—all these so agitated their minds that they did not trust themselves to speak.

Now they are drawing near the venerable pile. Its heavy battlements loom above them. The silence has become oppressive. They pause. Halket speaks.—

"Nunc animis opus, Ænea, nunc pectore firmo."

Jamie, who recognises the line, gives a murmur of assent; and again they move forward.

*　　*　　*　　*　　*　　*

"Hark! what's that?" exclaimed Jamie in an excited whisper.

Halket and he, after having with much difficulty thrid the dark passages, and clambered down the narrow stairs that led towards the secret dungeon, had come to the last door, which had been secured in a certain way with an iron bar,—the lock having grown unworkable with age and rust.

They were working to get the bar removed, when an indistinct murmur fell on the ear of the younger man, and drew forth his excited remark.

How their hearts beat!—The eerie surroundings had acted on their nerves. Then, from the very first, there had been signs that the place had been recently entered, culminating in the appearance that this last door presented; and the excitement and suspense, now almost unbearable, had worked their minds into a dreadful state of strain and tension.

Before the door was opened they heard the sound again. It was louder this time, and they were almost convinced it was a human voice.

At length the bar was removed; the door was opened; and Jamie, who carried the lantern, flashed its light into the dark dungeon, to which they had at last gained access. And now they can see a figure—evidently a woman—crouching down in the far corner.

Very slowly they approach.—It is Lily Douglas.

"O Fred," she said, "you've been long, and I'm so cold and hungry."

The hearts of those two strong men grew sore with a great and strange anguish. Tears would have been some relief.

Halket advanced, and took her by the hand.

"Come away, Lily—out of this," he said, hoarsely.

The poor creature tried to rise, but it was no use. Halket saw how helpless she was.

"Let me carry you," he said, tenderly.

He lifted her gently in his arms, while, with the low

sigh of a satisfied heart, she twined her arms about his neck.

"My Fred," she murmured, softly.

At sound of the hated name heard *then* and *there*, Halket shuddered in fearful wise; and a sudden storm of fierce and conflicting passions shook his inmost soul.

"Never say that name again!" he hissed in her ear. "Never!!"

And she never did.—For this is what happened.—

The strange fierceness of the tone in which she was addressed made her look in the face of the speaker, on which just then the lantern shone full.

One moment of strange bewilderment.—A flash of sudden and perfect intuition.—And she understood all!

A wild and unearthly scream rang through the dungeon, dying away into a moan of unutterable anguish, while fierce convulsions shook the frame that Halket held in his arms, until he quite expected it to stiffen into the rigours of death. His heart stood still, and his limbs trembled under him, till he almost collapsed on the dungeon floor; while Jamie staggered against the wall, and stood paralysed with perfect horror.

But the crisis passed.—

Life and reason were saved; but memory was gone. From that moment the past was to her an utter blank.

And now she grew calm as an infant.

"Who are you?" she asked, with the sweet innocence of childhood.

Halket started, and a strange feeling thrilled his heart.

"I am—George," he stammered, awkwardly.

"George," she repeated, in her own sweet way. "*George.*"

It was the first little bit of knowledge she had gained in the new life on which she had now entered.   .   .   .

"Jamie," said Halket; and his voice had now re-assumed some of its old practical tone, "Jamie, come with the light.   It's time we were out of this."

.   .   .   .   .   And they went.

CHAPTER X.

VENGEANCE.

" AND has that scoundrel been about Logie again ? "

The question was addressed by Halket to Bell, whom he had chanced to encounter on her way home from Kirkton, where she had been doing some errands. Bell had herself brought the conversation round to the point that prompted Halket's question. It referred of course to Fred Clark, and was not so much intended to elicit information, as to convey surprise and rebuke. Bell understood its import, and proceeded to explain.—

" Weel than, ye canna keep a body awa' when they're wantin' to come."

" He wouldn't come without encouragement ; and you know what sort of fellow he is."

"Fowk's maybe some hard on him," Bell ventured to say.

" Indeed ? " said Halket, drily.

" He says he—never did naething ava."

Bell was rather a halting apologist ; but Halket didn't like that she should take the fellow's part at all, or have a single word to say in his favour. It implied that he had still some influence with her. Halket didn't like it, we say ; but the old anxiety was pretty much gone, for he felt he could now grapple with the danger, and, being able, was prepared to take up the challenge.—

" O, nae doot, he's a fine innocent chiel," he said, sarcastically. " And folk's sayin' ill aboot him, are they ? —Weel that's a pity, and him sic a guid chap."

Bell sniffed a little.

"I'll maybe see him some nicht," Halket went on. "Him and me could speak the maitter owre."

"He says he's wantin' to see you," said Bell, with a little briskness. "He'll meet ye ony nicht ye like, and redd the thing up."

"Oh! I'm gled o' that. Naething could gie *me* mair pleasure; I hope the meetin' will be as pleasant to *him*."

Bell had in a manner undertaken to Fred to bring him and Halket together. Fred professed it was for the purpose of clearing up matters and vindicating his own reputation; but he had another and darker design behind that, and really wanted to ensnare Halket.

"And when micht this precious young gentleman be to be found aboot Millbog?" Halket asked.

"Maybe next Feersday," Bell replied. "I think he said he micht be passin' that aifterneen or evenin'."

Bell was herself anxious to have the two men brought together. She was curious to know what Halket had against Fred, and to see how the latter would meet the charge—the one was so confident, and the other so defiant. She was accordingly glad when Halket said he would come over to Millbog on the afternoon of the day mentioned.—And so the two parted.

As Halket walked along towards Cairnbulg in the quiet gloaming, the hard mood engendered by his conversation with Bell began to dissolve and wear away. It was now towards the end of February. The season had been unusually mild, and already in air and earth there were hints of spring. Halket was a poet and felt all these things, but somehow he had just now to confess to sensations more tender and sweet than he had experienced for many a day.

He moved along quite leisurely, noting things on either hand, but ever and again glancing ahead.

" I wonder if she'll think of coming to meet me," he said to himself.

He was evidently expecting someone ; and, when at length a figure appeared on the road ahead, he betrayed a feeling of very real satisfaction as he muttered,—"Yes, it's Lily."

With lightsome step and cheery voice she approached; and how different she looked from the Lily Douglas of old ! Since that dreadful night when she was rescued from a living death, she had been in almost every way a new creature. The crisis through which she had then passed, had cancelled for her all her former life, and with its memories had gone all its depressing and poisoning influences. Her health was restored in quite a wonderful way, and now she was as bright as any girl again.

She stayed with some friends of Halket's, where she made herself so useful, and was always so cheerful, that they had grown very fond of her. To Halket himself she remained ever specially attached, showing her devotion with an innocent and unsophisticated enthusiasm that was at times a little embarrassing. He couldn't well give people such an account of the matter as would fully explain her feelings towards him. All he cared to tell was that she had been a poor wanderer, and that he had rescued her on a certain occasion when exposure might possibly have resulted in death.

While his male friends were inclined to rally him a little, his female acquaintances set themselves to worm from Lily herself the secrets of her past life. But, of course, vainly. Lily had nothing to tell, and they were mightily puzzled. Was she a lunatic, or a designing adventuress? In ordinary matters of daily life she didn't seem either, acting always quite sensibly, although with a certain innocent inexperience, and being as to motive and intention perfectly perspicuous.

"Well, George," she said, brightly, "I am glad I've met you."

She turned to accompany him back, linking her arm in his. Halket was pleased with this little touch of friendly confidence, but at the same time he was rather thankful that twilight was settling down. It wasn't just a common thing for people in Buchan to practise this kind of courtesy. There was in it too much chivalry, and too little warmth, for native taste.

And now they began to converse quite freely. He told her about Logie, and said he would take her over some day to see the place.

"That's where Jamie stays?" she said, with some enthusiasm.

"Yes," replied her companion, "but you mustn't think too much about Jamie. He has got a lass of his own."

"I am not thinking much about Jamie: not half so much as about you, George." And she looked fondly in his face.

Now, Halket wasn't just a young man. He was fully as old as Clyacks. But he had a certain natural vigour of mind and body, and possessed the imaginative temperament that helps the spirit to retain its fresh and youthful standpoint. He had been a widower for a number of years, his wife having perished in a snowstorm between Fraserburgh and Rathen, leaving a young family of two sons and one daughter, who were now grown up and doing for themselves.

He was sensible enough to realise that to this girl of some twenty-five summers he must appear practically an old man. Yet her clinging confidence and loving ways were stirring emotions that he couldn't altogether repress. When he became conscious of this, he tried to persuade himself that the feeling was purely platonic. By-and-by he was driven from this position, and then he allowed there was some sentiment in it, and a little romance; but the sentiment was very harmless, and the romance was just sufficient to supply a poet with inspiration. At times, however, he caught himself day-dreaming with an earnestness that belied his philosophy. Waking up, he would see and confess how absurd it all was, and wind up the review with the sententious soliloquy, " There's nae feel like an aul' ane."

There was of course another aspect of the case that obtruded itself from time to time, although he might well be pardoned for often overlooking it.—Lily was not a free woman.

However he might try to persuade himself that the old ties were broken—as indeed they essentially were— the law and society would not take this view. Fred might be as dead to Lily as she was to him ; but in the eyes of the world the old bonds remained. And this consideration never failed to pull Halket up when fancy would stray too far.

As they walked along, they continued to talk about Logie and the people whom Lily would see.

"Then I must take you to lots of other places," said Halket. "You hardly know anybody yet."

And, just with the remark, came a thought, followed by a little pang. — As Lily's circle of acquaintance widened, he himself would be less and less to her; and who could say but she might erelong meet with one of more equal age and kindred tastes, who would capture her young affections? He gave a sigh. It wasn't so deep as would be the sigh of a young man in similar circumstances, but it was like to be often repeated. The pang was less severe than the said young man would feel, but it would longer persist.

Erelong they seemed to exhaust subjects for conversation, and walked on in silence. Night had now fallen. The quiet stars were above them, and in their ears the soft wash of the waves. Each was conscious of a deep joy. Lily felt it and was satisfied, and never thought of reasoning about it. Halket couldn't take it so. He saw lots of things that Lily didn't; but his mind gave them no very welcome entertainment.—Why should things be regulated by laws or principles? And what was the use of ethics and all that sort of thing? Why might not two people who were pleased with each other do as they liked?—He would reason no more. Let the heart alone speak. And its cry was, "O that for ever thus!"

. . . The very next night Fred Clark was at Millbog. Learning from Bell that Halket had accepted his challenge, he resolved to go to Peterhead at once and see Captain Campbell.

A great restlessness had now laid hold on him, and, since the night of the dark deed at Cairnbulg, he had hardly ever been quite sober. He promised himself a few jolly days at Peterhead, where he knew one or two congenial spirits. And they did have a wild time of it. For a day or two the debauch lasted, and at length, with bleared visage and bloodshot eye, Fred presented himself before Captain Campbell.

"Well, Clark," said the Captain, "what's up now?—Any more rebels with you?"

"Yes, d—n it!" said Fred, speaking thick. "There's that old d—l Halket still on the loose. We can catch him now. And then there's the young b—r Robertson."

"What?" interrupted the Captain eagerly, "Jamie Robertson—do you mean? The young gardener at Logie?"

"Just him, by G—d!" said Fred fiercely, striking the table on which he sat. They were in a kind of barrack-room that had been fitted up temporarily to accommodate the soldiers stationed in Peterhead during the suppression of the Rebellion.

"Have a drink, Clark?" asked the Captain in high good-humour. There was good news coming, and it was worth getting into the best possible form for enjoying it. —"Have a drink?"

"Don't mind.—D—n it, Captain!"

A quantity of spirits was brought in by an orderly, and both men took a good pull.

"Now, Clark, let's hear you.—You can prove that this fellow Robertson is a rebel—that he has been aiding and abetting the King's enemies, and all that sort of thing?"

"Yes, by G—d, I can!"

Hereupon he unfolded to the Captain his proofs. In the first place he produced a rusty knife marked with the initials " J. R.," which he had found in the cornyard at Millbog.

"Now," said Fred, emphatically, "this is the d—l's knife—"

"That he cut the rope with that night, to let Halket away," the Captain eagerly added, taking the knife and looking at it. "The very thing."

They were quite right. It was Jamie's knife, and with it he had cut the rope which bound Halket's feet on that memorable Hallowe'en night. But the direct and easy way in which they arrived at these conclusions was somewhat amusing. And, beginning so, they were not likely to find much difficulty with the rest of the evidence. From the coachman Fred had learned about Halket's intercourse with Jamie, and he now retailed the information, with such addenda as his fancy dictated.

The Captain expressed himself quite satisfied with the evidence. It would scarcely have supported a case in a law-court; but the military standpoint was less technical and squeamish. More depended on the attitude and spirit of the tribunal than on the guilt of the accused. And, in the present instance, that attitude was specially hostile and prejudiced. Captain Campbell had from the very first conceived a deep dislike to Jamie, and had come to hate him more and more as the man who, he was assured, was spoiling his suit with Miss Innes. Nothing would give him greater pleasure than to be able to crush this insolent clodhopper. And so he wasn't ill to please with the evidence against such an enemy.

"That's all right, Clark," said Campbell, when the interview ended. "We'll be along on Thursday afternoon,—Lieutenant Farquhar and myself with a trooper or two ; and, hang it, if we don't make a better job this time !"

Once more they applied themselves to the liquor,— this time drinking success to the project they had just discussed and arranged. After which Fred staggered away.

This was on the Tuesday. Fred remained in town till next day, and then set out to walk to Logie ; but, landing at an alehouse in St. Fergus, he drank himself stupid once more, and spent the night in a barn.

Next morning he was in the horrors. The dawn broke bright and fair, and the larks were singing overhead ; but in his soul nature's joy and peace found no place, nor awakened any echo. For there only dark passions dwelt, with their still darker shadows of remorse and despair, shutting out the sweet light of Heaven, and poisoning its vital air.

Coming to another alehouse by the way, he managed once more to drink himself into a mood of reckless abandonment ; and so moved on. He reached Logie about mid-day, and made his way to the stables. The coachman was away at Rattray with Captain Duff, who had driven there to make arrangements for going south the following week.

Fred got into the farthest stall, and, making a bed of straw, lay down and fell asleep. He wakened about mid-afternoon, and, pulling himself together as well as he could, walked away over the fields towards Millbog.

About an hour before, Halket, accompanied by Lily Douglas, had arrived at the farm. There was nobody in the house at the time but Marget, who was busy churning.

"Ay, guidwife," said Halket, walking in, "ye're jist at the kirn?"

"Ay, but there's little to kirn the noo, the cream's sae scarce.—But come awa' in by and lean ye doon." Then, noticing Lily, she added, "Ye've company I see?"

"Ay, this is a young frien' o' mine, Lily Douglas. I thocht I micht bring her owre to see you."

"We're unco gled to see the lass," said Marget heartily, prepossessed with Lily's appearance. "Come awa' in by."

Just then Bell came in, and to her likewise was Lily introduced, Halket being amused to note that neither she nor her mother recognised Lily.

Bell took at once to Lily, and invited her out "to see some lammies they had gotten,—awfu' bonnie craturs." And away the two went.

"And hoo's the bairn aye gettin' on?" Halket inquired, when Marget and he had got the kitchen to themselves.

"O, fine; but it's an unco wark. Some o's has aye a fest han' wi't; and syne its nae that little expense, and it'll aye be growin' mair."

"I believe that," assented Halket.

"Ye've never heard nae mair word o' the hizzy that left it?—I wish I could only get my hands on 'er. My certies! That's fat a body gets for bein' guid to that kin' o' gentry. That was a fine story—gaun awa' to Rathen. Fient a Rathen had she been near, the leein' limmer! But I'll gang to Mr. Lundie aboot it, and see fat he says. We're nae to be saiddlet wi' the bringin' up o' ither fowk's bairns, I can tell ye.—But there's the cratur' greetin', puir lammie.—I'm comin', wee wifikie, comin', comin'!"

And Marget, stopping in the midst of her churning, ran to the other end, and soon re-appeared with a fine healthy child in her arms, which she fondled in a way that seemed somewhat strange after the complaint she had just uttered.

"It's a fine bairn," said Halket, "it's mither winna ken't again."

Marget looked at her little charge with fond pride.

"But it maun be a gey handfu' to you and Bell; and ye'll be thankfu' to hear that it's mither's comin' to tak' it awa'."

"O, guidsakes!" cried Marget, almost letting the child fall in her consternation, "ye dinna mean't? She's nae comin' back is she?"

"Ay, is she," said Halket quietly, "and I thocht ye'd be gled to hear't."

"O, mercy on's! She winna get the bairn! Fat could she dee wi't? She's nae fit to be trusted wi' a chielie—never! Ye ken that yersel', Mister Halket. And min', gin she tak' it awa' and gie't a cheenge o' kye's milk, it'll dee,—the puir thing 'll dee. I winna aloo't, Mister Halket!"

Here she stopped to fondle the child, kissing it, and crooning over it with a voice in which tenderness and distress were strangely blended.—Halket was mischievously enjoying the scene.

"Weel, Marget, we'll see gin the mither will pass ye the bairn when ye're sae fond o' the cratur.—We can jist cry her in and see."

Marget looked utterly amazed as he rose and went to the door.

"Yon's nae her?—Yon's nae the deem that left the bairn?" she cried, breathlessly.

" Jist the same," said Halket, as he reached the door. Then, looking out, he called, " Lily, come here.'

Then he turned to Marget again.—

" It's her," he said, " and it's *nae* her.   Puir thing, the trials she has come through has a kin' o' turned her heid. She's weel eneuch noo in body ; but she has forgotten a'thing.   She minds naething aboot her bairn ; sae ye needna say onything aboot it,—unless ye like."

The look of relief on Marget's face was a study.— That baby was now almost dearer to her than her own children had been.

But now Lily and Bell entered, and the talk got on other subjects.

Meanwhile Captain Campbell and his men had arrived at Logie.   He sent Lieutenant Farquhar with a couple of troopers on to Millbog, where he expected to find Halket.   Two men were left, and these he stationed at the stables to be in readiness should he need them. He wanted to arrest Jamie Robertson himself.   Revenge is sweet, and he wanted to get the full good of it.

He must, however, in the first place wait on Captain Duff, and apprise him of his intention.   So he strode away to the House.

Captain Duff, as we have said, was from home.   A servant told Campbell this, and offered to call Miss Innes ; but he didn't want to see that lady just then, and, turning away, made for the garden.

Miss Innes was sitting in her boudoir, an upstairs room that overlooked the garden.   She saw Captain Campbell as he proceeded along the walk, and wondered what he could be after.   Watching him as he strode along, she saw him draw his sword, and a sudden apprehension that mischief was intended seized her.

Next moment she was on the stair. Gliding down with arrowy swiftness, she was soon outside. A private entrance to the garden shortened her way, and she hurried after the Captain with swift and almost noiseless steps.

Jamie Robertson was bending over a bed which he was preparing for some early seeds, when a loud voice made him start and look up.

"James Robertson, surrender! In the name of King George, I arrest you as a rebel against His Majesty's most lawful authority."

By the time this speech was done, Jamie had so far recovered from his surprise as to be able in some measure to grasp the situation. Nor was he far astray in his interpretation of it. He was being arrested on a trumped-up charge. Fred Clark was at the bottom of it, and Captain Campbell was, from motives of revenge, lending himself to the conspiracy.

All this flashed through his mind in a moment. His blood was up. Seizing the rake with which he had been working, he prepared to defend himself. Yield he wouldn't. Never!

The fight, however, promised to be a very unequal one. A rake was but a sorry weapon when measured against a sword. The Captain could not but admire Jamie's pluck. It pleased him too, for he should now have the keen delight of dealing his adversary a blow at first hand, and bringing him to his knees in quite a literal sense.

The sword gleamed on high, and next moment the blow would have fallen. But just then the Captain heard a step behind him and felt his belt suddenly twitched. Dropping his sword-point, he wheeled round ; and there stood Miss Innes, pointing his own pistol at his head.

"Touch him, Campbell, and—" There was no mistaking her meaning. The ring of that voice, the flash of that eye! They couldn't be misunderstood.

In utter helplessness, the Captain stood, and gazed at her. Astonishment, dismay, admiration—with each and all was he struggling. It was some moments ere he could find voice.

"Miss Innes," he stammered at length, "what on earth do you mean?"

"You see what I mean," she replied, without moving a limb or winking an eye.

"He's a rebel," he explained, "and I was arresting him."

"He *isn't* a rebel ; and you'll *never* arrest him."

How the Captain burned with anger and shame to be thus thwarted and defied! How, at the same time, he thrilled with admiration at that figure and face, perfect in outline and attitude, and instinct with intensest spirit and purpose! But all this time his enemy was looking on. He must make a desperate effort to comport himself worthily.

"Miss Innes," he said, "I am a soldier. If you defy me as you are doing, and threaten so—well—shoot! I am not afraid." And for a moment he looked calmly and fixedly at her.

"Put down that pistol," he went on. "As I say, if you persist in taking this way, you'll just have to shoot me. Speak as Miss Innes, and," dropping his voice, "I am your slave."

She put down the pistol.

"I take your word, Captain Campbell," she said.

"Now, what do you want?" he asked.

"I want you to go away, and leave—this young man alone."

"But if it is my duty to arrest him? You wouldn't interfere with an officer in the discharge of his duty?"

"There is no duty in the matter. You know very well he isn't a rebel."

"Well, but if the case has been reported to me, what can I do? Think of my position. I came here to arrest him. My men are at the stables over there. And how am I to get out of it?"

"Follow me," she said, imperatively. Then, turning to Jamie, who had remained a silent spectator of the strange and thrilling scene, she said, "Jamie, go on with your work."

Miss Innes was afraid to discuss matters further in Jamie's presence. She feared lest his impetuosity and high spirits might wreck the plans she was meditating for his safety.

The Captain followed her to the House, where the discussion was resumed. After some further show of arguing, protesting, and appealing, he at length agreed to let the matter drop, if Jamie would get out of the way. Miss Innes, who saw how the Captain would be compromised if he let his prisoner off *simpliciter*, undertook to see this condition carried out. Jamie could go away with Captain Duff and herself next week, lying low in the interim. And so the matter was settled.

"Ah, Miss Innes," said the Captain, as he parted from her, "to think of it! I never feared a foe in battle-field, and you—well you have made a fool of your poor Captain. Won't you think a little more kindly of me for it all?"

"I do think kindly of you, Captain; and will."

She gave him her hand. He bent and kissed it. Then, with a graceful obeisance, he was gone.

. . . . Let us now return to Millbog, and see what was happening there meantime.

We left Halket and Lily, and Marget and Bell, all talking together. During a pause in the conversation, Bell, who had been looking out at the window, suddenly said—

"O, here's Mr. Fred!"

"Would you take Lily away somewhere?" Halket said, with a certain anxious quickness, "to the other end!"

Bell, who thought that Halket merely wished to save Lily hearing or witnessing anything unpleasant, led her to the room-end, and, finding her a chair and a book, returned in time to meet Fred at the door and conduct him into the kitchen.

"Well, you old d—l," Fred began at once, "and you've been trying to blacken my character? Come on; where's your proof? Come on; or you can go to h—l for a d—d liar!"

Bell and her mother shuddered and drew off. But Halket, although pale, was calm and resolute.

"What have you done with your wife?" he asked.

Bell put up her hands, while an involuntary scream escaped her lips.

Fred's evil face was blanched; but he instantly burst out with a volley of awful oaths, and rushed at Halket. But Halket was prepared for him this time. He dodged the blow that was aimed at him, and then, ere his adversary could recover himself, he struck him a blow that sent him staggering back against the opposite wall.

The women screamed, and rushed into opposite corners. Fred stood a few moments leaning against the wall, stunned and irresolute. Then his eye caught sight of a big kitchen knife lying on the dresser. In an instant he seized it, and again rushed at Halket.

There is no saying what might have been the upshot ; but, just at that moment, Lily, alarmed by the noise, and fearing something was happening to her friend, appeared in the kitchen doorway.

Fred saw her just as he had raised the knife to deal Halket a deadly blow. The weapon fell from his hands, and he stood for one moment with his eyes fixed in horror on Lily's face. Then he staggered back against the wall again, and, with a cry of wild and abject terror, sank on the floor.

Marget and Bell screamed, and Halket felt a cold shiver run through his frame. Lily was the most calm of any. She saw Fred's horror, but couldn't understand it ; and she stood regarding the whole scene with a certain innocent surprise.

So much were all taken up with the scene that was being enacted, that nobody heard Lieutenant Farquhar and his men at the door. The lieutenant pushed past Lily, and, with sword drawn, advanced right into the kitchen.

Halket was the first to notice him. In an instant it flashed on him that he had once more been betrayed by Fred Clarke, and he gave himself up for lost. But Lieutenant Farquhar did not know him, and his attention was at once drawn to Fred Clarke as he crouched on the floor, still looking with horror-dilated eyes towards Lily.

Farquhar stood a few moments regarding the fellow intently, while all waited in silence.

"Jamieson, by G—d!" he exclaimed at length.

At the name Fred turned his eyes on the speaker, and a new terror appeared on his face. He struggled to his feet, and looked wildly about as if for some way of escape.

"Men!" shouted Farquhar; and in an instant the two men were at his side.

"Seize the fellow—Jamieson there!"

With a wild yell Fred dashed for the door. One of the troopers he knocked over, but the other caught him round the waist, and, after a brief struggle, Fred was on his back on the floor.

Lily had withdrawn when Lieutenant Farquhar entered, and, during the progress of the struggle, Halket unobtrusively slipped out. Bidding her follow, he hurried away, not in the direction of Cairnbulg, but away towards Strichen; not keeping to the roads, but cutting across fields. And not till they were many miles away did the two fugitives stop to gather their breath.

As the soldiers were pinioning Fred Clarke, Captain Campbell, who had followed with his men to see how matters were progressing at Millbog, appeared on the scene.

"Captain," said Farquhar, enthusiastically, "I have made a rare capture—Jamieson, one of the rankest Jacobites out. Never would have thought of finding him here. It's a long cry from Prestonpans to Buchan; but you never know where your man will turn up."

Captain Campbell wasn't in a very good mood, and, without a word, followed his lieutenant into the kitchen.

He looked at Fred as he sat on the floor, pinioned and helpless, sullen and silent.

"What?" he broke forth, "Clarke?—There must be some mistake about this. It was Halket—Where's he?"

"O hang it," said Farquhar, "we forgot all about him, boys; but never mind, this is better than Halket."

"But," Campbell went on, "what the deuce does it mean? I can't understand it?"

Whereupon Farquhar proceeded to explain. Campbell hadn't been in Cope's army, and didn't know about this Jamieson who had been in the Prince's army at Prestonpans, and had, after the battle, made himself so obnoxious by the cruel way in which he treated the Royalist prisoners. But, after hearing his lieutenant's statement, he agreed that Jamieson—*alias* Clarke, richly deserved to suffer.

The Captain was disappointed that Halket had been allowed to escape; but, as there was little use in trying to find him now, he decided to remain with his prisoner over-night at Crimonmogate, and return to Peterhead next day.

And so Fred Clarke left Millbog—left Buchan, never to return again.

CHAPTER XI.

CHANGES.

As soon as Captain Campbell had left the House, Miss Innes returned to the garden. Jamie was working away as if nothing had happened; but, when she came near, he stood up, and his embarrassment became very evident.

"Miss Innes," he began, "how shall I thank you?"

She felt the situation quite as keenly as he did, being conscious that she had, through the sudden crisis, been betrayed into an exhibition of her feelings for which she could not now but blush. So she hasted to take the matter off in as lightsome a way as possible.

"Never mind thanks," she said, interrupting the speech Jamie had set himself to deliver. "Never mind thanks, I want no gratitude: I only want obedience."

Jamie was himself relieved to be taken in this way, and readily followed suit.

"Well, and haven't you always got it?"

"Yes, you have done pretty well as yet; but I want you to promise that you will always be good and obedient—will you?"

"I will," he replied, taking off his bonnet and bowing.

"That's right: thank you.—Now see you don't forget your promise."

Although all this was accompanied with a pleasant smile, yet there was a certain insistence in the tone that led Jamie to apprehend that his fidelity and loyalty were to be tried in some way. Nor was he mistaken. For Miss Innes now proceeded to disclose the paction that had been entered into between Captain Campbell and herself.

Jamie's proud spirit rose in rebellion, and, with flushed face, he began to protest.

"Now, sir," she interposed quickly, "you are forgetting your agreement, and growing insubordinate."

"Well, but—"

"The 'well' will do; but I must have no 'buts.'"

But Jamie couldn't all at once tame his proud spirit. He must speak out. Miss Innes saw that it would be as well to let him have his say. He would be more likely to listen to reason after he had relieved his feelings a little. So she allowed him to go on; and very eloquent he was in vindication of the rights of the citizen, and in denunciation of oppression and injustice.

She heard him in silence, always looking more and more subdued and regretful as he went on; and when, after his philippic was over, she proceeded to reply, it was in a quiet pathetic tone that went to Jamie's heart.—

"Well, well, Jamie, I beg your pardon. I did it all for the best. I see I have been wrong. I have done you an injustice. I didn't mean to do it, and I hope you will try and forgive me."

Jamie's fire and fury had all gone. He was now quite meek; apologetic in fact; almost abject.—

"Miss Innes, pray forgive me. I've been most ungrateful, after all you've done for me. I am anxious to please you, and to do what you want; but you know how hard it is to yield in a matter of this kind. It *is* hard; but I will do it,—for your sake I'll do it."

In a sudden access of pleasure, she offered him her hand.   He took it ; and, at the touch, his whole being thrilled in a way that was almost startling in its rich novelty and keen unexpectedness.

O, the subtle magic that may reside in a hand!   How it may become the repository of the finer influences of being and personality; and what a pity that with so many this rare instrument of soul-revelation should become so dulled, and clogged, and spoiled, through hard and sordid conditions of life!

Miss Innes too was conscious that their spirits had met in a more decisive and unequivocal way than they had ever done before ; and she instantly reproached herself.   Where were all her good resolutions ; where all the results of the self-discipline so painfully applied during those weeks past?   Ah, what an amount of labour and effort may be cancelled and effaced by some simple action!   How sudden and easy may be the lapse that brings us down from heights that took us long and painful effort to reach!

Jamie hardly realised the crisis, startling as was the experience ; but his companion, with a woman's quicker intuition, did.   She could forecast the possible developments.   She withdrew her hand, and immediately strove to be very practical, giving Jamie directions as to how he must act meantime, and looking as if sentiment had no place in her mind at that moment.   Jamie, however, couldn't so quickly shake off the strange mesmerism that had enthralled him.   He listened like one dazed and half conscious, and his companion had to repeat some of her injunctions ere he appeared to grasp their import.

To begin with, Jamie must get out of sight, so as to

avoid if possible being seen by anyone about the place. The old tool-house in which Halket had hid would do meantime as a place of retreat. Then after nightfall he could come to the House, by which time Captain Duff would be back from Rattray, when a consultation could take place as to future plans and movements.

When the Captain returned, his niece gave him an account of the events of the day. Of course all the heroic element was eliminated from the recital. Especially did she take care to edit all references to her own share in the affair, representing herself as simply brow-beating the Captain with words and arguments, till he grew ashamed of himself, and agreed to fall from the business on condition that, to save himself getting compromised, Jamie should get out of the way.

Captain Duff was naturally disappointed that such things should have taken place about Logie. He would have been more so had he got a fair and ungarbled account of them. But, now that the matter had been settled, he was saved the trouble of taking any action; and for this he was thankful. In any case he was leaving in a few days, and needn't trouble himself much about anything now. And, as for Jamie, it wouldn't do him any very great harm to have to leave Logie a little sooner than he had intended.

To these reflections Miss Innes readily assented. But she had been thinking a bit since afternoon, and had got her programme extended and filled in. So she ventured to pursue the subject, and make a few sugges-tions on her own account.

Jamie, she pointed out, might now have some difficulty in finding a situation in that part of the country, leaving Logie as a suspect. Would it not be fair, or at least kind, to help him to find a situation somewhere else, where he could begin life under more favourable conditions? If, for instance, he could go south, he would not only get well away from the compromising influence of the circumstances connected with his leaving Logie, but there he would find a much better field for his ability and energy.

Captain Duff admitted the force and reasonableness of his niece's remarks. This was encouraging. Like a wise woman, however, she refrained from showing all her hand at once. Admitting that her uncle must be tired after his journey, she said they would bother no more about the matter meantime. On the following night he could have an interview with Jamie himself, when everything could be discussed in a quiet and leisurely way.

Miss Innes had got Jamie into a room in a wing of the House which, having the reputation of being haunted, was safe from the intrusion of the domestics after nightfall. Here she now visited him, and told him what she had suggested to her uncle. Jamie had now had time to get into a more quiet and reasonable mood than he had exhibited in the garden; and his adviser was much pleased to find him prepared to fall in with her suggested plans for his future welfare.

Next day when dinner, wine, and a nap, had put her uncle in a thorough good humour, Miss Innes returned to the subject of Jamie's future. She thought Edinburgh would be the best place for a young gardener; but Jamie she now remembered was poor, and could hardly find his way so far without assistance. Would it not be a kindly thing to offer to take him with them when they went south next week? Her uncle, being in that mellow mood when generous impulses come quite natural to one, agreed that it would be a nice thing to take the young fellow with them.

She was not long in letting Jamie know this latest proposal. The young fellow experienced a strange flutter when he thought of his good fortune,—getting away with Miss Innes, with the prospect of retaining her acquaintance and friendship, and enjoying further intercourse with her. He wasn't likely to hunt for objections to the proposal; and so, when everybody was pleased, the matter got arranged without any special difficulty.

So Jamie was going away to Edinburgh with Captain Duff and Miss Innes. And they were to sail from Rattray about the middle of the following week. The time was short; but he had no special preparations to make. When he had "roped his kist," he was about ready for any movement. Yet there were one or two things he must do, one or two people he must see, ere he left Logie—not to return for many days at least.

He must first see his friend Halket, and discuss everything with him. Having heard from Miss Innes of the events that had occurred at Millbog on the Thursday afternoon, he was prepared to encounter some difficulty in finding his friend. He set out early on the Sunday morning, and made his way to Cairnbulg. Inquiring among Halket's friends, he got directed to a croft lying in the direction of Mormond, where it was understood he had been residing for the last day or two. Thither Jamie directed his steps, only to find, on arriving at the place, that the man he sought had that morning gone away up the hill, without saying exactly where he was bound for, or when he would return.

Jamie had nothing for it but to follow after, in the hope that he might fall in with his friend somewhere on the hill.

As he paced along, it occurred to him to call at Betty's cottage. Halket might be there, or the inmates might have seen him pass. As he approached the door, out came the very man he was seeking, and, after a very friendly greeting, they passed together into the cottage.

Halket had come over to tell Betty about Fred Clark's capture. Deeply impressed with the account, she was sitting looking in the fire, when Halket re-entered with his friend.

"This is James Robertson, Betty," said Halket, by way of introduction. "Ye'll mind on Jamie?"

"O ay," replied Betty, rising and confronting Jamie, "I min' on him fin he wis a loon; but, my, fat a strappin' chiel ye're growin'! I widna hae kent ye again."

Jamie blushed, and murmured an acknowledgment of the compliment.

"Tak' a seat, Jamie, man," she went on, offering him a chair, "and Kirsty, bring the kebbuck and the yill. . . Ye maun be hungry aifter yer lang traivel. Ye'd come frae Logie the day? . . . . The kyacks, Kirsty, wumman, the kyacks.—Fa wid eat cheese wantin' kyacks?"

Jamie partook very heartily of the cheese and bread, and enjoyed a draught of Betty's home-made ale. Then they sat and talked together in a very friendly manner, indulging in reminiscences of bygone days, and tracing the careers of old acquaintances.

By-and-by, however, Betty began to betray some

uneasiness. She moved about a good deal, and looked ever and anon at the "wag-at-the-wa'." At last she planted herself in front of her guests.

"Weel, frien's," she began, hesitatingly, "I dinna jist like to interfere wi' ye in ony wye, but—but it's wearin' to kirk time." And she pointed to the clock.

"But we're nae gaun to the kirk the day, Betty," said Halket.

"I wisna maybe thinkin' ye wid be gaun; but—but I wis half thinkin' I wid maybe like to gang mysel'."

"You, Betty?" And there was surprise in Halket's tone.

Betty looked awkward.—

"Weel, ye see, we've been gaun to the kirk for a Sunday or twa, Kirsty and me, time aboot; and this is my Sunday; an'—an' I wid like to gang, if it wis a' the same to you."

"O surely, Betty; dinna lat us keep ye frae the kirk. Jamie and me are jist gaun awa' for a daunder on the hill; and, if ye would gie's a bit o' your cheese and breid, we wid manage wantin' denner for a day."

"Seerly," said Betty, with kindly readiness, "ye'll get a piece in your pouch."

Thus provided, the two men went away, leaving Betty to get ready for church.

"Ay, ay," said Halket, when they were outside, "and Betty's ta'en to gaun to the kirk?—Weel, wonders will never cease. I'm safe to say that, until this new maggot took her, she hadna been in Rathen kirk for twenty years."

"And what's ta'en her noo, would ye think?" said Jamie.

"Weel, unless it was a' this aboot Lily, I dinna ken."

Halket's surmise was right. The events connected with Lily's disappearance and rescue had made a deep impression on Betty's mind. When the truth of her dream was vindicated, she believed that the Deity had made a special and direct revelation to herself. This idea, along with the softening influence that the tragic pathos of the occurrence exerted on her mind, had stirred in Betty the religious sentiment that had lain dormant for many years. The first Sunday after Lily's rescue she appeared in church, to the great astonishment of both minister and congregation. And now every alternate Sunday, with well-starched mutch, and carrying her Bible wrapped in a clean handkerchief, was Betty to be seen making her way to Rathen Church, where she appeared quite a humble and devout worshipper.

It was a fine day in the early part of March, and, as Halket and Jamie reached the top of the hill, a wind from the west full of the message of spring blew freshly in their faces. They sat them down on a cairn of white stones that marked the highest point of Mormond's long ridge.

As yet Jamie had not referred to the crisis that had come in his own life and career. Now he began, and told his friend the whole story. Halket lent close and utterly sympathetic ear to the recital, only occasionally allowing himself an ejaculatory expression of feeling at certain moving points.

When Jamie's story was done, his friend had a good deal to say by way of comment ; and delivered himself with his usual vigour and incisiveness. When he had relieved his feelings in this way, he addressed himself to the more practical aspects of the matter.

" Ye're better to gang frae hame, Jamie," he said, "and gang a good bit, and aye, as the beggars say, be haudin' sooth. A young chap's better to see what the warld's deein'. It lats him ken his ain wecht ; and, if there's ony smeddum in him, he gets a better chance. We'll a' be sorry to lose ye, Jamie ; but ye maun mak' your wye in the warld ; and, when ye come back a great man wi' plenty o' siller, we'll a' be prood that we've kent ye."

Jamie blushed and smiled in a somewhat sad way, but said nothing. Halket judged there was something more on his mind ; and, as he remained silent, he thought he might encourage him to speak.

" And what aboot Bell ? "

Now Jamie wouldn't in ordinary circumstances have liked to tell the whole story of his connection with Bell, but the occasion was special. He might never see his friend again, and really he wanted to get his advice on this as on other less delicate matters. So he unburdened his mind in a very frank and confidential way ; referring specially to the hostile attitude taken up by the girl's parents.

" Weel, Jamie," said his friend, giving a sort of deliverance, " their ae objection to you is evidently your want o' siller. And this jist forms anither argument for your gaun awa'. Gin ye could mak siller and position, and syne come back armed with these recommendations, the day would be your ain. Clyacks is your only rival—noo ; and ye say he has promised nae to press his claim sae lang's ye're to the fore and willin' to tak' Bell. (And Clyacks is a man whase word is as good as his bond.) Your plan then is to gang to Millbog and see the auld folk, and tell them plainly and frankly what ye mean to be at. Bell's but young yet, and can easy afford to wait a year or twa."

Jamie wasn't at all sure that much good would come of approaching Bell's parents. He rather feared that he would but invite a more severe rebuff. Yet he could see that it was but fair to all parties that the old people be directly appealed to, and asked to give a definite answer to his questions and proposals.

It was now afternoon, and, feeling hungry, they produced Betty's cheese and bread, which they enjoyed very much, only regretting that they hadn't likewise brought a "preein' o' her hame-brewn."

And now, before leaving the hill, they stood a while surveying in silence the wide landscape. With Jamie it was touching thus to take what would be the last look of his native vale for years—what might be the last look for ever.

There were the fields over which as a boy he had wandered to pluck the gowan or seek for teuchits' nests; there the long stretches of breezy heather, and the low-lying moss where he had helped to dig and wheel the peats under the broiling sun; there were the winding burns, where with other light-hearted lads he had waded many a summer day; there were the lowly homesteads he knew so well, with the smoke now rising aloft in this quiet Sunday afternoon; and beyond all was the great sea, whereon he would soon embark to be carried to strange places, where Buchan would be but a memory and a vision.

Halket guessed what his thoughts were, and did not seek to intrude into his spirit's privacy. A true friend knows when to speak and when to remain silent. He hung about till Jamie, after a long look at the surrounding country, made as if to go away. Then, turning too, he appeared ready to leave; and thus, as if by common impulse, they set on together without exchanging a word.

Returning by the way they had come, they were passing Betty's cot again, when she appeared at the door, and, hailing them, invited them to come in and get "a bite o' something." Being in no special hurry, they turned aside, and were once more seated at Betty's humble ingle.

" Ay, Betty," Halket began, in his bantering way, " and did ye get a richt sermon frae Mr. Anderson the day ? "

" Ay, a fine discoorse," said Betty.

" Ye'll min' what it was a' aboot ? Ye micht gie Jamie and me the heids o't, when we werena at the kirk oorsels. Come on noo, *Firstly ?*—"

Betty stood a few moments, evidently trying to recollect at least the outline of the sermon.

" Weel, raley, Mr. Halket, I canna jist min' the noo fat the heids o' the discoorse war. But it wis a grand ane."

" Nae doot ; but that jist maks us a' the mair anxious to ken aboot it. What was the text ? And we'll maybe manage to mak' heids for oorsel's. Ye see I was lang in the lectern mysel', and got the guid o' the mealocks and skailin's o' inspiration frae the poopit abeen my heid. That gied me some special skeel in sermons, ye see. Sae gie's the text, Betty, chapter and verse, and I'll lat ye hear *my* diveesions."

" Weel, fegs," said Betty, looking quite crestfallen, " I canna jist min' the noo far the text wis."

" Nor the words o't ? "

" Nor the words o't, aither. But it wis a fine discoorse."

" And it did ye a lot o' guid, nae doot ? "

" Ay, I think it did.—I'm sure it did."

" Weel, weel, Betty ; it's a' richt gin ye think it. . . .
And hoo's the new dominie comin' on wi' his precentin'?
Has he gotten the length o' fower teens yet ?   And is he
aye in the wye o' rinnin' oot o' Dunfermline intil French?"

Betty, who now saw that Halket was in a bantering
mood, gave a laugh, and said "she couldna tell, nae
kennin' hersel' ae teen frae anither."   This exhausted the
kirk as a subject of conversation, at which Betty was
visibly relieved.

Other topics were discussed with more or less zest ;
but at length Lily's name was introduced, and then it
was easy to see what lay nearest some hearts.   While
Jamie showed quite a warm interest in the girl, Halket
and Betty seemed as if they couldn't have enough of the
subject, growing ever more enthusiastic as they proceeded,
till at last Jamie had to hint that it was now getting
dark, and that Logie was a good bit away.

After leaving Betty's house, Halket began again to
speak about Lily Douglas.   Jamie was amused.   His
friend had rallied him from time to time on *his* love
affairs, and now it was difficult resisting the temptation
to have a little bit of friendly revenge.

"Well, Mr. Halket," he ventured to say at length,
" it seems to me that, if ye had been a bit younger, or
Lily a bit aulder, there's only ae thing would hae keepit
you apairt."

" Jamie ! " was all the reply Halket attempted to

make ; but on the word there descended such a combination of accents, that the meaning was as difficult to unravel as that of a Delphic oracle. Yet, when the word had passed, there remained on the air for a moment a certain pleasant echo, which left on Jamie's mind the impression that the soft impeachment was not altogether ungrateful to the speaker.

Halket, who had been giving his friend a convoy towards Logie, now stopped.—

" Ye leave on Wednesday mornin' ? " said Halket.

" On Wednesday mornin'," repeated Jamie.

" I'll try to see you at Rattray afore ye sail ; but, for fear I shouldna manage,—goodbye Jamie, good-bye ; and God bless you ! "

" Good-bye," said Jamie ; and, with a warm grip of the hand, they parted.

Halket had proved to his own somewhat sinister satisfaction that Betty's professed appreciation of the sermon she had heard in Rathen Kirk was a piece of conventional humbug, and the idea she evidently entertained of good derived from it, a mere pietistic delusion. But, had he seen and followed Betty next morning, he might have found cause for revising his opinion.

It wanted a good hour of sunrise on the Monday morning when Betty was on her way towards Logie. Although she had scarcely been out of her native parish for a number of years, she knew the general direction to take, and pushed on with rapid steps, till she thought she must be in the neighbourhood of her destination.

Meeting some ploughmen going out to their work, she hailed one of them.—

" Far aboot's Clyacksneuk ? "

" O, yon's Clyacks," said the man, turning and pointing to the farm they had just left.

" An' is Clyacks himsel' at hame ? "

" Ay, we jist left him in the close."

Betty hurried on, and found Clyacks looking through
the byres. He had a large well-stocked farm, and plenty
of money; but, having a firm belief in the virtue of
personal management, he worked as hard as any of his
men, and was always indeed "the first-gaun gear aboot
the toon."

" Weel," said Betty, confronting him as he came out
of a byre, "ye'll be Clyacks ? "

" Ay," said Sandy, in his slow deliberate way, "and— "
He was going to ask who his visitor was, but she antici-
pated him.—

" Weel, I'm Betty Duncan frae the Hill o' Mormond."

Sandy knew Betty by repute; but had never seen her
before. He regarded her with a certain quiet phlegmatic
curiosity, while she went on.—

" And I've come owre by to see you aboot a sma'
maitter."

" Weel ? "

Betty was considerably excited, and Sandy wondered
what she could want with him.

" Ye kent Fred Clark—frae Rathen ? " she said.

" Brawly," said Clyacks. " Puir chiel, I doot he's like
to come till an ill end."

" Ay, that's sae," was Betty's solemn assent, followed
by an impressive pause.

" Weel, ye wis ance robbit ? " she resumed.

" Ay, dyod, I wis," he admitted, with a facial contor-
tion that was quite comical.

" And kent ye ever fa did it ? "

" Na. Gin I hid, there wid hae been mair wark aboot it."

" Weel than, I can tell ye."

" Yea ? "

" It wis jist Fred Clark."

" Dyod, wumman, I'm nae sayin' but ye're maybe richt. Some o's has fyles thocht that oorsel's.—But fat pat it in yer heid ? and— "

He was going to ask what interest she had in the affair ; but again she forestalled him.—

" Noo, Clyacks, ye maybe winna jist be owre angry gin I tell ye fat he did wi' some o' the siller ?—He gied it to me."

" To you, Betty ?—L—d's sake ! "

" Ay, to me. Shame tak' me that I sid hae to say't. But I'm gaun to tell ye the evendoon truth.—Fred gied some o' the siller to me, and I took it that sidna."

Sandy hardly knew what to say ; but Betty's volubility saved him the necessity of saying anything just then.—

" I've been gaun to the kirk for a Sunday or twa," she went on, " and the minister, that's Maister Anderson doon-by at Rathen, ye ken, he says, says he,—ye see he wis speakin' aboot fowk gaun to the sacrament,—he says, says he : It's nae eese gaun to the kirk, it's nae eese readin' your Bible or sayin' lang prayers, gin ye're nae deein' the richt gate yersel' a' the time. If onybody's strivin' wi' their neebors, says he, they maun gang and mak' it up.' Noo, says I, that's intil Widow Youngson and Mistress Elshender ; for they're aye fechtin' and tonguin' ane anither nae handy. Syne, says he, If

there's ony o' ye drinkin' and sweerin' and cairryin' on,
ye maun gie't up and turn owre a new leaf.   That pat
me in min' o' drucken Willie, the vricht, and I thocht he
micht weel be takin' till himsel'.   But syne he says, says
he, Gin ony o' ye hisna been honest, an' his fat's nae yer
ain, gie't back at ance.   An' I says, Noo Betty that's for
you—that's for *you*, wumman.   An' I says, Ye'll jist gang
fit-for-leg the morn's mornin' owre to Clyacksneuk wi'
that siller.—That's fat I said to mysel', jist sittin' in
the kirk yon'er.   And here I am, and—." Here she took
from her bosom a handkerchief carefully knotted, and un-
doing the knot, offered Clyacks the contents, evidently a
considerable quantity of silver.   He hesitated to finger
it.

" Here, man, tak' it ; it's yer ain and mair forbye.
Jist ye coont it.   There sid be sax poun a' but a saxpence.
He gied me aucht poun' ae time or ither.   That's a' that
I hid by me ; but ye'll get the lave as seen's I can get a
haud o't.—Twa poun' and that saxpence that I want o'
sax the noo, d'ye see ? "

" Ye're richt, Betty," said Clyacks, after he had counted
the money, " jist sax poun a' but a saxpence.   And ye
got aucht ; so that ye're due me twa poun' forbye a
saxpence."

Clyacks was "siccar."

" Noo," said Betty, looking as if a load had been
lifted from mind and conscience, " noo that's a' I can dee
wi' ye the noo ; and ye'll maybe lippen me a fylie till I
hae the lave by me ? "

" I'll dee that, Betty.   Ye've shown yersel' an honest
wumman, and I'll trust ye."

" I hope ye'll forgie me, Clyacks, for takin' the siller

ava," pursued Betty, not quite sure if she was yet properly absolved.

"O, fairly that, Betty, fin ye're peyin't back.—But come awa to the hoose and get a piece. Ye'll be famisht aifter yer lang traivel."

Betty was hungry; and, accepting Clyacks' invitation, got treated to a hearty breakfast.

As Betty was preparing to go, he asked in a hesitating kind of way, "And are ye—onything weel aff, Betty?"

"O, I'm rale weel, thank ye, Clyacks."

"Is yer meal guid?"

"O, nae that ill."

"I've some rale guid the noo, and I'll maybe mak' the men leave a bow o't fin they pass the smiddy yon'er."

"O, thank ye, Clyacks, ye're owre guid."

"Na, na; say naething aboot it."

"Guid-day than, Clyacks."

"Guid-day, Betty.—And min' its twa poun' and a saxpence ye're due me."

Betty, we may say, managed in course of time to make up the sum. Clyacks took the last penny; but he sent the meal, and once or twice a year he repeated the present till Betty's death.

Thinking the matter over after Betty had left, Clyacks resolved to give the money restored by her to Jamie Robertson. He had heard it rumoured that Jamie was going away, and judged that a little money would be not unacceptable to a penniless lad going out into the world.

"He'll be sair eneuch needin' some siller, puir chiel," soliloquised Clyacks, "and raley aifter a' he has the best richt till't. . . . I wonder far I could see him. . . Bell wid likely ken far he is. . . I'll cry in by at Millbog the nicht, and, gin I get a canny chance, I'll spier at her."

That evening Clyacks walked over to Millbog. As he drew near, who should he see enter the house but Jamie Robertson?

"That's lucky," said Clyacks to himself, "I'll jist hing aboot till he comes oot."

CHAPTER XII.

PARTINGS.

Jamie Robertson was naturally a very courageous young fellow. On a battle-field he might have been counted on to do daring deeds; to lead, sword in hand, a desperate charge, or, with his beloved bagpipes, to burst into a bullet-shower, and play his fellows—and himself—on to victory or death. But, in entering Millbog at this particular juncture,—quite commonplace and easy as the operation seemed, he had an ordeal to face that was in many ways more trying than those other feats would have been. Nothing, indeed, but the conviction that he *must* go could have nerved him for the task.

He would have liked to advise Bell of his coming; but no chance offered. Yet he didn't come unexpected. Bell was looking for him. When she understood he was going away, she knew he *must* come to see her; and, as he was to leave Rattray on Wednesday, he could hardly defer his visit till Tuesday night, when his hands would be full of preparations for going away. Monday was now his only available night; and, as evening approached, Bell was momently expecting him.

Since the day when Fred Clark had been arrested and Jamie had disappeared from public view, Bell had been in a wretched state. The exciting events of the day, with their terrible *denouement*, had given her nerves quite a shock. Self-reproach mingled with her feelings, and positive shame, when she thought of the way in which she had tried to defend, if not actually to champion Fred Clark. Ardently did she hope that Halket would never tell Jamie about it.

And now Jamie was going away—and in company with Miss Innes! Old jealousies were revived. At times she was wildly angry, like one who feels oneself deeply and wantonly injured. In calmer moods she almost admitted that it was a kind of punishment on herself for the part she had recently played.

Distracted with such feelings, she was longing to see Jamie, and yet hardly knew what to expect from the meeting.

The Millbog household had just finished supper and were seated round the ingle, where a big peat fire gave sufficient light for a crack in the quiet gloaming hour. In the midst of their conversation a knock was heard. Bell, sure it must be Jamie, jumped up, and made for the door with a speed that did not escape her mother's observation.

"Oh! it's you, Jamie?" Bell exclaimed, when she had opened the door and saw her lover. She put surprise into her tone, and tried to look as if she had hardly expected to see him.

"Ay; and wisna ye expectin' to see me, Bell?"

She knew that everything was being heard in the kitchen. So she gave a short laugh and said, "I dinna ken." But she gave Jamie a look that told a different tale. *It* wasn't seen in the kitchen.

"Are ye comin' in-by?" she added.

"Ay,—I wis a kin' o' wantin' to—see ye a'."

Bell understood. Marget heard, and she too understood. Old John heard, but thought little about it.

Jamie walked along the passage that led to the kitchen. It was a keenly trying moment when he faced the hearth. The light was not of the brightest, but it was clear enough to reveal the hostility of Marget's look. They hadn't seen each other since the memorable night in the cornyard, and neither had forgotten the occasion.

Standing irresolute a moment, and finding that neither John nor his wife was in any hurry to speak, he broke silence with the orthodox salutation, " It's a fine nicht."

" Ay," said Bogie, " nae that ill."

Marget was pleased that her husband should reply. However she might herself ignore the young fellow or " gie him a tonguin'," she wanted the head of the house to act in a dignified way. In his hands were the honour and reputation of the establishment.

Bogie, as he spoke, moved his chair a little. This was an invitation with the minimum of welcome in it to join the circle. Bell eked it out by placing a chair.

Jamie was glad to get seated. It was less awkward than standing. The relief, however, was but momentary. The business with its difficulties was all before him. And he soon found it was about as difficult to make his speech from a chair as it would have been to deliver it while standing in the middle of the floor.

O the distress of such a moment!—A young and bashful lover facing hostile parents in presence of the girl he loves. Only once in a lifetime can it be experienced in its full force. And once is often enough.

Jamie sat and agonised. How was he to begin? If somebody would but say something and break the awful spell! But nobody came to his aid. Bell couldn't, and the old people wouldn't. The embarrassment grew unbearably acute. He seemed to have been sitting there a long time, although the rest were only conscious of a rather awkward pause.

At last he achieved speech. How he managed he could never quite understand.

" I'm gaun awa," he said, in a sudden and breathless manner, like one who had rushed in to deliver an alarming message.

It was Marget's turn now.—

" Sae we've heard," she said.

She spoke in a cold and even cutting way. Jamie felt that this announcement was getting a rather frigid reception. He expected this. If, however, the subject were but taken up and discussed, he didn't mind so much meantime the spirit in which it was approached. So, when Marget contented herself with a cold and brief assent to his proposition, his disappointment was not so much with the tone of her reply as with its abrupt finality. She might at least have given him a cue. The matter had made hardly any progress. The difficulties of the situation remained, and had to be attacked pretty much *de novo*.

He wasn't so long, however, in toeing the line the second time.—

" I've come to speak to ye—aboot something."

" Yea ? " said Marget.

Bell grew alarmed. She divined what was coming ; and, dreading the scene that was bound to ensue, she slipped away " to the ben." Jockie, who guessed something was up, was now all ears and eyes, and his mother, noticing the youngster's keen interest and expectancy, judged it prudent to get him removed beyond earshot.

"Jockie," she said, "ye'll better gang furth and play yersel'."

"It's gettin' some dark," protested the youngster, "an' I'm feart."

"Weel than, gang to your bed."

"I'll rayther gang oot," said Jockie, hastily; and, taking his bonnet and whistling on the dog, he made for the door.

As he came along the passage, his sister appeared in the room door.—

"Jockie," she said, in a pretty loud whisper, "fat are they deein'?"

"Naething as yet," he replied, coming towards her. "They pat me furth afore they wid begin." Then, an idea coming suddenly into his head, he added, "Wid ye like to hear fat they're sayin'?—'Cause I could stan' ahin the door and hearken."

"Och, I'm nae carin', Jockie," said Bell, "but ye can dee't gin ye like. It wid be fine fun at onyrate."

"Ay, but wid ye gie me onything?—I'm sure it's you they're gaun to speak aboot."

"Oh, we'll see ; but awa' ye rin."

"Ay, but ye maun gie's something. I'll maybe get a lickin' gin they fin't oot. And I'm nae gaun to get a lickin' for naething. Na, fegs me!"

Bell was afraid something important might be missed through delay, and said hastily, "Weel than, fat wid ye like?"

"Wid ye gie's—a saxpence?"

"Ay, will I."

"Hauden, than!"

Slipping to the outer door, he opened it, let the dog

out, and then shut it with a good bang. Then on tiptoe he was making his way back towards the kitchen, when Bell again whispered to him.—

"Jockie, min' and come back ilka noo and than to tell me fat they're sayin'. Dinna bide owre lang at a time."

He nodded, and was soon posted behind the kitchen door. Pretty soon he was on his way back to Bell, taking rapid but stealthy steps. She stood in the room door, craning her neck towards him.—

"Weel?" she whispered, excitedly.

"He's seekin' you, Bell," was Jockie's impressive announcement. She felt it would be the orthodox and proper thing to slap his face. But she refrained. Next moment Jockie was back at his post. He remained longer this time.—"Mither's in an awfu' rage," was his next budget of news. "She says Jamie's mair needin' claes than a wife.—Feyther spiered fu muckle siller he had, and he said he had only a saxpence the noo."

Bell could have cried. The tears did indeed stand in her eyes ; but with an effort she kept them back. Jockie was soon back with a fresh instalment of news.—"Jamie says he'll gang awa' and mak' siller ; but mither says ye're better aff than he can ever mak' ye, though he work till his back's like an aul' heuk."

But Jockie's work as courier was done. His career was to be ignominiously cut short. Returning to his post with too great eagerness, he stumbled and fell against the kitchen door, which, opening inwards, landed him at full length on the floor. He got up with astonishing speed, but his mother was waiting him ; and, when at length he reached the outer air, he swore through his tears that he "widna dee't again—nae for a shillin'."

The interruption did Jamie good. The comical element in it had a healthy effect on him, and, when the discussion was resumed, he felt more like himself than he had done since entering the house.—

"Ye think I winna be able to mak' siller and get a hame for a wife?—Gie me a chance. Jist gie me a chance."

"And haud a lassie hingin' on and wytin' you?" sneered Marget. "And fa kens if she'll ever see ye again?—Na, na."

"Na, na," chimed in John.

"But if Bell's willin' hersel' to wyte?" pursued Jamie.

"Bell's nae in the coont," said Marget, quickly. "A lassie like her disna ken her ain mind. Ye wid try to blaw up her heid nae doot; but we maun see till her interests, and nae lat her spoil hersel'. It's oor duty, an' we'll dee't, Jamie Robertson."

"Ay, we'll dee't," echoed John.

"Sae ye winna listen to my proposal ava?" Jamie said, his voice growing louder, and his manner more animated.

"Jist nae ava. That's fat it comes till."

"Nor gie Bell a chance to speak for hersel'?"

"No. Ye've gotten a' the answer ye'll get.—We jist dinna want to hae onything mair adee wi' ye. That's the hale thing. And sae ye needna fash sayin' onything mair aboot it."

Jamie's face had been getting redder and redder. He was now quite angry.

"Well, friends," he said, rising to his feet, "I go; but I'll perhaps return."—

"As I said, ye needna fash your thoom," Margaret put in, scornfully.

"I shall not consider it necessary to consult any-body," said Jamie, loftily.　And poor Marget was snubbed.

Jamie had got on his high horse.　His was a nature full of great and untried possibilities, needing but an adequate challenge from without to make it assert its powers and predominance.　Defied and dared, his spirit swelled up ; and the two commonplace individuals who had a moment before been scorning him, now almost quailed before his overweening presence.

"I go," he resumed, "but I shall likely return ; and, if I do, you'll perhaps not scorn me then as you do now.— Good-bye."　And with lofty dignity he bowed, and turned to go.

Marget and John sat silent.　Even already they tacitly admitted his superiority.　His personality, thus brought out into strong assertion, had in a measure over-awed their lesser natures.

Bell, who had heard Jamie's final speech, delivered as it was in a high key, came from the room as he was opening the outer door.　She was in tears.

"Oh, Jamie !" she sobbed.

"Good-bye, Bell," he said, with emotion in his voice. "They won't listen to me."

"*I* canna help it," wailed poor Bell.　"But I'll—I'll—"

"You'll stick to me Bell ?—Is that it ?　You'll stick to me ?"

"I will."

"And wait for me ?"

"Ay, I'll wait for ye—as lang's ye like."

Of course the old people heard all this, and Bell knew it ; but she didn't care.　The occasion was desperate, and she and Jamie would say their say in spite of everything.

Jamie had now stepped outside, Bell following him. He took her hand. He looked in her eyes. How lovely she was in the gloaming light, with her flushed cheeks and eyes shining through a mist of tears.

"You will?" he asked. And both now knew how much the promise covered.

"I will," she replied.

"Good-bye then, Bell."

"Good-bye, Jamie."

He drew her towards him; and their lips met. One brief passionate kiss sealed the compact, and sanctified the adieu. Next moment he was gone.

So absorbed was Jamie in his own reflections, and so oblivious of his surroundings, that, although Clyacks was standing by the side of the road leading past the corn-yard waiting him, he would have passed without noticing him, had not the latter spoken.—

"Ay, it's a fine nicht the nicht, Jamie."

Jamie started and stopped.

"Ay, fine."

There followed a moment of embarrassment for both men.

"Ay, and—ye're maybe gaun awa'—I wis hearin'."

"I'm gaun awa', Clyacks," Jamie said, briefly, not trusting himself at the moment to say more.

"I'm sorry aboot it."

There followed another awkward pause.

"Ye hinna onything special in view, I suppose?" Clyacks said at length, and with evident hesitation.

"No," said Jamie, "naething. I'll jist hae to tak' my chance."

"Weel than, Jamie, I wish ye weel.—Ye'll come back some time and see a' your auld freens?"

" I will that, Clyacks. Good-bye," he added, thinking that Sandy had only meant to take farewell of him.

Sandy took the offered hand, and held it irresolutely for a few moments.

" I suppose ye hinna jist a lot o' siller, Jamie?"

" No, Sandy," said Jamie, with a short and somewhat sad laugh, " I've never had muckle o' that commodity. But ye min' what Patie says in ' The Gentle Shepherd?'

> ' He that has just enough can soundly sleep,
> The o'ercome only fashes folk to keep.'

That's aye my comfort and consolation."

" Ay, but *hae* ye eneugh, Jamie?" persisted Sandy.

" O weel, I canna say I've muckle, but I'll maybe manage till I mak' mair."

Jamie didn't feel it necessary to admit to Clyacks, as he had done to Bell's parents, that he had only a sixpence in the world. But Clyacks was sure that Jamie's finances must be " gey near the bane."

" Weel, ye see, I've aye been disappointed that I never got a chance o' deein' onything to show fu thankfu' I wis for you helpin' me yon nicht fin I wis robbit. Noo, there's something queer happened this very day."—

Here he gave an account of Betty's visit. He didn't mention the exact sum that Betty had brought back or admitted liability for ; but he allowed Jamie to suppose it was about half the sum that had been stolen.

" Noo, this ten poun'," he said, producing a handful of gold pieces, " this ten poun' is nae mine ava in a sense. I never expected to see the siller again, and had made up my mind to dee wantin't. Sae ye see it's nae mine. And, if it's nae mine, it maun be yours. It'll jist help some to mak' up for your loss—fat ye suffered ae wye or ither bein' aff o' wark and a' that."

He held out the money to Jamie. But the young man drew off.

"It's very kind o' ye, Clyacks, and I feel very grateful for your offer. But I canna tak' the siller; I winna tak' the siller. I did naething mair than ony neebor should hae deen, and I would be ashamed to tak' onything for't."

"Noo, Jamie, dinna be thrawn," said Clyacks, who thought Jamie was needing some "priggin'."

"Jist ye tak' it. Ye are weel deservin' o't; and, as I said, I'm nae for't mysel'. And, mind ye, ye'll be a' the better o't fin ye're gaun sae far frae hame. Mind ye canna gang far wantin' siller.—Hae!"

"No, Clyacks. As I said, I thank you for your kind intentions; but I winna finger the siller. I mean what I'm sayin'—I winna tak' it."

Clyacks now saw that Jamie was quite firm in his resolution.

"Weel than, Jamie, I'm sorry; but, if ye're nae for't, we'll say nae mair aboot it. But, mind, if ever ye should need onything, lat me ken.—The offer aye stan's; and the siller's yours whenever ye want to tak' it."

"That's a' richt, Clyacks. Thank ye."

"Guid-bye than, Jamie; and I wish ye a' speed and forder."

Clyacks watched Jamie as he strode away in the dim light.—

"He's a prood chiel, Jamie. To think he widna tak' the siller; and him sae sair needin't tee. Fegs, he'll fin' the want o't yet, or I'm sair mista'en.—Gaun awa' the length o' Edinburgh! But nae doot the Captain and Miss Innes will look aifter him—Fegs, I'll tell ye fat : speakin' o' Miss Innes, I'll see if she'll tak' the siller and keep it for Jamie. She'll maybe hae a chance o' giein' him the guid o't some time in spite o' himsel'.—I'll jist awa' doon-by to the Hoose and see her."

So soliloquised Clyacks, and made his way to Logie, where he had an interview with Miss Innes. She readily agreed to take charge of the money on Jamie's behalf, and use it for his good, in such ways as his needs dictated and his pride would allow. And then Sandy came home with a lighter purse and a lighter mind.

Next day there came a message from Rattray to Captain Duff, that, owing to certain unforeseen circumstances, the vessel in which they were to sail would not be able to leave before Saturday. The Captain and Miss Innes were much disappointed at the delay ; and Jamie at first shared their feelings. In course of time, however, he came to think that the hitch which had occurred wasn't such a bad thing after all. It put an idea in his head,—sweet and exciting.—Might he not see Bell once more before he went ?

They had said farewell, Bell and he ; but, now that he thought of it, it was altogether too hurried. There was a lot of things that they might have spoken about. And then the sweet pain of parting ought to have been spun out. They hadn't vowed with sufficient earnestness, nor ratified their compact with oath and pledge. Their leave-taking in short hadn't been near impressive enough ; and it ought to be done over again.

Such was the gist of Jamie's cogitations. He persuaded himself that he ought to embrace the chance circumstances offered of re-enacting the farewell scene in a more deliberate way, and with more impressive adjuncts. And yet he was wrong. The final scene between Bell and himself, being quite impromptu, was utterly natural ; and nothing could make more binding the promise uttered in absolutely good faith by a heart perfectly sincere and in dead earnest. Any deliberate attempt to work up feeling, to manufacture impressive adjuncts and devise unusual sanctions, would tend rather to weaken than strengthen the bond, by emphasising the element of distrust that lurks in all vows. And, apart from this, all experience shows how unwise and dangerous it is to re-open matters that have once been well closed.

When Jamie had decided that Bell and he must see each other once more before he left, he fell to considering how it could be carried out. He would have to send a message to her, telling her where and when to meet him. The tryst must be at night, and away from Millbog, where it would be liable to interruption. Bell and he had never met in this way before. Their trysts had always been tacked on to some other errand or expedition more or less bona-fide. He calculated, however, that the special and impressive nature of the occasion would lead her to set aside her scruples, and make for once an unequivocal assignation.

Jamie had now more freedom. It had come to be understood that Fred Clark was the moving spirit in getting the military brought to Logie ; and, as the instigator had himself been crushed and removed from the scene, there was now nobody specially interested in hounding on the Government myrmidons. Miss Innes saw this ; but, in accordance with agreement, Jamie's keeping out of sight was continued in a certain way. He was understood to be invisible, although most of the people about the place had at one time or other caught sight of him, while one or two had even spoken to him.

During the last few days of their stay at Logie Jamie's concealment grew more and more of a formality and a fiction. Being weary of his confinement, he strayed about a good deal, and Miss Innes, to make his life in-doors more bearable, had given him access to the library. Here he was in his element. He spent hours on hours among the books. He looked into every one, read bits of many, and perused not a few from beginning to end.

Some old works dealing with pagan mythology interested him very much, appealing strongly to his imaginative temperament. Very impressive, in particu-lar, was the account of the religious beliefs of the ancient inhabitants of our island—the rites and ceremonies of their worship, with the strange superstitions that dominated their lives. This kind of reading, falling in with his other train of thought, soon suggested the idea of interweaving with the farewell ceremony of which he had been think-ing, such forms and superstitions of the ancient ritual as lent themselves most aptly to the occasion and its purpose.

A certain coincidence, chance but striking, impressed him much. Friday was the night he had fixed on for his meeting with Bell, as being the last he would spend at Logie. To begin with, he found that Friday was the day of Freya, the Venus, or Goddess of Love of the Saxons; while, over and above, this particular day chanced to be, according to the most ancient form of the calendar, the first day of the year, unique in its aptitude for occult rites and binding ceremonies.

The place of meeting was the next thing to fix. With this he had little difficulty. The ceremonies he contemplated could only be carried out in some temple of the ancient faith. There were two Druidical circles in the neighbourhood : one on Netherton of Logie, and the other at Newark. The latter was nearer and more convenient.—They would hold their trysting there.

Having fixed all these things in his own mind, he must next communicate with Bell, tell her his proposed arrangements, and get her assurance that she would come on the night, and to the place appointed. She might have scruples in meeting him, as the tryst would have to be carried out without her mother's knowledge or against her wish ; or she might have some engagement for that evening. These possibilities Jamie foresaw ; but he felt sure he could override all difficulties.

He wrote a letter to Bell. It was really his first love-letter, and, as such, was a pretty long and forceful document. He unfolded his ideas and proposals, and told her what she had to do. Nothing must stand in the way. She must come to Newark on Friday night about nine o'clock. He would be waiting her there ; and come she absolutely must, in spite of everybody and everything. He put it as strongly as he could, winding up by saying that her coming would be the one and final test of her love and fidelity. If she failed !—

He didn't ask her to reply. It was unnecessary ; was in fact inconsistent. It would have admitted the possibility of the inexorable being questioned, of the inevitable being challenged.

By the hand of a trusty messenger the letter was carried to Millbog ; and, when Jamie was assured that it had been delivered into Bell's hands, he felt no more anxiety. All he wished now was that Friday night would come as quickly as possible.

CHAPTER XIII.

THE LAST FAREWEEL.

FRIDAY came.

Never before had Jamie looked forward to a day with such intense expectancy; never in his experience had a day got so individualised. The keen and consummate interest that it derived from its place in the chronology of his own personal history was emphasised by the other coincidences he had discovered and noted. As these contributory lines of interest were Pagan in their origin and significance, it is hardly matter for wonder that he should, in regard to this occasion, have caught some of the spirit of those old times, when life was lived for its own sake, when its joys were drunk without apprehension, without stint, without remorse.

The touch and message of the season told in the same direction. The stirrings of spring were in earth and air, and lush life revelled in the throbbing pulse.

It was an ideal spring day. The air was mild, with a genial pervasive influence that touched into livelier green, garden, and field, and wild wayside. The yerlins sang among the broom; the larks carolled clear overhead; while away over the fuming field the screaming lapwings wheeled and plunged. On sunny hillocks the lambs were frisking in their own abandoned way; and cattle roamed over the lea, restless in their new-found freedom.

Such was the day; and to it succeeded a gloaming still more rich and rare. O those gloamings, when the heart swells with the tide of a boundless life, and we feel well-nigh immortal!

Jamie left the house about sunset. He meant to have a long ramble, and take a kind of farewell of old haunts, landing ultimately at Newark in time for his tryst with Bell. He went through the garden, sitting down for a few minutes in the arbour, where in imagination he lived over again the hours of that Yule night, when Bell and he had renewed their love.

Then he strayed through the Drummledoor Park, and, striking the burn, wandered down along the bank, listening to its low gurgle as he had done many an evening in days gone by. Nothing about Logie would he remember better than that little stream. It had been almost a living thing to him, and he hoped when far away to hear in dreams its low sweet voice.

Crossing the burn at length, he struck through the policies of Crimonmogate. Thus round by many familiar spots he wandered, as gloaming slowly deepened, and away beyond Mormond the red was dying from the western sky.

He had taken a wide circuit, and now, as evening darkened in, he approached Newark. Everything was quiet. The birds had gone to rest. Not a breath of air was stirring. The sky was clear, and away in the south-east hung a low warm moon.

How utterly still looked that little clump of trees, hiding among its shadows those strange monuments of a bygone age and a vanished faith! Jamie walked round the enclosure to see that no one was about, and then, crossing the little ditch, entered the planting, and sat down on one of the stones that had fallen and lay on the ground. He was now waiting for Bell.

Knowing that he was somewhat earlier than the hour appointed, he didn't expect she would come just yet. But he sat and thought about her, his heart growing ever more fond. By-and-by, thinking she might now be coming, he rose, and, advancing to the edge of the enclosure, looked away in the direction of Millbog. It was now too dull to see far, so he betook himself to listening. No ear so acute as that of the lover who waits at the trysting-place; no sound so welcome as the step of the loved one.

Yet Jamie had to wait and listen a good while. Could it be that Bell was going to fail him? Had she shrunk from defying her parents? Had some untoward accident prevented her coming? He was getting quite dejected. What if he should have to go away without seeing her? He couldn't bear to think of it. He would grow desperate, and do some desperate deed.

In the midst of his thoughts his ear caught a slight sound as of some one crossing a fence. His heart almost stood still with hopeful expectancy. A moment later he was sure he heard a step crossing the road—the Park road which passed quite near.

Now he can descry a figure advancing towards him, and soon he assures himself that it is Bell. She drew near very timorously, not noticing him, and stopped a few yards away.

" Bell," said Jamie, in a low voice, " is that you ? "

" Ay, Jamie," she answered quickly, with a nervous fondness in her tone.

Jamie stepped over the ditch to meet her. Then

taking her hand, he assisted her to cross; and they retired together into the planting, sitting down on the seat that Jamie had himself lately vacated.

Bell began nervously to explain the difficulty she had had in getting away. It was the first time she had deliberately left home against the known wish of her parents. Her conscience troubled her, and then she had good reason to tremble when she thought of what waited her on her return. And yet all this but added zest to the situation, and gave a new thrill to love's keen joy.

But there was, to begin with, no word of love between these two, thus met for the first time in avowed tryst. There is always a certain reticence with young lovers. They need some time to overcome the natural shyness which is at once the charm and the good angel of young love. So, for a while, Jamie and Bell talked away on ordinary topics of interest as two acquaintances would—the weather holding chief place in their preliminary conversation.

In course of time they got on to more personal matters, and erelong Jamie was speaking of his plans and prospects. This gave Bell an opportunity of throwing out a hint about Miss Innes,—

"Noo, Bell, fat's the eese o' that?" protested Jamie. "Ye ken fine it's nonsense to speak aboot Miss Innes and me."

"Maybe it is, Jamie; but I canna help it."

"Ye ken fine I dinna like naebody —half sae weel's— yersel'."

He spoke in a tone of tender reproach, and it was the most natural thing possible to emphasise his declaration by putting his arm round his companion's waist. She leaned a little towards him.

"Weel than, Jamie, I'll tak' your word. But I canna bear onybody bein' onything till ye. And min', Jamie, fin ye gang awa', ye maun never haud a wark wi' nae ither body. Ye maun promise me that."

Of course Jamie promised; but soon added, with earnestness quite equal to hers, "And, Bell, *ye* maunna gang wi' nae chaps fin *I'm* awa'."

"I'm sure I never will, Jamie; never!"

Then the talk drifted back to practical matters, Jamie thinking it too soon to bring their vows and endearments to a climax. He explained that he was going first to Edinburgh.

"But fin I'm ance there," said he, "I'll maybe gang farer. They say there's lot's o' money to be made abroad; and I'll maybe gang owre the sea, Bell."

"O Jamie!" And Bell almost cried. "Ye'll maybe be drooned, or some o' the wild folk awa' there will kill ye and eat ye; and fat 'll I dee syne? O Jamie, ye maunna gang awa' there!"

Jamie had to draw her still closer to him, as a preliminary to further comfort and consolation.

"That's awa' in Africa, Bell, that the natives dee things like that. I wid gang to the Indies, far there's nae particular danger. It's a fine het place, and they grow lots o' sugar."

It was news to Bell that sugar was "grown," but she didn't like to show her ignorance, and so let that subject alone. She had no difficulty, however, in finding a fresh cause for querulous fondness.

"But ye'll be awfu' lang awa', Jamie ; and fat'll I dee a' the time ? "

"Oh, I winna jist bide awfu' lang—maybe four or five years."

"Five years ! " exclaimed Bell, with a distressful movement that sent her closer to Jamie.

"It'll gae deen quicker than ye think, lassie ; and of coorse I'll be sendin' ye hame a letter frae time to time, tellin' ye fu I'm aye gettin' on ; and ye'll maybe write to me noo and than, and tell me fu things is aye deein' aboot Logie. And the time'll be deen afore we ken o' oorsels ; and syne I'll be hame Bell, and—and—"

He didn't like to put in words the consummation that would then be reached. It was expressed—and much better—by a hearty hug and a warm kiss. And Bell couldn't very well continue her lament after that.

It was now Jamie's turn—

"But are ye sure ye can wyte me a' that time, Bell ? "

"Ay, Jamie. I'll wyte ye."

"Though your folk's nae willin', and want ye to mairry some ither body ? "

"Ay, Jamie, in spite o' a' that."

"Ye're sure, Bell ? "

"Perfectly sure, Jamie."

Jamie didn't say anything more for a little, but he hadn't left the subject.

"Wid ye sweer to that ? " he asked at length.

"Ay, wid I," answered Bell, not thinking that Jamie meant anything more than a strong assertion of her fidelity.

There was another pause ; and, when Jamie resumed, his companion thought he had got on a new line.

" This is a queer kin' o' a place to meet in, isn't it ? "

Bell had thought it was, and had meant to protest, but she didn't like to do it on her arrival ; and, after a while, it had passed from her mind. Now she remembered the impression.

" Ay, Jamie ; it's a gey queer place. Fat wye did ye think o' comin' here ava ? "

He first explained that it was advisable to appoint some out-of-the-way place for their meeting, so that they might not be spied on or interrupted. Then he added a reason that Bell soon saw was the chief one.

" And this bein' a fearsome kin' o' a place, I thocht, if we met here and plighted oor troth, we wid feel mair impressed like, and never daur aifter-hin to think o' brakin' oor word—D'ye see ? "

" O guidsakes, Jamie, ye'll scare a body ! "

" And min' ye, this is a special nicht, that the folk lang lang ago held sacred, and there's some spells that can be wrocht in this place—spells that—"

" Jamie, Jamie," whispered Bell in nervous alarm, interruping him, " dinna speak o' siclike things, or I'll gang oot o' my judgment. I ance got an awfu' fleg wi' that kin' o' thing mysel'."

" Yea ? " said Jamie, getting interested, " fan wis that? "

" Oh—jist ance—a file ago."

" But fan ? "

" Oh—aboot last Hallowe'en."

" And fat wye did it happen, Bell ? "

" Oh—jist some wye. I wis in the mull,—and—and—"

" Fat ? "

" Weel, something queer happened. That wis a'."

" But tell's aboot it, Bell."

"Och, it's nae worth."

"Ye didna say that at first.　Come on and tell's noo."

"Och, ye'll jist lauch at it."

"No, I winna.—Come on."

Thus they went on as lovers do in such circumstances, and with the usual result.—The story was told.

It was of course the episode of the kiln and the clew, which Bell had kept a profound secret since the eventful Hallowe'en when it took place.　Scarcely, however, had she finished her recital when Jamie broke in.—

"*I* hiv't !　I ken fa did it—fine ! "

"Fat d'ye mean ? " said Bell, astonished and evidently disappointed.　" Fa could hae deen't ? "

"It wis Halket.　I'll wager it wis jist Halket ! "

"Halket ? "

"Ay, jist him.　He'd been hidin' in the kiln at the time."

Jamie spoke with all the enthusiasm of a discoverer, proud of the acumen he has displayed in tracing things to their causes.　He was at the same time innocent enough to expect that his companion would share his complacency.　In this he was wrong.　She didn't want the fearsomeness of the thing explained away, if the dear delusion she had so long and tenderly cherished had to go with it.　No.　She couldn't well refute the destructive theory that was playing havoc with her dream ; but she resented the thing all the same, and was in a bad humour over the business, which a certain sense of shame and outraged delicacy didn't help to improve.

"Oh, maybe," was all the comment she made ; but the tone was that of sullen disappointment.

Jamie, however, failed to note how unwelcome his explanation was, and went on.—

" But this is a different kin' o' thing that I'm speakin' aboot.—The auld powers and deities that ruled things langsyne are aye to the fore, though we've a kin' o' shoved them aside wi' oor new faiths. And, if they hover aboot onywhere, it maun be in their ain auld temples, that hae seen mony a race o' kirks rise and fa', and are aye stanin' yet."

Jamie was getting eloquent, but he had an unsympathetic audience for once, and got pulled up in the midst of his flight.

" Ye needna care, Jamie ; I'll hae naething adee wi' that kin' o' things."

He reasoned with her in the most persuasive way he could think of ; but it wouldn't do.

" The thing's nae canny," said she, obstinately, " and I winna dee't. . . . And it's time I was hame. It maun be a' the hoors o' the nicht. . . . Lat's awa', Jamie."

She made as if to disengage herself from his arms. He detained her, which after all wasn't so very difficult to do, and asked in a tone of tender reproach, " Fat's adee ? "

" Naething ; lat's awa'," said Bell ; and, to show that there was nothing wrong, she began to sob.

A woman in tears is irresistible to the average man.

" Bell, forgie me," exclaimed Jamie, feeling sure he must have done something very far wrong to make the dear girl weep, although at the moment he didn't understand the nature of his offence. But very soon he did. The mind, when urged along some engrossing line of thought, may seem to overlook many collateral matters to which its attention is invited. These, however, leave an impression, unheeded though it be at the time ; and, if the mind is suddenly pulled up and has to retrace its way in search of an explanation for something, it may find in those unconscious impressions, material for new and definite ideas. Like chance seeds that seem to have been dropped in vain, they keep their vitality, and germinate when at length they command some fostering attention.

Thus did Jamie on review come to understand the cause of Bell's strange petulance. He saw it was the reception he had given to her pet little tale, connected as it was with her strange ebullition of passionate love on that same Hallowe'en night—the explanation of which he also now for the first time got hold of. He couldn't have put the thing in words, no more than Bell herself could have done—the whole emotional situation was so complex and elusive. But he *felt* it.

It wouldn't have been very clear to an ordinary listener what he was apologising for exactly, the whole performance being rather inconsequential and incoherent ; but the two understood each other, and that was enough. He tenderly kissed away her tears, and life looked bright once more.

Jamie could see, however, that he would have to revise his programme. The Druidical mysteries he had wanted to introduce into their leave-taking would now have to be omitted. It was a disappointment after he had filled his mind with the subject, and had set his heart on having their love-vows confirmed with the weird sanctions of an old-world ritual. But, in after years, it was a relief to think that he had been kept from doing it. *Dii laesi* are to be dreaded, even though they be the old divinities of an outworn faith.

One thing alone he now wanted to do which had a touch of symbolism in it.

"Bell," he said, after some endearments had made their reconciliation complete, "as ye said, we'll maybe need to be gaun awa'; but, afore we pairt, I wid like to gie ye something to keep for my sake."

"Weel, Jamie?"

"I've a saxpence here, and I'm to brak it in twa. I'll gie you ae half o't, and I'll keep the ither to mysel'."

"That's fine, Jamie," said Bell, delighted to have a chance of showing her readiness to acquiesce, and understanding, as every maiden did, the significance of the gift.

"We'll aye keep oor bits," said Jamie, "they'll mind's on ane anither, and on oor vows."

He knew it was unnecessary to enlarge on the subject, but, rising to his feet, he said, as he drew the coin from his pocket, "We'll get it divided on yon muckle stane."

He led the way to the altarstone on the south side of the circle—a huge recumbent boulder, whose rounded surface shimmered in the soft moonlight. As the slope on the further side of the stone was more clearly illuminated, he went round to that side, to have better light for the operation he had in view. Bell remained on the nearer side, leaning on the boulder while Jamie proceeded with his task.

It didn't take long, for he had taken the precaution to have the sixpence pretty well divided beforehand. When the bisection was completed, retaining one half in his left hand, he took the other in his right, and thus addressed his companion :—

" Noo, Bell, I'll gie you this half, and I'll keep this ane to mysel'. As lang's ye keep yours, ye'll be true to me ; and as lang's I keep mine, I'll be true to you.—And may God judge between you and me ! "

He held out the half of the coin to her. She, leaning forward on the great stone, stretched out her hand to take it. But she had placed her foot on a loose pebble, and the movement she now made caused it to slip. She lost her balance, and, rolling sideways, fell behind the boulder.

Then just in the space she had vacated there appeared, framed as it were between the two upright stones on the north side of the circle, a female figure, distant, shadowy ; and to it Jamie now found himself involuntarily stretching out his hand. The sudden start he got made him drop the piece of silver, which, slipping on the stone, disappeared on the further side.

Next moment the vision had vanished ; and Jamie's attention was recalled to Bell, who, more scared by the untoward accident than hurt, was rising to her feet. He hurried round to her help.

" Are ye hurtit, Bell ? " he asked, veiling his own nervousness in an exhibition of extra concern for her.

" No," she replied, with alarm and distress in her voice, " but— "

Jamie at once divined the chief cause of her disappointment ; and, feeling the omens were already sufficiently unfavourable, he decided instinctively and in a moment to conceal the fact that her part of the coin was lost ; while not for a world would he mention the strange and disconcerting thing he had just seen.

" Oh, never mind," he broke in, speaking in a tone of

confidence, though with misgiving at his heart, " it disna maitter. Here's your bit, and it's a' richt noo." And he gave her the half of the coin which he had meant to keep for himself.

He took her in his arms and caressed her tenderly, murmuring such sweet and cheering things as he could think of, but with a feeling that the disquieting effect of the incident couldn't be quite met by soft speeches and tender endearments. For Bell remained strangely silent ; and, if he couldn't re-assure her, there was little he could do for himself.

He thought it best to get away as quickly as possible from the eerie place. They would never recover their spirits there.—

" I think we'll maybe be gaun noo," he said, " it maun be gettin' late."

He took her hand, and together they turned to leave the circle. But now, when Bell began to move, she discovered that she had given her ankle a wrench which made walking painful. Determined to conceal this from Jamie, she walked on bravely for a little ; but it wouldn't do. She soon began to limp and drag in spite of herself, till Jamie noticed there was something wrong, and she had to admit that she had hurt herself when she fell.

He gallantly proposed to carry her ; but she wouldn't hear of this, and continued to limp along at an ever-slowing pace. Seeing this, he insisted that she should submit to be carried ; but she still demurred. When, however, they were crossing the fence on the other side of the road, and he was lifting her down, he took her gently but firmly in his arms, and, refusing to set her down, walked away with the dear burden through the field.

Bell, feeling the distress that assails people who imagine themselves an oppressive burden, protested a good deal and struggled a little; but, as she began to see with what firm ease her stalwart lover was bearing her, she got reconciled to the situation, which was in other respects supremely delightful.

Millbog was about a quarter of a mile distant over fields. About a hundred yards from the house there was a piece of waste ground, covered with a profusion of broom.

"Jamie," said Bell, "ye maunna come farer. I'll easy manage noo."

"Weel, than, I'll lat ye doon; but ye maun tak' a bit rest afore ye set oot." And so down they sat among the broom.

They had now recovered in great measure from the depressing effect of their experience at Newark. Their surroundings had become natural, and feelings that a little ago had either been repressed or directed into morbid channels, had now free play; nay, by a kind of reaction, were asserting their predominance in a more compelling way than ever. The pulse of youth and love again beat free and high.

But they didn't talk—not even of vows. They only felt.

After a long spell of silence, Bell at length spoke.—

"Jamie, I maun gang noo."

"Weel than, Bell, good-bye!"

At the word a great passion of unutterable fondness seized her soul. She threw her arms around her lover's neck, and on his face rained burning kisses. Him too the sweet delirium seized, and he strained her to his breast. . . . .

. . . . . Love touched them then with his immortal finger; and so still in that unforgotten hour, shine for them the star-heavens overhead, and through the long broom steals evermore the witchery of the westering moon. . . . .

. . . . . There and thus they took farewell. It was to be a long one; longer—much—than either of them wot.

CHAPTER XIV.

"O LOGIE O' BUCHAN."

AND so Jamie was gone from Logie. No more by garden and green at early morn would his stalwart form be descried. Not again would his stirring pipe wake the rural echoes; nor his "viol sae sma'" help in hoose or ha' to pass the evening hour.

He was much missed about the place, more than anybody would have thought possible,—so little do we realise the worth and weight of people while they are moving in our midst. For a good while indeed after Jamie's departure Logie hardly looked like its old self.

No one of course missed him as did Bell. She, poor girl, felt as if the light of life had for her gone out. What made the desolation of her heart all the greater was the fact that she had no one to whom she could confide its secrets and its sore. That last escapade of hers, when in the small hours of the morning she had returned from her clandestine meeting with Jamie, had led to a stormy scene at Millbog, which greatly widened the estrangement between her and her parents. Jockie in fact was the only one about the place to whom she could mention Jamie's name, and he, of course, wasn't old enough adequately to understand or sympathise with her feelings.

The first ray of comfort came through the receipt of a letter from Miss Innes, telling how they had arrived in

Edinburgh and were all well. Incidentally the writer mentioned—although of course the information was the real kernel of the letter—that Jamie was getting on well, but that his heart was still at Logie.

Bell was naturally flattered by Miss Innes's attention. A letter was a great thing in those days, and was always duly appreciated. Then it was delightful to hear about Jamie. Yet somehow or other the satisfaction and the joy were not altogether unmixed. There was a fly in the sweet ointment of her comfort.—

Jamie was near Miss Innes, and Bell could only hear of him through her. She tried to reason herself out of this unreasonableness, and accused herself of ingratitude. But after all the heart knows not reason—knows not anything but its own instincts; and these are inexorable—and infallible.

More real satisfaction and comfort came from a visit that Halket about a week after paid to Millbog. Bell chanced to be alone in the house when he arrived, and they had an hour's quiet crack together.

She was at first somewhat distant and reserved, being afraid that her visitor would return to the subject of Fred Clark. But, when he never offered to mention the fellow's name, she got re-assured, and began to talk more freely ; and, when he led the conversation to Jamie, she grew more and more communicative. It was such a relief and a joy to get some one to talk to about her absent lover. And she knew that Halket was thoroughly true and sympathetic.

There, sitting on her low " creepie," while Lily's child crawled on the floor, she told her old friend of her parents' opposition, and of Sandy's suit. Then she referred to the farewell. After a while she was emboldened to show Halket the half of the sixpence which Jamie had given her. Of one thing she didn't like to speak, and that was of Jamie's project of going abroad. She was fain to hope it would never be carried into execution ; and, as we are all apt to do with unwelcome possibilities, thought she would help to prevent it by ignoring it. She had further been considerably re-assured in the matter by the fact that Miss Innes had made no allusion to it.

Going home in that spring gloaming, Halket found himself dwelling on the episode of Jamie's leaving Logie. Along therewith his favourite old tune of " The Ripells " was running in his head. The sadness of the parting of the young lovers was interwoven with the hopefulness of the season ; and erelong he had, almost unconsciously, got the idea thrown into a quatrain to suit the measure of the air; and now, as he paced along, he was humming,—

> " He said, Think na lang, lassie, tho' I gang awa',
> He said, Think na lang, lassie, tho' I gang awa' ;
> The simmer is comin', cauld winter's awa',
> And I'll come and see thee in spite o' them a'."

He hadn't been thinking of finding in the incident a theme for a song. It came to him unsought, as all genuine inspirations do. No man need seek for a theme. It must find him, or it is no good.

For several days thereafter the thing stuck to Halket He had got the refrain, and gradually the body of the song was evolved and came into being. At length the lyric was completed. He had made his song; and it was going to make him. He christened it "Logie o' Buchan."

A week or two after he paid another visit to Millbog, bringing Lily with him. She wanted to see Logie, and Halket proposed that Bell should go with them. It was a delightful day in April. They took a turn round the place, and then strayed down the burn side. Coming to a natural hollow where between green sloping banks the stream slid along, they sat them down. The primroses were bright on bank and brae, and birds sang sweet on many a budding bush.

After they had sat some time in silence, Lily turned to Halket, and said in her sweet engaging way,—

"Sing us a song, please, George. I think music is so nice near water."

Bell started to hear her elderly adviser so familiarly addressed, and darted a glance at him. But Halket had got accustomed to Lily's mode of address, and seemed to take it as a matter of course.

"Well," said he, "I'll sing you a song that I don't think you have ever heard before."

And this was what he sang.—

> O Logie o' Buchan, O Logie the Laird,
> They ha'e ta'en awa' Jamie that delved in the yard,
> Wha played on the pipe and the viol sae sma',
> They ha'e ta'en awa' Jamie the flower o' them a'.
>
> > He said, Think na lang, lassie, tho' I gang awa',
> > He said, Think na lang, lassie, tho' I gang awa',
> > The simmer is comin', cauld winter's awa',
> > And I'll come and see thee in spite o' them a'.
>
> Tho' Sandy has owsen, has gear, and has kye,
> A house and a hadden, and siller forbye,
> Yet I'd tak' my ain lad wi' his staff in his hand,
> Before I'd ha'e him wi' his houses and land.
>
> > He said, Think na lang, lassie, etc.

My daddie looks sulky, my minnie looks sour,
They frown upon Jamie because he is poor ;
Tho' I lo'e them as weel as a daughter should do,
They're nae half sae dear to me, Jamie, as you.
      He said, Think na lang, lassie, etc.

I sit on my creepie and spin at my wheel,
And think on the laddie that lo'es me sae weel,
He had but ae saxpence, he brak it in twa,
And gied me the half o't when he gaed awa'.

      Then haste ye back, Jamie, and bide na awa',
      Then haste ye back, Jamie, and bide na awa'.
      The simmer is comin', cauld winter's awa',
      And ye'll come and see me in spite o' them a'.

Halket had a good voice, and, what was of more consequence, sang with taste and feeling. The notes rang sweetly in the hollow, while the gush and ripple of the burn made a soft accompaniment. Bell sat with eyes fixed on the water, and they were full of tears. Lily, who began to understand the song, glanced at Bell, and, seeing her in tears, put her own hand in hers, and thus sat till the song was finished ; after which no one said a word till they had left the spot and were on their way back to Millbog.

Thus for the first time was " Logie o' Buchan " sung. How many thousands of times has it been rendered since then ; how many thousands of times will it be sung in days to come! Songs rise into sudden fame—blaze for a day—then die and are utterly forgotten. This song is for all time.

. . . . Such is the episode of " Logie o' Buchan " ; and such the end of it for most people. And, indeed, as far as the lyric is concerned and its message, no addendum is needed—no sequel called for. The mind rests there. For ever does the maiden utter her sweet plaint; for ever waits the return of summer and of her lover ; for ever contrasts him with the older suitor; is for ever faithful though parents frown and threaten. The hearer is pleased with the lay, and wants no more. Like a picture it selects and fixes the situation, and there it stands unchanged for all time—ideal, perfect, satisfying.

And we too would like to stop here, if we well could. But the story-teller is neither lyrist nor painter. No single scene or situation, however pregnant, however suggestive, will cover his task. He begins before it ; he goes beyond it. The completeness of his work is the completeness of evolution.

And so we must go on—on at least for a little.

CHAPTER XV.

FIVE and a half years have elapsed since Jamie left Logie ; and now away among the sugar plantations of Jamaica he stands, looking out on a tropical sea. Wistfully he gazes, for he knows that away beyond the wide Atlantic lies his own native Scotland. He is thinking of Buchan as he often does—oftener now in fact than he used to do. He sees the great flocks of rice-birds that have come over sea from Carolina to feed on the seeds of the Guinea grass, and he wishes he had wings like them to fly away—fly away over to Scotland,—to Buchan,—to Logie.

And yet many people would have thought he had little cause to wish himself back in the old country. There he was Jamie Robertson, the apprentice gardener, with scarce a sixpence to bless himself, obscure and condemned to hard manual labour. Here he is Mr. Robertson, the " Massa," looked up to by all as the overseer of the estate, with a big salary and plenty of comforts. Life in fact had gone well with Jamie since coming to Jamaica. He had verified Halket's prediction, being already well on the way to position and fortune.

Then, how rich and generous is the clime he is now in compared with the bleak land he left ; how much fairer and grander is Jamaica than Buchan !

Mormond with its few hundred feet of elevation is but a mound compared with those mountains away inland, which rise thousands of feet to lose their heads among the clouds. The uplands of Buchan were mostly bleak wastes, with nothing growing but heath and whin. But here on all the hills wave groves of pimento, with their rich deep tints, while many a glade discloses a woodland carpet of rarest verdure. The streams he knew in other days—the Logie, the Ailie, the Ugie—were but poor burns creeping along to a cold sad sea. Here from romantic valleys pour a hundred rivers, which flash in the tropic ray, and leap in mad joy right into the arms of a sunny sea. How dreary were the flats of moss away in Buchan, and even the cultivated ground was tame and monotonous. In this new home of his Jamie sees the great savannahs stretch on every hand—rich plains where the sugar cane grows in wide plantations.

Such was the contrast, all in favour of the new land wherein his lot is now cast, all against the old country he came from ; and yet he is sad and longs for his native shores. With that other exile he could have sung,

> " I sigh for Scotia's shore, and I gaze across the sea,
> But I canna get a glimpse o' my ain countree."

Again with fancy's eye he can see the Logie, and the House and the garden and all the surroundings; again he can picture that quiet homestead at Millbog, with the girl of his early love moving about among the cattle and the poultry, or sitting spinning by the evening fire.

More wistfully now than ever, we have said, did he recall those far-off scenes. For he had had no word from anyone about Logie for nearly two years. During the first three years of his residence in Jamaica he had written to Halket and received a reply from him about once a year ; but when, after waiting a year, he had got no answer to his last letter, he had written to another acquaintance. That communication evoking no reply either, he had at last written to Bell herself. But not even that letter had been answered as yet.

No wonder that he felt anxious and wistful. And it has to be remembered that the longing for home was much greater in those days, when few went abroad, when communication was slower and more difficult, and travel attended with more discomfort and danger.

In all outward respects Jamie's life, as we have already indicated, had been very successful. When he came out to Jamaica, he had, through the influence of Miss Innes's friends, who had a considerable interest in the sugar industry, got a good situation on a plantation.

He had a capital equipment for success. His was, to begin with, the general and thorough-going advantage of being young and poor. Then, his natural abilities were great, and had now good scope for their exercise and display ; while for this particular line of occupation on which he had entered his early training as a gardener fitted him exceptionally well. Above all, there was the resolution he had made and the determination he cherished, to succeed and make for himself position and fortune.

Very soon this combination of advantages began to tell. Step by step Jamie worked himself forward, and in less than three years he had become overseer of the estate. He had now got appointed to the charge of another and larger plantation, lying nearer the sea ; and he had just arrived to take duty.

It was autumn, and the season of rain and storms was beginning. Unfortunately yellow fever, which often recrudesces at this time of year, now broke out on the estate. Besides the usual complement of negro slaves, there were some assigned hands, who had been transported to the Indies for their connection with the Jacobite rebellions in the old country. One or two sad survivors of the Fifteen were there, along with a few who had been sent out after the suppression of the Forty-Five. Among these wretched whites the disease erelong began to work special havoc.

In such outbreaks little attention was, as a rule, paid to the sick, unless they were free men and held some position on the estate. Those that had sufficient strength of constitution to battle successfully with the disease would recover. The others had just to die, and be treated to hasty and unceremonious burial.

Little humanity remained in the heart of the average planter. The sentiments that prevailed in the old country underwent considerable revision in these latitudes ; and those who, on their first coming to the Indies, felt shocked at the ways and practices of the planters, came in course of time to fall in with them and think nothing about it. Most of those employed on the estate were negro slaves. The nigger was regarded pretty much as an animal would be—useful and all that, but with no rights or feelings to be consulted. Nor were the convicts reckoned at any great figure. In some respects, indeed, their lot was harder than that of the black slave.

Jamie's feelings, however, had not been so blunted. As a master he was kind, although firm ; and in this way he got an amount of work out of his estate hands that surprised other managers, who depended mainly on the lash and strong language for keeping their people in order and at work.

Hence, when the fever broke out,—as it did immediately on his arrival at his new plantation—he set himself to devise means for having the patients well treated. He got a wooden erection put up on a piece of uncultivated ground beyond the bounds of the estate, and to this hospital all who were attacked with the malady were conveyed.

It was difficult to get those who were well to go near the sick; but for a while he did manage to get his plans and wishes to some extent carried out. When, however, the dread disease was seen to be spreading rapidly, and one victim after another was struck down; when many graves had to be hastily dug in the deep brown mould, and the population of the district was visibly shrinking —then did a panic seize those that were still in health. The paid hands slipped away, retiring inland to the higher grounds, where conditions were healthier and the risk of infection less; while the blacks who had to remain got demoralised with fear.

The result was that Jamie was left to combat the outbreak pretty much single-handed. Very trying was the situation, and it would have been little wonder if he had consulted his own safety and ease and followed those who had gone away. But Jamie wasn't the man to quit what he considered his post of duty, be the danger what it might.

Many a dull and anxious hour he passed during those days. Thoughts of home and far-off friends mingled with his other sad reflections. Yet he didn't yield to despair, as many might have done in such a combination of distressing circumstances. Every day he visited his hospital, and did what he could for his patients. It wasn't much, but not a few poor wretches died happier from having seen "Massa" and got some little attention at his hands.

One evening, after being away all day, he returned to his lonely residence more tired and dejected than ever. He didn't get a light, but sat in the gloom. It suited best his mood just then.

The air grew still and close. A great weight and oppression seemed to sit on everything. But this wasn't for long. A sudden flash lit up the whole landscape, and there followed a mighty peal of thunder that seemed to shake the universe. The storm got momently worse. The lightning became a kind of continual blaze, and the thunder like an uninterrupted cannonade. Soon the wind began to rise, and erelong a mighty hurricane was raging that threatened to sweep everything to destruction.

Jamie had seen not a few such storms, and was not particularly alarmed. He sat still, almost enjoying the wild uproar of the elements. It seemed to fall in with his train of thought, and to suit the unrest of his spirit.

Casting his eyes round the room, he started a little to see a dark figure lying on the floor near his couch. The strange dazzle of the lightning prevented him seeing the object at all clearly, so he got a light and went near to examine it.

It was a man and evidently one of the convicts. He moaned as Jamie drew near, but did not attempt to rise ; and Jamie had little difficulty in seeing that he had been struck down with yellow fever. But how came he there ? —Looking more closely, Jamie saw that he had a big knife in his hand, which only made the whole affair more strange and suspicious.

The man was lying with averted face; but, when Jamie spoke to him, he looked round. Jamie started back : there was such a mixture of hate and terror in that evil look. But more than that,—that face and that look have a strange attraction for him. His eyes are fixed on the man with a kind of fascination ; and now something is dawning on mind and memory.—

He has seen that face before. . . . Where ? . . . When ?

Can it be—Fred Clark ?

Yes : 'tis he. Changed ; yet he.

" Fred Clark, by Heaven ! " exclaimed Jamie, when his thoughts had reached this point.

The sick man replied with a fiendish look, which bodily pain and weakness caricatured into something unspeakably revolting.

" What are you doing here ? " Jamie asked, yet hardly expecting a reply.

But the man seemed to gather himself together with a supreme effort.—

" I wanted to kill you ! " And, as he spoke, he raised aloft the knife which he held in his right hand.

But the exertion and the excitement were altogether too much for him ; and the next moment he had quite collapsed, and lay speechless and unconscious on the floor.

Jamie stood for a few minutes like one paralysed— the affair was so strange and startling, even in a place where the exhibition of wild passions and the commission of dark deeds were common enough. It was not, however, the mere fact of his life having been in danger that impressed him so much. It was the way in which the strange experience connected itself with the past.

It was some time before the tumult of feeling thus excited was sufficiently allayed to permit of reflection When he was able to think, he set himself to find an explanation for the strange occurrence. And this was what he had to be content with meantime, until his theories could be confirmed or corrected.—

Fred had come to Jamaica among those who had been transported for their connection with the Rebellion. He was evidently an assigned servant on this very estate, to the management of which Jamie had just been appointed. Dreading to meet his new master, Fred had contrived to keep out of sight, which, under the circumstances, was not so difficult to do, for a time at least. Taking advantage of the deserted condition of the estate, he had resolved to murder Jamie ; and, after his intended victim had left in the morning, had gained access to the house, and had there secreted himself to wait for his return. But already the fever was on him, and in the course of the day the disease had made such progress that, by the time his victim came back, he was unable to carry out his dark design.

Such was the general theory that occurred to Jamie in explanation of the strange incident. He stood looking at his enemy, too prostrate and helpless now to invite the treatment that might have been meted out to him in other circumstances. Yet he couldn't help deriving a certain grim satisfaction from contemplating a villain thus struck down by Providence in the midst of his dark designs.

The storm without was abating, and Jamie began to

consider what line of action he would adopt for the night at least. He decided just to leave Fred where he was. It was a good deal to leave him alone in comfortable quarters, and Jamie couldn't help reflecting with some complacency on the magnanimous part he was playing. He would just let him alone, and say with the old Hebrew, " Let not my hand be upon him." If he died, it would be the work of Providence, and—well there wouldn't be any great loss. If he got well, there would be an opportunity to consider his case and see how the ends of justice could be met.

Reflecting thus, Jamie moved away and shut the door. He went to another house on the estate that was then unoccupied, and, entering, got a light, and sat down to further moralising.

The incident had brought back to memory more vividly than ever the old life about Logie, with its experiences and interests,—its joys and sorrows,—its love and its hate. He sat thinking over these things for a long time, reviewing the various events, and living over again the old days, now rendered romantic by time and distance. At length, feeling it was late, he determined to turn in for the night. This recalled the fact that he had been driven from his usual quarters, and again he thought of Fred Clark lying yonder all alone in the clutch of the dread distemper. The more he thought of him, the more effectually did pity challenge all other feelings. Distress recollected usually appears more pathetic than it did when actually viewed.

Jamie tried to throw off these softer feelings. Considering what the villain had meant to do, he was being treated shamefully well. He had deserved death, and he was being left unharmed and in circumstances of greater comfort than many another more deserving man was enjoying. No, no: the scoundrel didn't deserve any pity.

But, as Jamie lay and thought, and as the great silence of the night bore in on his spirit, he found his arguments more and more powerless to resist the voiceless appeal of pain and suffering. He tried to forget about it all and go to sleep. But it wouldn't do. Sleep refused to come.

After lying a while and finding that he couldn't get the matter out of his head, he rose and moved about. But this also failed to restore his equanimity, and at last, in a kind of desperation, he went outside. He didn't just intend to go anywhere in particular, but somehow or other he found his way back to the house he had left, and in a little was standing once more by the side of the sick man.

There was no change in Fred's position; he was evidently in a state of collapse. There was no one near to render any assistance, but Jamie managed by dint of strength and some engineering to get the patient to bed, where he made him as comfortable as possible, and gave him such medical treatment as the circumstances would allow.

Jamie knew well the extreme risk he ran of infection, but somehow or other he felt he couldn't help himself. He just *had* to do it. After doing all he could, he returned to the place whence he had come, and again lay down, when sleep came sweetly and soon.

In the morning Jamie made it his first work to visit his new patient. He found the wretched man raving.

Jamie had got well accustomed to rough scenes and rough words, and wasn't just the squeamish lad he had been in former days at Logie; but the ravings of this man appalled him, revealing as they did so much of his career of crime and his dark feelings and impulses.

Jamie soon got thoroughly interested in his patient. Humanity had urged him at first, but erelong it was the physician's enthusiasm as much as anything that impelled him to work so hard for Fred's recovery. This, too, made him almost forget that he was doing all he could to restore to health and activity an implacable and most dangerous foe.

Luckily for himself, he enjoyed the physician's immunity from contagion, and passed personally unscathed through all the trying time.

At length Fred took a turn for the better, and, as often happens, an apparently worthless life was preserved, while many lives that appeared useful and worth preserving were extinguished—just as the weed often survives when the fair flower is nipped by the blast. When Fred was sufficiently conscious to understand the situation and see who was nursing him, he relapsed into a sullen indifference and reserve. He would say nothing to Jamie, nor reply to any of his questions.

This, of course, was rather trying to Jamie's temper and he could hardly be expected to stand it with perfect good humour. He had some patience with a convalescent man, and was inclined to credit Fred's sullenness to a kind of embarrassment which he was bound to feel when he first came to realise what had happened. But, when no improvement took place in his demeanour, Jamie was tempted to devise some disciplinary machinery for his special benefit. He first tried a lecture, and then threats ; but all to no purpose.

By this time Fred appeared well enough to rise, and Jamie at length ordered him to get up. When he paid no heed, Jamie got exasperated, and went off for a negro or two to compel obedience. Before he returned, however, Fred had gone. And not only had he quitted the house, but, as far as could be ascertained, had left the estate altogether.

Jamie was relieved to think that the fellow was gone for good. He certainly would make no effort to find and bring him back.

The epidemic being now over, Jamie set himself to have the estate put once more in working order. This involved a good deal of labour and anxiety, so great had been the dislocation caused by the visit of the fell disease. In course of time, however, he got things set right, and began to look ahead with some hopefulness.

But now a new trouble began to show on the horizon. —Away among the mountains of the interior lived the Maroons, a predatory tribe, who, like the Scottish Highlanders of old, made a good deal of their living by plundering their richer lowland neighbours. When, nearly a century before, the island of Jamaica, then in the possession of the Spaniards, was given up to the English, the negro slaves of the Spaniards fled to the mountains. Their descendants continued to live there, and were called Maroons. They often made descents on the English plantations, committing great depredations. On such occasions severe fighting would take place between them and the planters.

For some time they had been quiet, but now, taking

advantage of the weakened condition of many estates owing to the ravages which the fever had made, they had resumed their incursions. Several plantations lying further inland had already suffered, and there was no saying when the Maroons might find their way to those places that lay nearer the sea.

Jamie proceeded to prepare for possible attack. He sent to Kingston for a good supply of arms and ammunition, drilled his hands, and took such other steps as occurred to him for putting the place in a defensive condition.

It was while attending to these matters that he learned something which did not tend to allay his apprehension. One of the assigned hands had ventured the remark in Jamie's presence that their estate would need to make special preparations for defence; and, when asked for the grounds of his opinion, the man, after some hesitation, divulged the fact that Fred Jamieson (as they knew our old friend) had said that he would some day run away and join the Maroons, which this man believed he had now done.

And so Jamie could understand how special was the danger that now menaced him and his estate.

CHAPTER XVI.

THE FIGHT

FRED had indeed made for the mountains. He had had such a step in view for some time; but recent events had precipitated the execution of his design. For now he felt he couldn't stay on the plantation. He must get out of the way. He couldn't bear Jamie's presence Wild and turbulent as were his feelings before, they were rendered still more so by the conflicting emotions which his enemy's treatment of him generated. Only some desperate step would create an adequate diversion. And such a step he was now taking.

He had to make the journey in easy stages at first, as his strength was not yet equal to the task of bearing any great exertion; but, as he got to higher altitudes, he regained vigour at a rapid rate.

He knew the Maroon country pretty well, having already visited it once or twice on an embassy of peace, when, some three years before, the planters were negotiating for a treaty. Away beyond the pimento walks the country got more bare and wild. The finely wooded hills were left behind, and great jagged cliffs began to rise on either hand. Following a river valley, he came at length to a transverse ravine, where the scenery was still more wild and desolate. A small torrent brawled down the hollow, but everything else was still.

Fred had now to pick his way among great rocks and round jutting crags, making but slow progress. All at once he heard a shout above him, and, looking suddenly up, he saw a Maroon sentinel posted on a rock, with a flint-lock which he was aiming at him. Fred knew the signal to make to indicate that he came on a friendly errand, and, when the sentinel came down from his lofty station, Fred explained that he wished to see the chief. The Maroons could speak a kind of broken English, sufficient for general purposes of communication between them and the planters.

Fred's Maroon guide conducted him up the pass. It was narrow and difficult to tread, for the mountains now rose steep on either side like two great walls, and many loose boulders were lying about. After proceeding about half a mile they fell in with another scout, into whose hands Fred was surrendered, to be conducted to the chief, while his first guide returned to his post. The Maroons, dreading reprisals now that hostilities had been resumed, were taking special precautions against being surprised, although it would have been exceedingly difficult for any body of men to force their way up the pass.

At length the pass seemed to come to an end. A great mountain barrier frowned before them, buttressed by beetling crags, seamed and splintered, and insurmountable to human foot. A stranger would have judged it impossible to proceed further in that direction; but the guide led the way round a mass of rock, and now there appeared a kind of natural stair, by which they climbed up to a ledge wide and safe.

From this ledge a view of the pass for some distance could be got, and several Maroons were lying lazily about, waiting to see who the stranger could be that they had just seen coming up. As Fred and his guide proceeded along the rocky table, they seemed to be getting in beneath the mountain; but erelong they came to an aperture in the great rocky wall, which had been artificially narrowed till no more than three men could enter abreast. The Maroons had several other retreats among the mountains; but this was their chief stronghold when danger threatened, being considered by them almost impregnable.

Fred followed his guide, and soon found himself inside a vast cave. When his eyes got accustomed to the gloom, he could see in one end a number of Maroons busy storing up a quantity of booty,—the fruits presumably of a recent raid. Far away in the other end blazed a great fire, where cooking seemed to be going on.

From this main cavern there were passages leading in various directions. Along one of these Fred was now led, until they reached a chamber which seemed to be lighted by a shaft. Here the chief of the Maroons was seated with his counsellors, discussing future plans of action.

The chief recognised Fred, but, thinking he came with overtures for peace, which they were in no mood for entertaining just then, the great man received in him a rather distant and haughty manner. When, however, Fred let him know that he came as a personal ally, the chief assumed an air of great graciousness, and invited him to join their council and take part in the deliberations.

Fred had arrived most opportunely for them; for they were just planning an attack on the estate with which he was familiar, and his service as guide and general director of operations would be of the very highest value. Fred at once professed his willingness to undertake the business, and there and then it was decided to make an early attack on the seaward plantations.

In ordinary circumstances it would have been rash thus to adopt as an ally an untried man, and give him right away an important commission. But the Maroons knew what they were doing. Fred was a convict, and it was very natural that he should wish to be free, and equally natural that he should embrace the chance of revenging himself on his old masters. There were already, in fact, several of these runaways among the Maroons.

And now the savoury things they had been cooking in the main cavern were ready. The best of these were brought through, and the chief and his counsellors feasted in royal style. Thereafter a supply of rum was produced.

Fred had partaken sparingly of the eatables; but now he fell to and did pretty fair justice to the latter part of the function, with the result that he found an impromptu bed on the floor of the cave, where among his snoring comrades he lay till well into the following day.

Meantime the planters were not idle. Realising the danger that menaced them, they cast about for ways and means of defence. Jamie was specially active, and set himself to organise a scheme for mutual help. He got a kind of alliance formed among the seaward estates of which he was by acclamation constituted head. For Jamie was a born leader—one of those men that are instinctively trusted and followed in any enterprise. The arrangement was that, whatever estate was attacked all should gather to its defence.

There followed a period of suspense. Everybody was on the alert and anxious. But, when a fortnight had elapsed without the enemy showing face anywhere, the most of the planters began to think that the danger had passed away, and that the Maroons, having heard of the defensive alliance, were judging it safest to remain meantime among their mountain fastnesses.

Not so Jamie, however. He knew Fred Clark too well to believe that he would let the matter rest. He was sure he would do all in his power to bring the Maroons on them. And in all likelihood the delay was part of the plan and intended to put them off their guard so that the attack, when it came, might be the more irresistible and overwhelming. Viewing the matter thus, Jamie was not likely to relax his vigilance. And the event proved the wisdom of his actions and attitude.

Jamie had an impression that the enemy would come by night, that his estate would be selected for attack, and that the first assault would be on his house. Fred's chief purpose would be to get the design carried out through the Maroons which fate had prevented himself from executing. Everything else would be subordinated to this. In brief, Jamie realised that his own life would be the first thing aimed at.

These considerations had guided him in devising and arranging his defences. He saw the necessity above all things of having his house well fortified. The walls up to his own height he rendered bullet-proof by placing bags of sand along the inside. Loop-holes were made all round, so that an attacking force could be fired on from any point. All the muskets, many of which were kept constantly loaded, were stored in the house along with the ammunition.

Into the house he introduced some four or five of the trustiest hands on the estate. A watch was maintained every night, these men dividing the duty among them, while a special mode of egress had been devised by which a messenger might, in case of sudden attack, manage to leave the house to give the alarm.

When these arrangements were made, Jamie found it at first very difficult to sleep at night. He was ever and anon waking up with a start, under the impression that he had heard some alarming sound. But a few nights put him more at ease, and he was able by-and-by to sleep pretty comfortably and soundly. But he never remitted any of his care and vigilance.

At length one night, an hour or two before dawn, he was wakened by the man who was on watch for the time being shaking him in an exited manner. Jamie was on his feet in a moment. There was no light in the apartment, and for a few moments he was too dazed to understand the nervous whispering of the man who had so suddenly roused him. When he had gathered his wits, he was prepared to hear it was the enemy.

In an excited whisper the man told him that he had heard footsteps outside, and that he was sure it was the Maroons reconnoitring the house. Jamie made no reply, but, listening intently, could hear for himself sounds as of people moving cautiously about.

His heart beat with the excitement of the moment, but he retained his presence of mind. Hastily whispering to the man to rouse the others and to see that they made no noise which might be heard outside, he proceeded to get the guns ready, quietly placing one or two beside each loophole.

And now he could hear the enemy gathering about the door, doubtless preparing to deliver an attack on it. But it was strongly barricaded and Jamie knew it would withstand a good deal of violence. And he really hoped they would concentrate their attention on it, as he would thus have a better chance of getting a messenger despatched by the exit at the rear.

Jamie had one of his men ready to slip out and spread the alarm, so as to bring reinforcements on the ground at the earliest possible moment. He was waiting, however, until the attack began, so as to assure himself that it was really the Maroons. The raising of a false alarm would make him look somewhat ridiculous in the eyes of his neighbours, and Jamie was too proud to run such a risk.

The suspense was of short duration. Suddenly a great thundering at the door began.

" Be off," said Jamie to the messenger; and out the man slipped into the darkness. " To the front, men, and fire out," was his order to the four that were now left with him to defend the place until help should arrive.

It was a desperate moment; but Jamie had grown quite cool. It was perfectly dark, for the Maroons had chosen their night. But Jamie had his plan of action so well rehearsed that he and his men found their posts and everything they needed with great speed and certainty, and not many blows had been delivered on the door ere a blaze of musketry lit up the scene, and one or two of the assailants fell wounded or dead.

A yell of rage greeted this unexpected reply to their

assault, and with redoubled fury they dashed against the door, only to evoke another volley, which was even more destructive than the first. The assailants retired, but in a few moments they opened a fierce fire on the front of the house. One of the bullets chanced to find the loop-hole at which one of Jamie's men was standing, and the poor fellow fell dead.

Again Jamie's muskets, now reduced to four, replied ; but the enemy were farther off and more scattered, and it was doubtful if the discharge had done any execution this time. And soon the sound of shooting all round the house showed that the foe had changed their tactics. But Jamie and his men were equal to the occasion. They moved from loophole to loophole, firing shots from each and all, some of which took effect.

The enemy were furious with rage, and yelled like so many wild beasts. They had counted on storming the house in a few minutes, and now they were like to be utterly baffled in their attempt, while the sound of the shooting would be sure to rouse some of the estate hands, who would soon spread the alarm and bring on them a host of planters and their men ; for the estates in this part were thickly planted.

Fred who was leading the attack, now called them off. A plan had just occurred to him. If some of them could get on the roof, they would be able to enter by the windows there. He knew where ladders were kept, and, bidding a desultory fire be kept up, he hurried away with a couple of assistants to fetch them.

Returning with the ladders, he got them placed against the wall of the house. A fire was kept up on the opposite side so as to divert the attention of those inside, and soon Fred with some ten or a dozen Maroons was on the roof. He was bold enough in a way and wanted the honour of being leader in the attack, but he preferred to send the Maroons before him in this instance. Sword in hand they dropped from the roof-light into the room; and, so unexpected was the manœuvre, and so loud the rattle of musketry inside and out that some half-dozen Maroons were in the house ere Jamie and his companions knew the extreme danger that now menaced them.

When Jamie's men understood that the enemy had got inside, they gave up all for lost, and, hurrying into the other apartment, cowered down in the darkness, awaiting their fate in mortal terror. Jamie followed and hearing their pitiful groans, ordered them to get up and fight, or he would shoot them on the spot. And, such an ascendancy had he gained over his men, that they got up at once. They were now more afraid of him than of the enemy.

Luckily a number of loaded muskets had been left in the room. He shouted to his men to get hold of them and fire on the Maroons, who, in the other apartment, were groping about to find the foe. Jamie discharged his musket, and a mortal yell proved that he had not fired in vain. The other Maroons, now seeing where their enemy was, made a rush for the end whence the shot had come; but a volley from Jamie's men checked their career. One man indeed rushed into the door-way, but the flash of the guns had revealed his whereabouts, and next moment Jamie had struck him to the floor.

The Maroons now found the mistake they had made in entering the house without firearms. They couldn't get out, nor could they let their friends outside know what was wanted. It was madness in the dark to rush upon an enemy who seemed to have an unlimited store of ammunition. So they desisted from further attack, and remained in the corners of the room, furious, but for the moment baffled.

Jamie, who felt that his assailants were hanging back told his men not to fire. It would be a mistake to waste their ammunition in chance volleys.

Oh, how fervently he wished that help would come! It was a critical moment. If more of the Maroons found their way into the house, he and his little band would be overpowered. Yet he would fight to the last, and die hard.

The Maroons outside, judging that their comrades must by this time have got into the house, ceased firing and listened. They expected to hear sounds of fighting inside, followed soon by the opening of the door and the announcement of victory. But all was strangely still. They couldn't understand it.

After waiting a little in grim silence they grew impatient, and the chief ordered some of his men to ascend the roof and see what was ado. Jamie, who was still standing in the doorway gun in hand, saw the figures fill up the dull lighted space that represented the opening of the roof-light, and heard Fred's voice shout to them, "Bring guns you d—ls!" They didn't seem to understand the order, and Jamie didn't give them the chance of asking it to be repeated. For, aiming as well as he could in the gloom, he fired. There was a yell, a thud and a scramble, and light appeared again.

One had fallen into the room shot, bringing one or

two of the unwounded after him, while the others had hurried back along the roof and descended to join their comrades.

What was to be done? The Maroons were baffled, and soon rage began to give way to alarm. Dawn was approaching, and every moment there was an increasing chance of the arrival of help for the besieged. Had they known that a special messenger had been despatched to rouse the neighbouring estates, their apprehensions would have been intensified.

The chief decided that another attack be made on the door. The reception they had already got from the foe inside made the Maroons hesitate, but their leader's order was repeated in a way that admitted of no question or debate, and again they rushed forward. They quite expected a volley from the inside, but, when no shot was fired, they got bolder and fiercer in their efforts to break into the house.

Jamie heard the thundering at the door.—Oh, if he could only get once more to the loopholes commanding the front of the house! But this he couldn't do without disposing of the dozen or so of Maroons who were in the room ; and these, encouraged by the sound of the renewed attack their comrades were making, were again beginning to show fight and shouting in a menacing manner.

The situation was more desperate than ever.—Where were the expected succour? If they did not come very soon, they would come in vain.

Now he hears the timbers straining and breaking. A few minutes and the enemy will be into the room. He gives all up for lost. There is nothing for it now but to die like men.

He turns his head and shouts into the room behind him, " Men, be ready ! "

There was no reply to his call, nor indeed any movement—Were they paralysed with fear ?

" Men," he shouted again, in a voice that rang fierce with angry reproach, " Men, where are you ? "

Yet no reply.

Suddenly it dawned on him that they were gone.— And they were. When the attack on the front door was renewed and they judged that the enemy would be all gathered on that side, it occured to them to seize the opportunity of slipping out by the exit at the rear. This they had done, getting safely away in the darkness.

When Jamie realised what had happened, a sudden gust of fierce indignation swept his soul. A moment later came the temptation to imitate their example, which was instantly scorned and dismissed. He would defend home and property to the last.

But now even flight would have been impossible, for dawn had begun to show, and soon it was quite light. Crash went the door at length, and the Maroons swarmed in. Fred, who was standing against the side wall, pointed to Jamie as he stood in the doorway between the two rooms. He thought it best to let the new comers make the charge. Forward they rushed, Jamie's gun rang out, and the foremost man fell dead. He seized another and tried to raise it to his shoulder, but it was beat down before he could fire.

He took a step back into the room, and, seizing his gun by the muzzle, raised it high in air. The first man that pressed through the doorway he felled to the floor.

Some behind would have fired, but the rush and crush prevented them.   The fight was hand to hand.

Jamie fought like a tiger.   One man after another he felled ; but the rest behind pressed on, and he was gradually borne back.   From one of his assailants whom he had knocked down he snatched a sword, and, backing against the wall, prepared to make his last stand.

Right and left he struck and hashed, and soon a little heap of dead and wounded gathered in front of him. But, making a lunge at one of his assailants who was pressing in on him, he slipped on the bloody floor, and fell.

A yell of triumph greeted his fall, and some of the foremost pressed forward to deal him the fatal blow, when suddenly Fred Clark, who had been, though out of sword reach, always hovering near, sprang in before them—

"Back !" he shouted, stretching out his arms in front of the Maroons.

They fell back at the word, and Fred, with sword raised on high, stood over his fallen foe.

CHAPTER XVII.

AT LAST—FAR OFF.

" Now ! " exclaimed Fred, as he caught the upturned eye of his victim.

Jamie heard and saw, and knew that his doom was come. Yet in his eye was no flinching, nor in his heart any fear.

One glance had showed him how things stood. There was his deadly foe standing over him, and round him was the crescent of ugly dark faces, peering forward with brutal expectancy and delight to see the fatal blow dealt. His mind grasped it all ; yet he seemed to have time to think of a thousand things besides.

While the physical powers are capable of marvellous extension under adequate stimuli, the mind and spirit acknowledge practically no limit. In that supreme moment when death is faced by one whose powers are unimpaired and unclouded, the mind can not only canvass the present, but can minutely review an extended past, or contemplate the possible situations of an elusive future.

This Jamie did ; and every emotion touched his soul—save fear.

And Fred ?—He hardly thought. He simply surrendered himself to the mad joy of the moment, and let his spirit revel in the fiendish triumph he had gained.

All this took but a moment. The next, a sunbeam striking through a side casement fell on Jamie as he lay.

Somehow it made Fred notice the position his victim occupied on the floor—just the very same as he himself had occupied on that night when fever struck him down in the midst of his diabolical designs! There he too had lain, and—

. . . . . One moment's pause : the most intense moment in his life. Scarcely yet did he think ; but his soul awoke.

. . . . . He bends over Jamie. The Maroons think he is going to stab his foe to the heart, and crowd closer. Jamie's arm is raised in self-defence,—instinctive, if vain.

Fred, keeping his sword in his right hand, tries with his left to take hold of Jamie's uplifted hand. Jamie eludes his grasp, whereupon Fred suddenly seizes him by the wrist. And now the eager circle has drawn a deep breath, ready to greet with savage shout the deadly thrust that will next moment be given.

But they were baulked—they and all other fiends!

Jamie struggled to free his wrist, but, with sudden energy, Fred exclaimed,—

" Jamie, you d——l, to your feet, by G—d! And to h—l with the black ——— ! "

An awful speech. Yet was it heard with joy by the argels, who forgot to wince at its profanity. And Jamie mistook not its meaning. In an instant the spirits of the two men had rushed together, impelled by the instinct that rules the high places of our nature.

Next moment Jamie was on his feet, the Maroons falling back in sheer amazement. He reached for the sword that had been forced from his hand as he fell, and he and Fred together now faced the common foe. These had simply been bewildered at first ; but now a yell of savage rage proclaimed that they understood what had happened, and a rush was made on the devoted pair.

But their victims were ready. Each faced his own half of the dread curve that was closing in on them, prepared to do and die as " brither Scots." On Fred was the most savage attack made ; but he was fresh, was an expert swordsman, and, above all, had the triple armour and inspiration of the man that fights in a good cause.

The foremost of the Maroons fell. But, now that the fighting was resumed, more pressed in from the room beyond, their place in turn being taken by those who were massed about the front door. Had the enemy been able to make room in the apartment where the fighting was going on, they could easily have shot down their two opponents. Only swords, however, could be used in the circumstances, and even for these weapons the conditions were much too hampered.

Both men fought with magnificent courage, and skill, and resource. They could hardly be said to hope or to fear. They simply fought. On that were all energies of mind and body bent.

Anyone, however, could have seen that this couldn't last long. A single false stroke or step might be their last ; and, fight as perfectly as they might, there was a limit to human endurance. Very soon they must get tired out by the physical strain involved, and go down before the foe.

Already, indeed, their blows were being delivered with less force, and their defence was becoming more feeble and uncertain ; for both were wounded and had lost not a little blood. Jamie was the first to show signs of exhaustion. Although of splendid physique and staying power, he had been pretty well used up before this last encounter began ; and only the inspiration of a supreme occasion could have nerved him to do what he had already done.

Fred, who felt that his companion was failing, tried to take on his own shoulders some of his work ; but this couldn't long help matters, especially as he was himself beginning to flag. The end was manifestly near.

At length a big powerful fellow of a Maroon, getting hold of a musket, had heaved it high, in order if possible to strike Jamie a blow on the head. Jamie held up his sword in defence ; but so feeble was now his arm that the force of the blow would have been but little affected by the interposed weapon ; and doubtless he would have been felled to the floor, and then easily despatched.

But at that moment a loud volley of musketry rent the air, coming on the ears of the combatants with the stunning effect of a mighty thunder-peal. Every arm was stayed. The surprise was followed by a brief pause of uncertainty and apprehension. Next moment all was understood.—Succours had arrived for the planters. And now a shout of English voices confirmed it.

The volley had dealt death among the Maroons gathered round the house. The rest, discharging a few straggling shots in reply, turned and fled, as with a ringing cheer the rescuing force bore down on the scene. A panic seized the enemy. Those inside the house struggled to get out, and Jamie and Fred were suddenly left without assailants.

Jamie, utterly exhausted, sank down atop of some of the dead bodies of the enemy, hardly able to think or even feel. Fred, however, had a little strength left, and

followed the retreating Maroons, slashing among them
with considerable effect. In the congested doorway he
was doing special execution, when, all of a sudden, a
Maroon whom he had stabbed from behind wheeled
round, and, ere Fred could do anything to defend himself
from the unexpected attack, the fellow had dealt him a
fatal blow. Fred staggered backward, and fell across his
prostrate companion.

There the two were found when the rescuers, after
killing or capturing most of the enemy that failed to
escape at first, entered the house to see how matters
stood. Both were quite conscious and able to speak.
Jamie directed his friends where to carry him. As they
were taking him away, he pointed to Fred and said,
" Bring him along."

Some who recognised Fred said they would see to
getting him taken to the hospital.

" No," said Jamie, " he comes with me." And they
had to do as they were told and say nothing more about
it, although there was any amount of wonder expressed
in their faces.

The wounded men were carried to a building which
Jamie, designing to use it as a kind of summer-house
when the warm season returned, had fitted up in a
delightful and artistic manner. Here in a lightsome room
were two couches placed for them, and the medical man
who looked after the health of the estates in that quarter
was soon in attendance.

Jamie's wounds he pronounced not just dangerous, if
proper care was taken, and he was proceeding to have
them dressed when Jamie told him to look at the other
man before doing anything further. When the doctor

saw the kind of patient he had on the other couch, he looked his astonishment. Very soon he saw that Fred's wounds were mortal, and said so.

"Can nothing at all be done for him?" asked Jamie, with pathetic anxiety.

"Nothing, I fear," was the reply.

"That's about it," Fred himself chimed in. "I know I'm a gone coon."

"Make him as comfortable as you can, surgeon, and then you can see to my injuries."

When the doctor had done what he could and had gone away, both men lay for some little time silent. Fred was suffering great pain, but he was manfully repressing all exhibition of feeling. But at length an involuntary groan escaped his lips.

"Fred," cried Jamie, "can I do anything for you?"

"Nothing, old man—this time."

"Do you suffer much?"

"Oh, not so much."

There was silence again. Fred was struggling with other things besides physical pain and weakness. At length he spoke.—

"Jamie!"

"Well?"

"Have you heard from—Logie, of late?"

"No." This was Jamie's audible answer, but along with it there was in his mind a curiosity to know why the other should ask such a question.

"Do you know why?" was Fred's next question; and, without waiting for a reply, he added, "I destroyed your letters."

"Destroyed my letters?" exclaimed Jamie, as,

stepping from his couch, he staggered to Fred. "Sir, what can you mean?" And he seized him by the wrist. But the feeble look in those dying eyes checked him, and he relinguished his hold.

"Yes, kill me out," said Fred. "I quite deserve it."

"But—how?—when?" Jamie stammered, painfully agitated.

"I knew the nigger who was in the way of carrying the up-country letters to the coast. He used to stay here overnight."

Jamie groaned, and, leaning on the front of the couch, hid his face in his hands.

"But we needn't bother about all that now," Fred continued. "The thing was done, and I did it. I saw my chance and took it. . . . . You know what I was after?"

Groans were still the only comment Jamie could offer on the painful recital. But now a servant entered to announce that the clergyman had called, and wanted to see Mr. Robertson.

"Help me back to my couch," said Jamie to the man, feeling now too weak to return to it unaided.

This being done, the visitor was introduced. He was one of the regular beneficed clergymen of the island, an elderly gentleman of courteous bearing and benevolent mien. He made a nice little speech, congratulating Jamie on the brave part he had played, and exhibiting kindly interest in his welfare. After which, glancing towards Fred, about whom the doctor had just told him, he said, "Might we not manage, Mr. Robertson, to make some more special and—proper arrangements for your comfort?"

Jamie knew what he meant, and instantly replied, "Oh, no. It is very good of you to think of it, but this will do very well meantime."

The clergyman, gathering from Jamie's tone that he was quite decided, didn't offer to pursue the matter further. But he wondered a bit mentally. He was a good man, but had certain ideas on the subject of caste, and couldn't well understand the manager of an estate electing to lie alongside an assigned hand.

Realising, however, that he had himself certain duties as a clergyman towards Jamie's companion, he said, "You will excuse me, Mr. Robertson, while I devote some attention to this—man, using such offices as our church hath prescribed in the circumstances?"

The reply came from Fred, who had been lying silent but attentive.—

"No, no, minister: you needn't mind me."

"But—but—you are dying, young man, and will soon have to meet your Maker. Doubtless you realise you have been a sinner, and—"

"I have been a devil."

The good man started, and instantly changed his tactics.

"Ah, but we have a Father who is of infinite mercy and willeth not—"

The dying man raised himself on his elbow, and said, speaking slowly and calmly,—

"Look here: I know all that kind of thing, but it isn't for me."

There was such a finality about the way in which he delivered himself that his spiritual adviser had not a word to say. But Jamie, whose heart was sore, couldn't

refrain from making reply, although deeply conscious
that preaching wasn't in his line.—

"Fred," he cried, in quivering tones, "don't speak
like that. We have all a Father in Heaven, and, however far away we wander, he'll bring us all back."

"Yes," replied Fred, "I know I'll go back. I'll *have*
to. I feel that it's all before me; and it will be a long,
long job.—You can't help me. I'll have to retrace every
step myself, and deuced rough will many of them be,
and sore, *I* know. All my old sins and ill deeds will
chase me along; and all the folk I have cheated and ill-
used will lash me as I pass. There's you, Jamie, and
Lily, and Bell, and Halket—"

"Fred!" protested Jamie, with tearful voice.

"You needn't speak, Jamie. You can't forgive me—
yet. You'll all help to drive me along. And I'll go on
—and on . . . . And at last . . . . after a
long, long time . . . . ages, maybe . . . .
I'll . . . —"

The exertion of speaking was too much for the dying
man. He collapsed in the midst of it, and fell back
unconscious. And a great awe fell on the two men who
had heard him.

Whatever length of way might lie before the poor
spirit, doubtless it had at least turned its face towards
Home. The sudden revulsion of feeling that took place
when he saw Jamie at his mercy was no doubt the turning point with Fred. Yet the change was not so sudden
as it seemed. His last escapade—about the most
diabolical of all—was the final paroxysm of the possessed,
when the evil spirit, having already heard the exorcising
call of divine love speaking through an enemy's unselfish

deed, was tearing its victim in its baffled fury, ere it should come quite out of the man. It came out; but the soul was in ruins. The prodigal turned to go home; but he was in a far country, and had a long way before him. How was such a soul to be repaired? How was that journey to be accomplished?—Suddenly?—Miraculously? —Hardly so. But oh, somehow, surely; and sometime.

Fred did not again recover consciousness. Now and again he seemed to rave, and, from chance words and phrases that could be caught, his mind appeared to have gone back to school-boy days. Jamie listened, and the tears fell free and fast. Once he called out, "Come on, lads, to Katie's Wallie: I'm awful thirsty." Whereupon Jamie crept from his couch, and cooled with water the fevered lips that spoke.

By-and-by his utterances grew more and more incoherent, until only a chance word could now and again be caught. Occasionally he would mutter the name of some friend or companion, when Jamie could tell that he was with them in dreamland, living old times over again. All reminiscences seemed to be of earlier and happier days, except once when Jamie could see that Fred was again fighting the Maroons, and could hear his own name uttered in encouraging tones.

The afternoon was now well advanced, and Fred had sunk into a kind of stupor. The sun shone in through a western casement, and the light fell on his couch. Outside the breeze was stirring lightly among the sugar canes, and from palmeto groves beyond came the mellow cooing of the ring-doves.

Just as the sun was setting, Fred began to stir, and Jamie, who apprehended that the end was now come, again dragged himself to the side of his couch. The dying man suddenly threw up his hands as if in appeal to someone ; and on his face appeared an agony of remorse and doubt, merging into a passion of infinite longing, as he cried, " *Lily !* "

Just then the beam that had been slowly travelling over couch and coverlet shone right in his face. It seemed to chase from his features the pain and the longing, leaving there a look of peace and satisfaction. He even smiled.

Thus he lay, while the sunbeam passed slowly from his face. He did not move again.

" Fred ! " murmured Jamie, while the hot tears rained to the floor.

But Fred heard not. For now, with face fixed on the sunlit heights of the distant Fatherland, and in such heart for the way as that calm look betokened, had the wanderer set out on his long journey Home.

CHAPTER XVIII.

THE RETURN.

AUTUMN has again come round, and Jamie Robertson is once more in Scotland.

Let us go back and explain how this came about.—
Fred's dying confession to Jamie that he had intercepted his letters was at the moment keenly distressing, and created in Jamie's mind a feeling of vague alarm. But the occasion was so intensely exciting, and gave rise to such a strange complication of deep feelings and awful reflections, that he couldn't fix his attention on the matter long enough to grasp its significance. How could he turn aside to think of such things when a poor fellow mortal was struggling there with Death and Darkness? What were such petty concerns alongside the dread issues that loomed up from the far horizon of that awful Beyond?

For many days Jamie lay feverish and ill, thinking of nothing but Fred and the tragedy of his death. But health and strength returned, and, when calmer moments supervened, he was able to review the situation. The matter of the intercepting of the letters now claimed attention, and, the more he thought about it, the more alarmed he grew. The strange silence of Halket and his other Buchan friends was now explained, and, with the explanation, came a great dread. He hardly dared put it in words. It was too terrible.

If for two or three years his friends about Logie had

heard no word of him, it would be little wonder if they concluded he was dead, or at least that he did not mean to return. Then he remembered the sort of bargain that Clyacks had made with Bell. Was it not likely that he was now claiming the fulfilment of her promise? She might put him off for a time, hoping against hope; but how could she be expected to hold out?

He would write home at once, and explain matters to Halket. Perhaps his letter would be in time to prevent the catastrophe he dreaded. But with the writing of this epistle came no relief. He wouldn't know how the matter rested, nor have his doubts resolved, until a reply came from the old country; and that would be a long time. How would he manage to live in the interim? The suspense would be almost unbearable. It would poison his life, and unfit him for the discharge of his duties.

Nothing would do but to return himself to Scotland. Yet Jamie knew well the sacrifice such a step would involve, as far as worldly prospects were concerned. He was now in an excellent situation, and had, besides, through the investment of some capital, got a direct interest in the sugar industry. Had he been able to stay in Jamaica a year or two longer, he would have reaped the advantage of these things. He felt, however, that material gain could never compensate mental distress and heart troubles.

Convinced that it would be best under the circumstances to return home, he began at once to make arrangements for leaving the island. There was much regret at his departure. He had always been a favourite, and of late he had grown quite a leading man, while his brave conduct in connection with the Maroon raids had given him something of the character of a hero among his fellow planters. He had the satisfaction of leaving the estate with which he was connected in a very prosperous condition ; and for the quiet and satisfactory state of the island in general he could take to himself no small credit. For the Maroons, after their repulse, were glad to make a treaty with the planters ; and, indeed, they remained quite peaceable till the end of the century.

He did not tell his Jamaica friends what took him home to Scotland ; but he gave them to understand that there was considerable likelihood of his returning—an announcement that gave keen satisfaction.

Though Jamie had, as we have said, made a considerable sacrifice in leaving Jamaica just then, he found, on realising everything, that he was, as regards money, quite a well-to-do man, and could not help contrasting his present affluence with the miserable state of his finances when he first landed on the island. While all this was very gratifying to himself on direct and purely personal grounds, he derived very considerable satisfaction from reflecting how his success would tell on other people and affect his relations with them. There were, to begin with, friends like Halket, who had had confidence in him and his future. It was pleasing to think that he had justified their confidence, and, in his career, had verified their kind predictions. There were others who had treated him as of no account, and as never likely to be anything better than a common gardener. For these he had now his answer ready, and he judged it would be pretty conclusive and triumphant. The satisfaction that came from this reflection was of course a little less worthy, but Jamie, you see, was human, and couldn't help enjoying a bit the prospect of silencing his detractors. In any case, whatever might wait him beyond the sea, he felt the confidence and security of a man who is pecuniarily equipped, and can speak and act from the vantage ground of an assured worldly position.

There was still another train of reflections suggested by the favourable complexion his fortunes were assuming. He hardly gave these thoughts definite form and presentation. They were of that sweetly hazy kind that thrill and excite in a strange and almost indescribable way. Needless to say, they centred round Miss Innes.

Having business communications with some of her friends in Edinburgh, he learned incidentally that she was still living in that town,—and unmarried. Now, as we have hinted, Jamie never said anything definite to himself. He contented himself with stating a problem. And with a repetition of that enunciation we must, meantime, content ourselves :—Miss Innes was beautiful, accomplished, and well-to-do ; she must have had many suitors ; why was she not married ?

Now, some people will wonder why Jamie should think at all about Miss Innes, especially when, apprehensive as to the issue of his love-affair with Bell, he was hurrying home in the fond hope of being in time to save her from being snatched from him for ever. It is strange, we admit ; but the student of the human heart must be prepared to find it a perfect encyclopedia of problems and puzzles, of inconsistences and contradictions. Not otherwise can he hope to make progress with his studies and investigations.

At length Jamie was ready to leave Jamaica. The

last spot he visited was Fred's grave. It was in a quiet hollow on the outskirts of the estate, and was marked by a stone which Jamie had caused to be put up. Here, kneeling on the lonely mound, he dropped a parting tribute of silent tears, and plucked a little flower to bear with him as a memento of poor Fred.

At length he set sail. He expected to be in Scotland by the month of July; but the ship in which he sailed had bad luck. Unfavourable weather delayed its course for some time, and then it got caught in a fierce storm, which drove it far out of its track. The captain was glad to put in at the Canaries, where, his vessel being much disabled, he had to wait till it could be made seaworthy.

In this way much time was lost, and it was the end of autumn ere Jamie arrived at Greenock.

From this place he proceeded north by stage-coach, till he reached Peterhead. Here he left the conveyance, and, resolving to do the rest of the journey on horseback, hired a good steed.

He decided to call first on his old friend Halket, and learn from him how matters stood. The result of this preliminary inquiry would guide him as to his future plan of action. Accordingly he made his way to Cairnbulg, where he hoped to find his friend, or at least learn of his whereabouts.

Harvest was now over, and the country had the bare look it assumes when all the crops have been gathered in. At no time of the rural year is the bleakness of the land-scape so keenly noted and felt. The contrast between waving fields of grain and bare stretches of stibble rig is sharp, and the transition has been suddenly made. At all other seasons of the year changes proceed more slowly.

The road was good and level, and for several miles Jamie rode briskly along. The movement was exhilarating, and inspired him with hopefulness. But, when the horse slackened pace and took to walking, somehow the rider's spirits fell. A cold wind was blowing from Mormond. This, with the bleak look of the surrounding country, encouraged the sad train of thought to which he now felt inclined. It was a lonely part of the road; nobody was in sight; and, to relieve his feelings, he took to singing. Often thus, when "lying on a foreign shore," had he eased a sad heart. And this was what he sang.—

> The summer days are gone,
>   And autumn nights grow chill;
> 'Tis bare and wide on Ugieside,
>   And bleak on Mormond Hill;
> All bare and wide lies Ugieside,
>   And bleak is Mormond hill.
>
> And soon shall Ugie moan
>   In dark ice-fretted flow,
> And wild across hill, field, and moss,
>   The wintry winds shall blow;
> The winds across hill, field, and moss,
>   Shall drive December's snow.
>
> So pass the changeful years,
>   So slips our time away;
> Nor fairest life, with pleasure rife,
>   For wish or prayer will stay;
> Youth's golden life, through toil and strife,
>   Comes to the winter day.

Reaching Cairnbulg, he made his way to one of the houses which Halket used to frequent. Here he learned that his friend was now schoolmaster at Memsie, to which situation he had been appointed some three years before. All the troubles arising from the Jacobite Rebellion were now over, and pretty well forgotten. In fact all the Jacobites, with the exception of some eighty of the leading men, were by an Indemnity Act, passed in the summer of 1747, relieved from all penalties and disabilities, so that Jamie was hardly well away from Logie when his friend was able, with absolute freedom and safety, to resume his place in society.

To Memsie Jamie went. The school and the dwelling-house, as was usual in those days, were under one roof. When he knocked with his riding-whip at the door of the house, he was hardly surprised to see it opened by Lily Douglas, who looked as sweet and engaging as ever.

She evidently didn't recognise him; but, before he could introduce himself, out came Halket himself from the schoolroom, bareheaded, with a quill stuck behind his ear. He had seen the horseman ride up, and wondered who he could be. And now he stood staring at Jamie.

"Well, Mr. Halket," said Jamie, smiling, "don't you know an old pupil?"

Halket looked at him dubiously for a moment or two.

"Jamie Robertson!" he cried at length, in something like dismay, holding up his hands, and backing against the wall.

"Jamie Robertson!" echoed Lily, running forward and seizing Jamie's hand.

"Yes," said Jamie, smiling to Lily. "But," looking to Halket, "why should you look so horrified?"

"Man—we thought—you were—"

"Dead?"

"At least we thought—you were—never coming back," stammered Halket. Then, coming forward and taking Jamie's hand, he added, "But I'm awfu' gled to see, you, Jamie,—awfu' gled. Come awa' in-by and tell's a' aboot it."

"But you are engaged, I see," said Jamie, looking towards the school, whence a growing sound was proceeding, the youngsters taking advantage of the master's absence to have a little fun.

"Engaged?—Nae when an auld frien' comes owre the sea.—

> ' Ye'se be fou and I'se be fain,
> Carle, sin the King's come.'

Jist wait till I get a nickum o' a loon to haud your beast."

He disappeared into the school, and soon returned with a big raw boy.

"Noo, Willie," said Halket addressing the lad, "tak' the horse doon to Waulkie's, and they'll pit him in. And," shouting after the boy as he went off with the animal, "mind and tell them to gie him a feed."

"Noo, Jamie lad," he said, turning to Jamie, "gang awa' in-by wi' Lily till I send the scholars hame."

"But," protested Jamie, "that's a pity."

"Fient a pity!" broke in Halket. "We're nae lang intil harness yet, and half a day's naething. I'll wager the loons winna think it's a pity."

"Well, well," said Jamie, with a laugh, "if that's the dominie's orders, I suppose we must e'en submit." And he stepped into the house.

Very soon a noise like the rumbling of thunder was heard. It was the scholars pouring out. And now, as they emerged into the open air, they could be heard shouting, " Hurray, hurray ! We're gettin' hame ! Hurray, hurray ! "

Jamie stepped to the door.

" Hi, loons " he cried, resuming his Doric, " ye're gettin' a holiday, are ye ? "

" Ay," shouted a number of them.

" Weel than, here's something to haud it wi'." And, taking from his pocket a handful of silver and copper, he scattered it among them.

Well—it was a sight ! The shout, the scramble, the high jubilee !—It was something to remember.

Laughing, Jamie retreated into the house. Very soon Halket appeared.

" Fat's yon ye was deein' ? " he demanded, with an affectation of severity. " They say a feel and his siller is easy pairted, and I think it looks some like it."

The only answer was a merry laugh, in which Jamie's censor soon joined.

The little pleasantry over, Halket looked at Jamie —long and earnestly ; and now the glad light of welcome which shone in his eyes seemed to get suffused with a certain haze of anxiety. Jamie noted this, and somehow it alarmed him. Halket in turn perceived the effect his scrutiny was having on the subject of it, and hastened to take the matter off.—

" Man, Jamie," he exclaimed, " but ye're greatly changed ! "

" For the better ? " queried Jamie, with an effort at lightsomeness.

" Yes, for the better. I wid hardly hae kent ye again, wi' that swarthy complexion and big black beard. And ye look like a man o' the world that has travelled far and seen lots o' things,—gey different frae the bricht innocent lad that used to keep things cheery aboot Logie.—Ye were gettin' on fine when I last heard frae ye, and I can see your fortune hasna ebbed since then.—Ye'll hae to tell's a' aboot it."

Lily was sitting meantime perfectly happy, looking alternately from one to the other.

"And you, Mr. Halket," said Jamie,—"why you look as fresh and vigorous as ever."

"Hardly, Jamie, hardly.—

'Damnosa quid non imminuit dies?'

But I canna complain, man ; canna complain."

Both men felt that they were hanging on the outside of things. Both wished to touch the heart and kernel of the matter that was uppermost in their minds.—And both dreaded to do it. But it was difficult keeping up a conversation on these terms, and erelong they relapsed into silence.

The situation now grew embarrassing, and Halket, rising to his feet, said,—

"But you must see my surroundings and general amenities. You come too late in the season to see us to any advantage, and, after being accustomed to tropic luxuriance, you'll think little of our bare place."

"On the contrary," said Jamie, rising, "it is a relief to get back to Buchan, with its quiet sober look. Man, I wouldn't give the sight of the heather on Mormond for all I have seen in the Indies."

"But Jamie must be hungry," protested Lily, when she saw them preparing to go out.

"Weel, lassie," said Halket, "ye can hurry up wi' the

dinner, and cry us in when ye are ready. We'll only gang the length o' the yard." And the two men stepped forth.

Reaching an arbour, they sat down.

"You have a nice place here," Jamie remarked. "How long is it since you came to Memsie?"

"Let me see.—Something better than three years."

"Indeed?"

A pause followed. Halket then took it up.

"How long is it now since you left Logie, Jamie?"

"Between six and seven years."

"Dear me! Who would have thought it?—

'Eheu, fugaces labuntur anni.'

It's a long time, especially in a young man's life."

"Yes; and lots of things take place in half a dozen years.—I should think there must have been a few even in Buchan."

Jamie affected the most matter-of-fact tone, but his heart was beating with the pain of suspense. Halket, hardly less moved, tried to appear equally indifferent.

"Yes, a few—baptisms, marriages, and deaths.—You see I used to keep the register, and got into the way of thus classifying all the events of the parish."

"Well, I haven't much interest in the first class—the baptisms."

"Maybe no," said Halket.

Jamie glanced at him; but he went on.—

"Then as to deaths, there's been a few—old Bogie, for instance; and ane or twa mair."

"And—marriages?" suggested Jamie.

"Jamie!" exclaimed Halket, suddenly seizing his companion's hands, "why didna ye write—or come hame?—Oh, man!"

Halket's restraint had all at once given way, and his pent-up feelings now burst forth. Jamie grew deadly pale.

"What?" he stammered; but Halket went on.—

"And to leave poor Bell to bear a' the blame, and the flytin', and a' that!"

"Good God!" cried Jamie, jumping to his feet, "what do you mean?"

"O Jamie, how could you?" Halket went on, taking no notice of his companion's ejaculation or question. "And to come now!—It should have been in time—or never."

But the uncompromising blame galled Jamie's spirit, and he said with some severity,—

"All that can be explained. You will find there are good reasons both for my silence and my delay in coming home."

"Oh, I'll be glad if there is," cried Halket. "But, man, it's a sair business!"

"And Bell," exclaimed Jamie, excitement again getting the better of him, "is she—?"

"Yes, she's married."

"And to—?"

"Yes, to Clyacks."

With a groan, the poor fellow sank on the seat, and buried his face in his hands.

Halket was deeply touched, and felt keenly for Jamie. But, knowing how irritating speech is to a spirit that is wounded, he offered no further remark, only placing his hand on Jamie's shoulder, as a token of friendly sympathy.

Thus they sat for some time. At length Jamie sat up, pale but calm.

"And when did it happen?" he asked, turning to Halket.

"Just this summer,—sometime in July, if I remember right."

Again Jamie groaned. Had his homeward voyage been undelayed, he would in all probability have arrived in time to prevent what he would have called the catastrophe. Then did he remember Fred's dying words, and owned to his own soul that he did not yet forgive the man who had caused him to lose his heart's desire.

He got up from the seat, and walked restlessly backwards and forwards. Halket looked at him, much moved. Here was a tragedy—the sad shipwreck of two young hearts. Why should Fate be so cruel? Why should our destinies be so wofully misplanned?

But, as he gazed, he was more and more impressed with Jamie's appearance,—his look of capacity, his address, and that note of distinction which, in certain men, is as unmistakable as it is impatient of definition. Jamie was born to position and influence, born to be a leader among men. Then Halket thought of Bell, the douce commonplace woman, happy among her cows and poultry, with few thoughts beyond the farm-yard, and incapable of the mental expansion and refinement needed to bring her into the world in which her old lover now moved. And, as he thought, more and more did the conviction grow on him that, great as was the tragedy of the separation of Jamie and Bell, their union would in all likelihood have been a greater tragedy. Sentiment of course is tempted to exclaim against such a view, but sentiment has a trick of recommending and urging transcendental situations, and then running away when the disaster comes, leaving reason to do its best with the sad entanglement.

At last Jamie sat down beside his friend. He was now wonderfully calm and collected.

"You greatly blame me in connection with this sad affair," he began, "and I shall not attempt to extenuate my fault. But first hear my story."

"Go on," said Halket, waving Lily away with his hand, who had come out to announce that dinner was ready.

Then Jamie began, and told him the story of Fred Clark. Halket listened, and, as the tale proceeded, his mind passed through all the varying phases of horror, indignation, pity, and even admiration. For Jamie made little of his own share in the drama, Fred being the main figure. Yet he told the story temperately. He had been too deeply impressed with the tragedy to treat it in any rhetorical manner.

Its effect on Halket was all the greater from the restrained and severe character of the recital; and, when Jamie produced from a small pocket-book the tiny withered flower he had plucked from Fred's grave, the two men, with bowed heads, joined their tears over the poor little souvenir.

Then Jamie put the flower carefully back.

"Now," he said, "you have heard my story. I have yours. And now I want to see the end of the drama.—Will you come with me to Clyacksneuk—to-night?"

"I will," was Halket's brief answer; and, rising, he led the way to the house.

CHAPTER XIX.

TOO LATE.

As they came round the house, Halket, who was leading the way, suddenly stopped, and, facing his companion, said,—

"When exactly did all this happen?—I mean your fight with the Maroons, and Fred's death. Could you remember the exact date?"

"Yes," replied Jamie, "I made a note of the day; but I hardly think I could have forgot it in any case." And he gave the date—a day towards the end of December.

"And," pursued the other, "it was about sunset with you?"

"Yes," assented Jamie, wondering what his companion was driving at.

"And that with us would be about say ten o'clock at night? Yes," pursued Halket, reflectively, "that agrees with it—exactly agrees with it.—Strange!"

"What do you mean, Mr. Halket?" asked Jamie.

"Well, I'll tell you.—On that very night, about the hour I've mentioned, which would agree with the time you had it in Jamaica,—about that time we were sitting round the fire, Lily and I. I can remember it was a cold dreary night. The wind was whistling without, and now and again showers rattled against the pane. I I was reading, while Lily sat looking in the fire. She had sat in this way for some time, quite silent, and appeared to be dreaming. All at once she spoke, murmuring in a low tone, and with great tenderness,— 'Yes, poor laddie, it's all right. Go to sleep now, you are tired and ill; but you'll be all right in the morning.' —I didn't understand it then; but I think I do now.— Very strange, isn't it?"

"Yes, very."

"Ay, there are more things in heaven and earth than are dreamt of in our philosophy."

To which Jamie mentally assented; and together they went indoors.

The dinner which Lily had prepared had been somewhat spoiled by the delay; and, like any other good housekeeper, she was disappointed that her cooking should appear to disadvantage. But she could understand from the looks of her guests that their thoughts had been on matters more grave than eating, and she prudently made no remark. Lily possessed the two saving gifts of loyalty and sense.

The meal was partaken of in silence. But by-and-by conversation was resumed, and soon became wonderfully hearty. Jamie wanted to bring his knowledge of local events up to date. The changes that had taken place in the district since he left were duly canvassed; and the careers of old friends and companions were reviewed. In this way many familiar places were referred to; but Millbog was never mentioned. Lily noted this, and she had little difficulty in understanding why all reference to it was so studiously avoided.

An hour or two was spent in this way, and then they prepared to set out for Clyacksneuk. It was felt that Halket would need to get mounted to be able to accompany Jamie, as he had undertaken to do. Waulkie was appealed to, and he readily lent one of his horses— " An awfu' canny beast." Halket, who had seldom been on horseback, felt very nervous over the business, although he tried to look brave, and spoke as if he had a full and intimate acquaintance with horsemanship. Unlike certain Pickwickian heroes, however, he came through the ordeal with a respectable measure of success, going and returning without accident.

They timed themselves to arrive about gloaming, so that their visit might not attract any special attention. A good bit of the way was made in silence. At length Jamie spoke.—

" And—Bell's at Clyacksneuk ? "

It was a euphemistic way of putting a sore matter.

" She's there," was the laconic answer. Halket had too much to do keeping on the back of his horse to indulge in extended speeches.

" And—she thinks I am dead ? "

" Yes."

Jamie of course knew all this already ; but he re-capitulated the position so as to prepare the way for a further excursion. But his courage failed him, and he relapsed into silence.

They were now coming near the end of their ride, which brought their minds to practical matters.—

" How shall we do ? " was Jamie's query.

His companion had been thinking over the matter, and was ready with a suggestion. But, as he couldn't quite explain it in a monosyllable, he judged it wise to get off his horse, finding from the experiments he had already made that one thing—either riding or speaking—

was enough at a time. Of course this wasn't the reason he assigned to Jamie for dismounting.

"Weel, to begin wi', you maunna show face at first. It would be owre great a shock for Bell, and Clyacks too."

"But," interrupted Jamie, "we must see Bell alone first."

"Weel, I'll arrange that.—Then I'll tell her that I've gotten a letter frae you. This will prepare her for the rest o' the news, and we can wear the thing on, bit by bit. Syne, when a'thing's explained, ye can come on the scene yersel', and I'll retire.—Will that dee?"

"Yes, very well. I can just hang about outside for some little time until you get the matter broached. But do it gently—very gently and kindly."

"Ye may depend on that."

They were now nearing Clyacksneuk, and Halket, feeling he would compromise his dignity and reputation as a horseman were he to arrive walking his steed, prepared to get once more into the saddle. It was a pretty difficult operation; but the horse was quiet and tractable, and his rider, drawing him close to a dyke, managed to clamber on.

When they arrived at the farm, they parted for the time being, Jamie going along the road a bit to pass the time, while Halket turned into "the close," and, giving his horse in charge to one of "the men," walked away towards the house.

On a stone at the door sat a bright-looking boy of some five years of age, peeling a rowan wand.

"Ay, Jamie lad," said Halket, approaching and laying his hand in a kindly way on the youngster's curly head, "and ye're nae beddit yet?"

"Na," said the boy, looking up with a frank smile.

"And what's this ye're makin'?"

"A stick to herd the nowte," answered he, holding up the wand.

"Weel, weel, it'll dee fine for that. . . . And is your mither in?"

"Ay, is she," said the little fellow, rising and leading the way into the house.

Halket followed, and was relieved to find Bell sitting alone by the kitchen fire.

"Weel, mistress," said he, "and hoo's a' wi' ye the nicht?"

"Oh, we're a' fine, Mr. Halket," said she, rising and offering her visitor a chair, "and I hope ye're weel yersel'. . . . . Fat's come o' ye this lang time? We've been thinkin' lang to see ye, Sandy and me."

"O weel, ye see," replied Halket, taking a seat, "the hairst's sic a busy time wi' you fairmer folk that a body disna jist like to come and bother ye when ye're a' sae thrang. But I thocht I would tak' a step owre noo that your hurry's feckly by, and see hoo ye were a' deein'. . . And I've gotten some news lately that I thocht ye micht maybe like to hear."

Bell's face grew pale, and she trembled a little. A certain dread something was ever on her mind.

"News?" she echoed. "Far frae, maybe?"

"Frae foreign. . . . But dinna get excited," Halket added, as he saw the colour come and go in her cheeks.

"Is't aboot—? Oh, tell's!" she exclaimed.

"Ay, it's aboot him."

"An'—an'—is he livin'? Mercy on's, is he livin'?"

she cried, almost hysterically, as she rose and came towards Halket.

"Jamie, my man," said he, ignoring her appeal, and turning to the boy, "ye micht rin awa' to your bed, like a fine loonie."

The youngster obeyed.

"And noo," said Halket, turning to Bell, and speaking with the tone of voice which his professional training had taught him how and when to employ,—"noo ye maun jist sit doon quaet and compose yersel',—or I winna tell ye anither word."

Thus admonished, Bell resumed her seat, and tried to appear calm and composed, although the wild gleam in her eyes, and the nervous way in which she worked her hands, showed what a tumult of feeling was surging in her breast.

"He's livin'," said her informant, speaking in quiet measured tones.

"O me!" wailed Bell, hiding her face in her apron. Great indeed was the conflict of emotions in her heart. A sudden pulse of wild joy had thrilled her whole being to think that her lover was still alive, but there had followed immediately a pang of dismay, when she remembered that she was now the bride of another. Great was the conflict—but short. Despair remained master of the field.

"Fat'll I dee?" she went on, rocking in her seat and weeping. "And me promised to wait for him.—O me!"

"That canna be helped noo," said Halket, in a calm voice, although his heart was being stirred by the tragedy. "Ye didna mean to be false to him."

But Bell only cried more bitterly than ever.

"And will he ever come back?" she wailed, hardly knowing herself which answer would please her.

"He *is* back," said Halket, quietly.

"O me! And will I see him?" And again was her heart divided. She longed to see Jamie again—*must* see him. And yet she dreaded to meet him— dreaded that above everything in the world. Such strange creatures are we. Her question was the cry of a longing heart; but, before Halket could answer, she had added—"I couldna face him aifter fat I've deen. O me! My heart will brak' in twa at this rate!"

"Noo, Bell," said Halket, firmly, "ye maunna gang on like that. It's nae eese noo. The thing, as I said, canna be helped, and ye maun bear up."

"Oh, but I canna face Jamie. I promised to wait for him, and mairry him when he cam' back frae Jamaica, and noo—"

"Bell," said Halket, interrupting her wail, "jist listen to me.—Ye are noo anither man's wife, and maun think on your duties to him. Sandy didna seek ye till a' hopes o' Jamie comin' back was by; and he took ye," speaking significantly, "jist as ye were, and made nae word aboot onything. Ye were willin' to tak' him, and vowed to be his ain true wife. The which ye maun be noo, hooever muckle ye may regret in your ain mind that Jamie Robertson didna come hame in time to claim ye."

Bell listened patiently to the lecture, and began to feel penitent.

"I ken I should be true to Sandy, for he's noo my man, and he's as guid and kind to me as ony man could be." But again the old feelings surged up, and she went on.—"But fat wye didna Jamie come hame—or write? He surely wanted to cheat a body, and gar them mairry Clyacks!"

"There's a reason for a' that," said Halket. "I can assure you Jamie's nae to blame, as ye'll alloo when ye hear his story. In fact naebody's to blame, and sae a'body will jist hae to mak' the best o't. Jamie himsel' will try to bear up like a man, nae doot."

"But does he ken a' this?" Bell exclaimed, eagerly,—"that I'm mairriet, and—a' the lave o't?"

"He kens a'thing," Halket replied, with calm decision.

"And, oh, was he in an awfu' wye aboot it?—Tell me that."

It didn't occur to Bell to wonder how her companion's information came to be so full and confident. But, so long as he was able to satisfy her curiosity, she would continue to appeal to him as to an omniscient oracle, without troubling to inquire how he came by his information. So, when Halket assured her that Jamie had been much put about, she proceeded to ask another question.—

"And did he blame me awfu'?"

"No, how could he?" Halket said, adding, "and he understands how ye cam' to mairry Clyacks, and sees ye couldna help yersel'."

And now Bell's mind began to travel ahead.—

"And is he gaun to mairry—Miss Innes?"

"Bell!" Halket exclaimed, reprovingly.

"Weel than, he maybe will.—I'm near sure he will, and ye couldna blame him." So said Bell, and then, with a woman's logic, went on,—"I was aye sure he would mairry her, and I would lose him. He wisna for the like o' me."

"There's something in that," Halket hastened to say, glad that this way of viewing the matter had occurred to Bell herself. He judged it advisable, indeed, to emphasise it.—

"Ay, there's something in that.—Ye see Jamie has grown a great man sin' we saw him. He has plenty o' siller, wears grand claes, and speaks fine English noo. I widna jist say that ye would fin' yersel' very comfortable wi' him, Bell."

But Bell had pride, and, like most people when they indulge in self-depreciation, did not just like to be taken at her word. Giving her head the least bit of a toss, she said,—

"Oh, maybe no. But folk needna jist cairry their heid owre heigh for a' that."

Halket, a little nonplussed by Bell's briskness, was casting about for a line of reply, when the door opened, and in stepped Jamie himself. He stood a moment looking at Bell. She didn't recognise him, but rose to her feet in embarrassment, thinking it was some gentleman calling to see her husband on some matter of business.

Halket waited a moment to see if she would recognise her visitor. When there was no indication of this, he rose, and, moving past Jamie, said,—

"Bell, this is Jamie Robertson."

A wild cry from Bell greeted his announcement; but he passed quickly out, and shut the door.

.   .   .   .

Halket had been greatly relieved to find on his arrival that Clyacks himself was not about, and now congratulated himself that the scene was likely to pass without that worthy man being brought directly into contact with any of its distressing circumstances. But things after all were not quite as he supposed. To explain which, we must go back a little.

Sandy had been in the barn threshing when Halket arrived. Working busily at the flail, he was making too much sound himself to hear what was doing in "the close." When, however, the failing light made him relinquish his task, he took a turn through the stable, and, finding a strange horse there, inquired of one of the men whose it was. Learning that it was Mr. Halket's, he went away to the house to see his friend.

Bell was in the midst of one of her outbursts when he opened the outer door, and neither she nor Halket heard him enter. Bell's excited tones arrested him, and he stood still in the passage. Then he caught something which still further fixed his attention, and he continued to listen.

Sandy was about the last man to play eaves-dropper, but now he didn't know what he was doing. Only one thing he knew; one dreadful fact held him spell-bound and helpless—Jamie Robertson was alive!

There are situations that turn on a single fact— which established, the whole matter is at once fully and irrevocably settled. And this was such a case. When he knew that Jamie was living, he knew all. Details were of little consequence.

Like one dazed, he staggered out and walked away, heedless where he went. Some fifty yards from the steading he encountered a man on horseback. Looking up, he could see the figure of the rider pretty clearly against the twilight sky. Full of a certain idea, he was able to recognise Jamie with a readiness that would in ordinary circumstances have been quite surprising.

Sandy was hardly astonished. He was prepared for almost anything now. And, as he grew more familiar with the dreadful aspects of the revelation that had come to him, he found himself able to think a little.

Sandy was one of those sensitive souls whose excessive conscientiousness is a great burden to them. They do not harden as most people do, but remain to the end like shy sensitive children. They are ever ready to think themselves the aggressors, and magnify to a morbid degree all the little delinquencies that conscience may charge against them.

Poor Clyacks now felt as if he had done some great wrong to Jamie and to Bell. His conscience accused him of asking her to marry him before he had assured himself of her former lover's death. Bell's cry of despair had cut him to the heart; and now, when he thought also of Jamie's anguish, he was almost ready to look on himself as a murderer.

Remorse for some time held him in its iron grip; but, after a while, he was driven by degrees to take up something like a new position.—What right had he to stand between Jamie and Bell? They belonged to each other, and he had no right to prevent them claiming each other.—

"She's Jamie's," he soliloquised, "she's nae mine. . . . We're nae mairriet ava. . . . It was jist a mistak', and we maun get it pitten richt. . . . I'll gang to Mr. Lundie and see him aboot it. . . . It wisna a richt mairrage, and winna stan'. . . . Na, na, it winna stan'."

He was making for the Manse of Lonmay, but, when about half way, he chanced to meet Mr. Lundie himself.

"Well, Clyacks," said the minister, cheerily, "how are you all keeping?"

"Oh, fell weel, minister," was Sandy's reply.

"And how's the goodwife?"

"Fa—d'ye mean?" said Sandy, in a strange unnatural voice.

"Why, your wife of course, Sandy," replied Mr. Lundie, somewhat astonished.

"Wife?—I hinna a wife, Mr. Lundie. Ye've made a mistak' there."

"Sandy!" exclaimed the minister, quite alarmed at his parishioner's strange manner and still stranger speech, but speaking in as restrained a tone as he could command, "you're surely joking. I am referring to Bell, your wife. I hope she is well."

"Ay, I suppose Bell's maybe rale weel.—But there's something aboot that, Mr. Lundie, that I maun explain to you.—Min', I'm nae mairriet. We were only a kin' o' funnin' yon time. Bell, ye ken, was Jamie Robertson's lass, and I had nae business to mairry her. It was a mistak'. Noo Jamie he's come hame, and ye maunna say nae mair aboot us bein' mairriet. Bell and me will burn the linie, and ye can jist scrape it oot o' your beuks and say naething aboot it. I can pey ye onything that's needed. It was a pity to bother ye; but it was jist a mistak'—jist a mistak', Mr. Lundie."

Mr. Lundie stood listening in helpless amazement. At first he thought something had touched Sandy's brain. Now he began to understand it all, and was deeply moved.

"Sandy," he said, seizing Clyacks' hand, "you mustn't speak like that. Bell is your lawful wedded spouse. Nobody can come between you. I understand about Jamie Robertson; and perhaps, if he had returned sooner, you might have agreed to surrender your claim in Bell and let her marry Jamie. You cannot do that now. By the law of the land no less than the law of God you and Bell are man and wife, and no one can now put you asunder. Nor need you have any regrets in the matter, my good friend. You acted throughout most honourably—quite generously in fact, and have nothing to regret. I can to some extent understand your feelings, now that Jamie has returned. They are like you, Sandy, and do your heart at least infinite credit. But the thing you suggest is, as I say, utterly impracticable—absolutely impossible. You and Bell are now united as man and wife, and nothing but death can dissolve the bond.—You understand that, Sandy?"

"And ye canna cheenge't than?"

"Nothing can but death."

"Weel, weel, minister; thank ye. It's a pity.—Good-bye."

And Sandy turned without another word, and walked away back.

"Nothing but death," he repeated to himself, as he went along. "Nothing but death."

Sandy's intellect was a slow one.

"Naething but death.—Weel, I suppose that maun be me. Ye see it widna suit if Bell wis to dee, for syne Jamie couldna get her. . . . . It maun be me; for ye see, gin *I* wis to dee, Bell and me widna be marriet syne, and she could tak' Jamie . . . Ay, that's it."

Musing thus, Sandy pursued his way. He went past Millbog. There was a new tenant there now, whose acquaintance Sandy had hardly yet made. In any case however, he would not have called just then.

Proceeding along the path that went by the well, he reached the small natural loch that filled the hollow at the foot of the field. It was an ugly looking pool. The depth of the water was not so very great, although that was sufficient to be quite dangerous ; but the bottom was a bog, soft and spongy, which would suck in anything that should rest on it. There were traditions of one or two tragedies having ended here, and the place had an evil reputation.

Just now in the gloom of the still autumn night it looked sullen and sinister. One end was deeper than the rest, and it was past this point that the path lay.

Here Sandy paused, and stood gazing down into the dark water ; and ever, as he gazed, its fatal fascination grew on his soul. It seemed to offer what everything else had denied : the resolution of all his difficulties— and peace.

From the marshes beyond came the scream of some waterfowl. Then an owl hooted away about the gardens at Logie, and he heard a dog howl in reply. He knew it was his own faithful Rover, but he heeded not. His eyes and his heart were still on the dark waters.

But now he hears a sound as of voices in conversation. He looks up, and thinks he can descry two figures coming over the rising ground on the left.

.   .   .   .

A soft hollow plunge breaks the quietness of the autumn night; the stars dance for a moment on the circling ripples; and then all is still once more.

CHAPTER XX.

THE PLEDGE.

WHEN Sandy recovered consciousness, consciousness of a vague, hazy kind, he was lying in a room in Logie House, and round him were Jamie, Halket, and the laird. And this briefly is how it came about.—

We go back to Clyacksneuk.—

When Halket passed out of the kitchen there, leaving Jamie and Bell face to face with each other, he shut the door on a scene too intense for words to describe. Imagination itself scarcely cares to deal too minutely with such things. Life has sanctuaries into which it is something like sacrilege for the alien and stranger to penetrate.

Meanwhile Halket, afraid that Sandy might come inopportunely on the scene, had gone away to see if he could find him and engage him in conversation, till Jamie's interview with Bell should be over. But he didn't find Clyacks, and so he just hung about the steading till his companion reappeared, which was in about half an hour.

Evening had now set in, and for this both men were very thankful. It helped somewhat to relieve the keen embarrassment they felt in meeting after the tragic ordeal that had just been gone through. Halket hastened to make a suggestion, so as to save Jamie the necessity of saying anything on his own account.

" I think we'll go down to Logie," he said, leading

the way to the stable where their horses were. Jamie followed without a word, glad now to get away from the place. In silence they took out their horses, mounted, and went on to Logie.

When they arrived at the stables, Jamie, who saw that his old acquaintance, the coachman, was still in office there, kept in the background, so as to avoid running the risk of having to undergo the ordeal of a recognition with all its attendant explanations and reminiscences, for which he was in no mood just then. But the groom who came forward to take his horse addressed him in such a frank and cheery, albeit quite respectful way, that Jamie was tempted to break silence, and, following the young fellow into the stable, got into conversation with him. Inquiring his name, Jamie was pleased to find that he had run across his old friend Jockie. But, if he was pleased at the meeting, Jockie was simply delighted. He began at once to ply Jamie with questions about the foreign places he had seen— about savages and wild beasts, and all the dreadful things that were associated in his mind with countries beyond the sea. Jamie, amused at the enthusiasm of his young friend, promised to see him again when he had more time, and satisfy his curiosity on these interesting points.

Halket and Jamie now strolled away across the burn and round by the garden and House. It was so interesting, and even pathetic, thus to revisit the scene of former days and duties. The soft light and quiet air of the autumn evening intensified the feeling, till Jamie's heart was well-nigh full, and his eyes began to grow dim.

His was the romantic imaginative temperament to which such things appeal with peculiar force.

After spending some little time here, Jamie suggested that they should take a turn round by Millbog, and together they set out across the fields. And now they began to talk a little, dealing with the changes that had taken place about Logie, where a new laird had introduced not a few new things, and certain altered ways.

Conversing thus, they were approaching the pool by the side of which Clyacks was standing, when Jamie thought he saw a dark object disappear from the path towards the water. As this was followed by a dull splash, he rushed forward to see what had fallen into the pool.

By the time Halket came up, Jamie was in the water struggling to reach the bank with Clyacks, whom he had managed to get hold of. The depth of the water and the treacherous nature of the bottom made this so difficult a matter that, despite his heroic efforts, it began to look as if Jamie would not only fail to rescue Clyacks, but even lose his own life in the attempt.

Luckily, however, Halket carried a walking-stick, and by means of this was able to help Jamie to reach the side with his unconscious burden. As the drowning man was now quite helpless, it was an exceedingly difficult thing to get him dragged out, even after his rescuer had managed to bring him to the side ; but at length this was accomplished ; and now, as the man lay on the bank with Jamie panting beside him, Halket was able to see that it was Clyacks they had saved from a watery grave.

After adopting such means as could be taken on the spot to resuscitate him, and finding to their joy that he was likely to come round, they began to deliberate as to what they should do next.

It was a great shock to Jamie and Halket to find that the man whom they had rescued was Clyacks. Though neither referred to the matter, each in his own mind at once connected the distressing circumstances with what had already taken place that evening at Clyacksneuk. They felt sure the poor man had in some way or other come to learn what had happened, and that his excessive sensitiveness had driven him to a despair from which he had sought to escape in this last dire way.

Although this theory, held by both men, was not put into words by either, it influenced them in their deliberations as to future action. For, feeling that the events of the evening had already created sufficient distress at Clyacksneuk, they deemed it a pity to add to it by taking Sandy home under circumstances that would suggest a connection therewith, as direct as it was lamentable. It would be an intense relief, if they could get matters so far put right as to be able to keep all knowledge of the tragedy from Bell, or, failing that, to minimise its gravity and significance. So neither of them thought or spoke of taking him home meantime, but both, by a kind of simultaneous inspiration, decided that it would be best to carry him to Logie, where efficient restoratives were most likely to be had.

Their way of viewing the matter was natural, and seemed right; and yet the opinion may be ventured that the shock which they wanted to spare Bell would have been possibly the best antidote for her somewhat selfish distress.

So they carried Sandy to Logie. Jamie entered the mansion with feelings that astonished himself, when he remembered how deferential and almost awe-struck he used to feel in former days when he had to pass its august portals ; and to Mr. Gordon, the laird, who was quickly summoned, he explained matters with the easy manner of one who almost addresses an equal.—So great a change can a few years make !

Mr. Gordon knew Clyacks well, and had come to regard him as not only one of his most successful tenants, but as a most estimable, if rather diffident man. His sympathies were thus at once and strongly enlisted, and he set himself to do all he could for the patient, applying such restoratives as he could think of, and despatching Jockie the groom on horseback for medical aid.

Of course neither Halket nor Jamie hinted at what they thought the real explanation of the unfortunate occurrence, but both treated it as a pure accident, and were even inclined to invent details in support of their theory. One difficulty they did indeed foresee.—When Sandy should be sufficiently recovered to give his own explanation of the affair, it was just possible that he might be more frank and honest than they were, and tell the plain distressing truth.

And now the laird noticed Jamie's condition, which had hitherto escaped attention. His clothes were all soiled and wet, and Mr. Gordon kindly invited him to avail himself of the facilities his own private wardrobe offered for getting himself comfortably rehabilitated. Jamie was very glad to fall in with the thoughtful suggestion. The laird chanced to be a tall man, and his clothes fitted Jamie wonderfully well, so that our friend escaped the caricature that so often results from changes of this kind; and for this, as we shall see, he soon had reason to feel very thankful.

As he came along the corridor on his return to the apartment where Clyacks lay, he heard voices in a room which opened on the passage.—

"Clyacks, poor man! I am so sorry. Where is he? I should like to see him."

It was a lady who spoke, and she was addressing a servant who had just told her of the accident. Jamie stopped involuntarily, for he thought he knew the voice, and his heart gave a great bound. Next moment out of the room came the lady. As she stepped into the shaft of moonlight that now from a side window struck across the passage, Jamie saw that his surmise was correct. The lady noticed him, and started slightly.

"Miss Innes!" said Jamie, advancing and holding out his hand.

One moment she hesitated. The next she had taken the proferred hand.—"Mr. Robertson!"

Fain would she have said "Jamie," for Auld Lang Syne, but, with a woman's wide-awakeness, she noted that the servant was near enough to hear.

"How in all the world come you to be here again?" he asked.

"I have still more reason to ask that same question of you, and to wonder how you come to revisit thus the glimpses of the moon." Then, as a sudden light dawned on her mind, she added, "Oh, I see! you are the strange gentleman who so bravely saved poor Clyacks from drowning?—But—but.—Well, really, I don't know how to begin."

"Well," said Jamie, smiling, "I have almost as great a host of questions to put to you. But you haven't answered the first one. How come you to be here once more?"

"Well, although I haven't the old footing here, I have been staying with my kinsman, Sir James, over at Tyrie, and have come to know Mrs. Gordon, who has kindly invited me to stay a few days at Logie; and so here I am. That briefly is the raison dê'tre of my presence at Logie. Now, what about thyself, sir?—thou who from the far Indies dost suddenly appear on Buchan soil."

"Well, it is a long story, and in some ways a sad one. But I can hardly tell it in a draughty moonlit passage."

"Well, I was going to see how poor Clyacks is progressing. I am so distressed about him."

"If that is your errand," said Jamie, interrupting her, "I can tell you that he is as well as can be looked for, and we have every hope that, when medical aid arrives, he will come round. If that satisfies your present interest in our friend, I should propose that we take a step out into the moonlight, where we can have an uninterrupted talk—All this, Miss Innes, if you care."

"If you—very much want it," she said, hesitatingly. "And if you think our friends wouldn't—wonder," she added.

"No: I don't think they will trouble over the matter. In any case, I should think we are old enough, and, in the present circumstances, free enough to act for ourselves. I shall, however, tell Mr. Halket, who is with Clyacks in the other room, that I shall be away for a little." And he went along to apprise his friend of his intention.

Very soon Miss Innes and Jamie were stepping along in the soft autumn moonlight. Jamie now tried to explain how he came to be back at Logie; but he found the task so difficult and delicate that he judged it necessary to appeal to his companion in an apologetic kind of way.—

"But I weary you with these things," he said, "and, selfishly perhaps, count on your interest?"

"Jamie!"

The old name, uttered with the inflection of kindly protest, was irresistible; and on he had to go once more. He made a brave effort to tell an honest tale, but again the embarrassment grew on him; and at last in despair he said,—

"But you have been in the district, and know the gossip?"

"Some of it," she answered, quietly.

"Well, then, let me just add the bit you perhaps don't know,—the events of the last hour or two." And he gave a brief and mild version of what we have already related. Brief and mild it was, but for Miss Innes it was enough. She fully grasped the situation, and neither asked question nor added comment.

After this they walked for a while in silence. They were proceeding along the Park Road, and had come opposite the Newark druidical circle. And now Miss Innes stopped.

"Do you know," she said, "I remember the last time I was here?"

"Indeed?"

"Yes, it was just the night we left Logie for Edinburgh. I took a stroll out this way, feeling restless and disinclined for sleep. It was a fine moon-light night."

"It was," interjected Jamie.

"You remember it too, do you?" she said, noticing the interruption.

"Yes,—very well."

"Well, I walked out as far as this. Then I stood for a little while looking over to the circle yonder, and thinking what an eerie place it was at such an hour—it must have been about midnight,—when I thought I heard a slight noise in the grove. It gave me a start, coming at that particular moment; and I can assure you, although I didn't just run, I made my way back with considerable speed. Now, I am not superstitious, but I have often wondered what that sound could have been, for, although it was neither loud nor distinct, it affected me in a strange and altogether inexplicable way. In fact, standing here, I almost think I begin to feel something of the same sensation, only I am not afraid—when you are here."

Jamie had been listening to the recital with intense interest, and, in fact, had considerable difficulty in restraining himself from interrupting it with the explanation which he felt he could so easily give. But, when he got the opportunity to speak, he discovered more difficulties than he had expected. The situation was again so delicate.—

"Miss Innes," he began, "I think I could explain the sound you heard. It wasn't at all supernatural. Yet I can hardly tell you."

"Oh, had you any connection with it?"

"Yes. It is altogether a delicate matter to handle;

but I have made you my confessor to such an extent to-night already that I may as well go a little further. I assure you I feel heartily ashamed of asking you to listen to such recitals; but I have been to-night so upset that I can hardly feel the restraints of ordinary prudence and good taste. No doubt I shall swear roundly at myself to-morrow for acting so very foolishly."

"If you are to swear at yourself to-morrow, forbear now. I don't want to encourage profanity, sir."

"Well, I must do my best in the awkward circumstances, and tell you as much at least as will explain the start you got, and restore your confidence in the arrangements of the universe."

Here he gave an account,—a very diluted, stammering, and awkward account of his interview with Bell. Most trying is it for a man to tell one woman of his relations with another. Miss Innes, however, was a very sensible person, and her interest in Jamie and his affairs was most genuine. This helped matters to some extent, and Jamie somehow or other got through the ordeal. Then he added,—

"Will you come across to the circle, Miss Innes, and see if we can find anything uncanny to-night?"

"Yes: after your explanation I think I may; and when I have your company."

Reaching the altar-stone, Jamie paused, and said,—

"Now, it was here I let fall the half of that sixpence. It must have fallen just here."

He stooped down behind the stone, and, lifting a handful of loose rubbish from the ground, riddled it through his fingers. This process he repeated with one or two handfuls, and was at length rewarded by feeling

in his hand something that corresponded in shape and
size to what he sought ; and erelong a vigorous rubbing
proclaimed the little semicircle to be the half of the
sixpence he had lost on that memorable night.

Miss Innes had been leaning on the great stone,
watching with more interest than she cared to show
Jamie's search for the lost pledge. Now, when it was
found, she felt instinctively that Jamie was going to
address her—in some quite special way indeed ; and,
resting her chin on her hand, she looked away to the
great moon that was slowly climbing up the eastern sky.
Her attitude at that moment was striking ; her faultless
profile was finely shown ; and, as a dreamy look gathered
in her eyes, Jamie thought he had never seen so en-
trancing a vision. It was to him the reverie of a goddess.
And somehow he felt inspired as he had never been
before.

" Now, Miss Innes," he said, " years ago I offered
this pledge—unwittingly at the time perhaps,—offered
it to a lady distant and visionary, whom the fates must
have brought thither. She fled, and would not take it.
Now the same lady is before me, real and near."

He paused. Miss Innes made no reply. She
hardly looked as though she heard. But Jamie grew
bolder.

"Well, Miss Innes, I am not worthy to offer you
anything. You know my history. I do not ask you to
listen to me now. I only ask if you will allow me to
try to prove myself worthy to approach you at some
future time and plead my cause. I return to Jamaica.
There I shall stay for a year or two longer, so that my
prospects, which are at present good, may become still

better.   Now, if you are willing to grant me a period of
probation, I shall endeavour to prove myself worthy to
return and approach you then with my heart's request.
If you are willing thus far to encourage me to hope, may
I ask you to keep this little piece of coin for my sake?
Fate seems to have destined it for you.   As once before
I offered it to you as in a vision, so now I repeat that
offer in a real and actual way—Miss Innes, will you
take this little pledge?"

She turned towards him.—

"*Miss* Innes takes no pledges of this kind."

He understood her in a moment, and his heart
thrilled with an overmastering delight.—

"Will *Rose* Innes take it then?"

"She will."

And she took from his hand the little bit of silver.

CHAPTER XXI.

FATE'S DECREE.

WHEN Miss Innes and Jamie returned to Logie, they found the doctor arrived, and also Mr Lundie.

The minister had been alarmed by Sandy's manner and speech, and, after arriving at the manse, had been unable to dismiss the matter from his mind. The result was that he soon set out for Clyacksneuk. He felt it his duty to see what was happening,—being concerned about his parishioner, and apprehensive lest in his despair he should do something ill-advised.

When he arrived at Clyacksneuk, he found Bell alone, and evidently in deep distress. He asked where her husband was, and she confessed she hadn't seen him for an hour or two. The minister was now more concerned than ever. Bell did not fail to note his anxiety. It had not occurred to her to wonder what had become of her husband, but now, when she thought of it, it was strange that he hadn't come to the house, as he always used to do when the day's work was done. She began to share the minister's concern.

Bell looked altogether so distressed that Mr. Lundie invited her to confide to him her trouble. And then the poor girl, with a burst of tears, told him what had happened—the general run of which he either knew or had surmised already.

When the sad recital was over, the minister set himself to talk to her on the subject. He set her duty in such a clear convincing light, and spoke with such evident feeling and sympathy, that Bell's better nature responded to the appeal, and she felt gathering in her mind and heart a resolution to do the right and bravely cast off the chains that bound her. It needed a great effort to face the task ; and yet the task was even greater than she imagined. And so it always is when duty and inclination run diverse ways. Did people know what they were undertaking in such cases, they would often shrink in dismay. The way will prove longer and more painful than they think. But, if they only get grace and nerve to make a beginning, there is hope that they will continue, and vanquish one by one the difficulties which, if contemplated in mass, would possibly have daunted their spirits. In duty, as in everything else, short views are best. Do the immediate task. It will be time enough to face the next when this is done.

Mr. Lundie now went away to look for Sandy. Somehow or other he couldn't rest till he knew where he was and what he was doing. Inquiring about the stead-ing, he found from some of the men that their master hadn't been seen since gloaming.

The minister was now at a loss what to do or where to go. But, after standing irresolute for some time, it occurred to him that Jamie Robertson might have some connection with the matter, and, on further inquiry, he ascertained that a strange gentleman had gone away with Mr. Halket in the direction of Logie. So to Logie the minister went ; and, there learning what had happened, was soon in the house, standing with the rest round poor Sandy. The doctor also had arrived. He was at first quite puzzled with Sandy's case, for the patient seemed physically able to rally, and yet was making no progress in that direction. When the medical man gave utterance to his difficulty, Halket took him aside and told him what he knew and what he suspected with regard to Sandy's so-called accident.

This put a new complexion on the matter. The doctor now felt that the case was very grave; in fact he opined that, unless something drastic could be done, his patient was likely to lose either his life or his reason.

On Jamie's re-entrance Sandy recognised him, and muttered, as if in apology, that he would soon be "oot o' the road."

"Cheer up, Clyacks," said Jamie, brightly, "you will soon be all right."

"Na, I'll seen be deid. I thocht I wid be oot o' the road by this time."

The pathos of the reply came home to the hearts of all who heard him. Miss Innes burst into tears. Jamie tried to bear up and speak cheerfully.

"Come, come, Sandy, you mustn't speak of dying."

"Ay, naething but death, naething but death," was the reply, delivered in a quiet matter-of-fact tone that was more hopeless than a wild burst of despair would have been.

The minister was deeply grieved, and he also spoke to the doctor of the strange interview he had had with Clyacks. This more and more convinced the doctor of the gravity of the case. The poor man was determined not to recover; and it was clear that never, with such a dread weight on his spirit, with such a horror facing his soul, could he hope to preserve sanity at once of body and of mind. Something must give way.

But now in came Bell, a look of wild alarm on her face. While the rest of the company were greatly disconcerted by her entrance, Jamie and Halket were positively dismayed. They hardly knew what to think or expect.

On the minister's departure, Bell had sent the men to look for her husband. At length one of them returned with the news, got from one of the Logie servants he had chanced to meet, that Clyacks had been nearly drowned, and was lying in Logie House. Thither she had hurried with all speed, and now appeared on the scene.

She darted a swift glance at Jamie and Miss Innes, who stood together, and then moved to her husband's side. But, when he saw her, a look of keen anxiety gathered on his face, and, with a movement of the hand as if to push her away, he said,—

"Gang awa' to Jamie, Bell. Ye're nae mine; ye're his."

"But she can't do that," interposed the minister ; and then, remembering his conversation with Bell, he added, appealing to her,—"And she doesn't want to go.—Do you, Bell ?"

"No: I dinna want to leave Sandy," cried poor Bell.

But Clyacks only shook his head ; whereupon the minister ventured to add,—

"And Jamie doesn't want Bell."

"Ay, but he does," said Sandy, with quiet doggedness, "and I'll seen be deid and oot o' the road."

All felt baffled and were in despair. They stood looking in helpless grief and pity on the poor man. In that critical moment, however, there came an inspiration to one of the company. Miss Innes stepped forward, and, approaching Sandy, said,—

"But Bell can't get Jamie. Jamie doesn't want *her*."

"Fa does he want than?" asked Clyacks, with just the least trace of interest in look and tone.

"He is going to take *me*."—With what an effort she spoke!

"Ay, Jamie's gaun to mairry—*Miss Innes*," Bell repeated.—And with a still greater effort spoke *she!*

A look of relief dawned in Sandy's eyes, but it soon passed.—

"Ye're jist sayin' that to cheat me."

"Not a bit," cried Miss Innes. Then, turning to Jamie, she said,—"Isn't it true, Jamie?"

"Yes," assented Jamie. He hardly knew what he said, but he took her hand. Then did poor Bell know what a task she had undertaken in renouncing her claim in Jamie and schooling her heart to surrender him to another. Then did she know the anguish of soul that must be borne ere the bitterness of death be past.

But Sandy, still incredulous, turned his eyes on Mr. Lundie.—

"Are they to be mairriet, minister?" he asked.

"It seems so," was the cautious reply.

"Are ye gaun to mairry them?" was the next question.

"I—hardly know," said Mr. Lundie, with evident hesitation, as he looked towards the couple whose intentions and plans were being canvassed.

"Weel than, they're only pretendin'," said Sandy, in the old dogged way.

Whereupon Miss Innes broke in once more.—

"Yes, we are to be married," she said; and then, glancing at Jamie, whose look seemed to bespeak unlimited acquiescence, she added, "and just now, if the minister will do it."

But Mr. Lundie looked dubious.—

"I am not so sure about that—just now," he said, hesitatingly. "It is somewhat precipitate, you know. We have certain forms to go through, and—"

"For God's sake do it if you can," exclaimed the doctor. "It is his only chance!"

"Well," said Mr. Lundie deeply impressed by the appeal, "*in rebus extremis* one may be justified in doing things that were otherwise inexpedient. And I shall consider myself justified in the present crisis in doing what you request, if the parties concerned are willing, and none of the company knows of anything that may hinder the proposed union."

He looked round. No one spoke. Sandy was keenly watching all that took place. Bell moved to his side, and took his hand.

Then did Jamie Robertson and Rose Innes stand forth in presence of the company, and, taking each other by the hand, were united as man and wife, for better for worse, till death should them part. And, though this improvised ceremony was afterwards supplemented by a grand wedding in an Edinburgh church, it was there at Logie and in this simple way that those two lives, which had long and unconsciously been growing towards each other, were first merged.

*   *   *   *   *   *   *

That very night Sandy was able to return with Bell to Clyacksneuk. He hardly knew what to think, but peace had returned to his spirit, and hope to his life. Bell too had attained a wonderful degree of calm, and was beginning to take refuge in the philosophy that represents the attitude of the rustic mind towards matrimony and the fates that preside over it.—" It has jist a' been ordained that wye," was her reflection.

With which reflection and the philosophy underlying it we too must perforce rest content.

CHAPTER XXII.

CONCLUSION.

THERE are one or two things to record, and one or two observations to make, ere we take farewell of Logie.

Our old friend Halket, now assured of Fred's death, married Lily Douglas, and lived very happily with her for a number of years. He died at Memsie, and lies buried within the old churchyard of Fraserburgh. He needs no monument to perpetuate his name. His song is his monument—*aere perennius*.

Bell settled down to her life at Clyacksneuk, and became such a model farmer's wife that Sandy would on special occasions, when an extra tumbler of toddy had made him communicative, admit to his cronies that she was "growin' as guid's his mither." The tragedy of her life gradually got into perspective, and she came more and more to see the inevitableness of it all, and to realise and admit that Jamie was not for her. That is, the Jamie of later years—the man of wealth and social position. But the Jamie of early days was still hers— the bright young lover who had won her young heart. No one could rob her of that dear image and the sweet memories that clung around it, for they were enshrined deep in her heart of hearts for evermore.

Yet was she loyal to her husband; for her real and present existence was associated with his, and therein she was ever the faithful spouse. It was a separate kind of life she lived in the reveries that would visit her from time to time. She thought Sandy didn't know or suspect anything; but he was more penetrating than she imagined, and knew quite well, when Bell would sit silent of an evening looking abstractedly in the big peat fire, that her thoughts were in the past. But it didn't trouble him. He was very happy and contented to feel that Bell was in all essential respects a good and true wife to him.

Thus life flowed on for Sandy and Bell. Their days were of the quiet uneventful order that marks existence in our rural parts, with prosperity beyond the common lot. They were long spared to each other, and now rest together in Lonmay churchyard.

And Jamie.—He and his fortunes are now permanently transferred to the south, and he ceases in large measure to be a Buchan man. He breaks with his antecedents, and, leaving the old narrow life, passes out into a larger world, where he attains wealth, position, and influence. Yet how strange is the irony of fate, and how little we know sometimes where our real strength and significance lie. For, although people may be interested to learn how Jamie "burst his birth's invidious bar" and achieved high worldly success, yet will they ever hark back to the Jamie of early days, to the apprentice gardener who delved in the yard at Logie. Indeed, as the merely prosperous man of the world, Jamie Robertson would have been forgotten long ago. As the poor lad who "had but ae saxpence," he has achieved a fame that is imperishable. As the man who married a rich and cultured lady and found his way into polite society, he would have remained unknown to posterity. As the young gardener lad who won the heart of the country maiden, he is immortal.

We have tried to tell his story—carrying it, in deference to the exigencies of plot and plan and in the light of supplementary information, beyond the scope of the song on which it is based. But further we will not follow our hero, nor seek to trace his career in that wider world into which he has now passed.—For us let him ever remain the Jamie of "Logie o' Buchan."

*   *   *   *   *   *   *

Something like a century and a half has elapsed since the events we have been narrating took place. All the characters have long since gone from the earth, and not a few changes have taken place in the scenes and localities.

Logie House has disappeared. Its foundations, however, can still be traced, as well as the site of the garden, about which still stand some of the old trees. The old life of the place is stilled and gone, and none of the voices of yore can now be heard save that of the little burn, which still slides by its alder-shadowed banks, singing the song of long-ago.

Millbog too has disappeared, and its fields have been absorbed in the neighbouring farm.

Yet, with all these changes, the outward air and aspect of things remain pretty much the same. Mormond still heaves his long bare ridge, and away on the eastern horizon still shimmers the distant sea. The same quiet rural air is about, and now, as of yore, while "simmer is comin' and cauld winter's awa," the larks sing aloft, and on fuming fields the lapwings wheel and cry. . . . . A quiet scene—with no outstanding feature and with little of outward interest. Yet stands it glorified for all time,—glorified by one simple lay of pastoral life and love.

Speaking of another locality immortalised in Scottish Song, the poet, while admitting that everything of concrete circumstance and charm has well-nigh gone, adds triumphantly,—

> " But the blithe lilt o' yon air
> Keeps the Bush aboon Traquair,
> And the love that once was there,
>   Aye fresh and green."

And so shall it be with Logie.

THE END.